Praise for Joely Sue Burkhart's
Hurt Me So Good

"The way Joely Sue Burkhart describes the feelings and the dynamics, the hunger and need, is mesmerizing."

~ *Pearl's World of Romance*

"Ms. Burkhart has certainly put herself in a class above the rest with this story. To be able to write such intensity, emotion and drama, and to have the characters remain loving and devoted, was amazing to see."

~ *Blackraven Reviews*

"The sex is hot, the foreplay edgy, and lots of dominant/submissive action got my total attention."

~ *Naughty in the Backseat*

"Hats off to Ms. Burkhart as she has once again proven herself a master of developing complex, likeable characters in a world most view as unpalatable."

~ *The Romance Rev*

Look for these titles by
Joely Sue Burkhart

Now Available:

A Jane Austen Space Opera
Lady Doctor Wyre

The Connaghers
Dear Sir, I'm Yours

Hurt Me So Good

Joely Sue Burkhart

SAMHAIN
PUBLISHING

Samhain Publishing, Ltd.
11821 Mason Montgomery Rd., 4B
Cincinnati, OH 45249
www.samhainpublishing.com

Hurt Me So Good
Copyright © 2011 by Joely Sue Burkhart
Print ISBN: 978-1-60928-281-3
Digital ISBN: 978-1-60928-215-8

Editing by Tera Kleinfelter
Cover by Scott Carpenter

First Samhain Publishing, Ltd. electronic publication: October 2010
First Samhain Publishing, Ltd. print publication: September 2011

Dedication

For my beloved sister

A huge thank you to beta readers Sherri Meyer, Pearl, Nicole Tom, Susan, Christine Lovejoy, Stephanie Christine, Marie R. and Sharon Muha for helping me make this book shine.

Sherri: Brandon is forever in your debt.

Chapter One

Dear Blogland:

The last thing the internet needs is yet another anonymous sexy blog detailing a submissive's journey to complete and utter surrender to her Master, but I promise you, this blog will be different.

For one thing, my Master doesn't know He's mine.

For another, He's my boss. Yeah, cringe at the political-incorrectness inherent in my situation. Now compound my insane attraction with the fact that I'm not only a submissive but also a masochist.

I don't just want my boss; I want Him to hurt me. I want Him to hurt me real good.

Oh, don't worry for my sake. I'm not going to do something stupid like stalk Him at work or strip in His office...although if He were to ask, I'd do it in a heartbeat. I'd do anything He wanted. If He asks, my answer will always, unequivocally, be yes.

Yes, Master V. Please make me yours.

I want to tie a big red bow around my waist and deliver myself to Him like a present, so that's why this blog is titled "V's Gift".

"We have a spy," Victor Connagher said in a professional,

measured tone. Despite the betrayal roiling inside him, the CEO of Dallas cable channel VCONN kept his emotions masked, when what he really wanted to do was slam his fist on the sleek table.

He paused the show playing on the large flat-screen television hung on the wall behind him. *Secret Fantasies* blazed in neon across the screen with the tagline "On the internet, any secret fantasy can be a dream come true".

"It's certainly no coincidence that KDSX is running a spot announcing a new show remarkably like our new fall lineup, down to the same idea of secret identities and baring all secrets online. What's the name of our show still in production?"

"*Internet Secrets.*" Malinda Kannes bit off each word. Victor knew she'd take the news the hardest as the show's producer. "I'm sorry, Victor. We've kept the show very quiet, even inside VCONN. It had to be someone on my production staff or the show itself."

He leaned back in his chair and steepled his fingers. Inside, though, he burned. He'd built VCONN up from a third-rate cable channel running *Grandma's Cooking* and *Bob the Garage Guy* to a smoldering, risqué adult channel that everyone in Dallas tittered about—and tuned in eagerly each night to be shocked, appalled, and yes, aroused. *Internet Secrets* was supposed to be their premier fall show to conquer KDSX, their number one copycat competitor.

Evidently copycat wasn't good enough for them any longer; they had to steal his shows outright.

"*Internet Secrets* is scrapped," Victor announced.

Mal didn't argue, although two red blotches blazed on her cheeks.

He leaned forward and pinned each of his employees with his gaze one by one. Mal met his gaze evenly, but the others paled and dropped their gazes after just a few seconds of his intensity. Out of guilt? Or simple respect to the years of power he'd built here as CEO? He couldn't be sure.

"We need a new show," he said softly. "Only a handful of people will work on it. That way it'll be very easy for me to identify our spy." He couldn't help but smile then, even though he knew it betrayed the consummate businessman mask he wore. He'd relish punishing their leak with his own hands. "And we need this new show in production *today*."

"Luckily," Mal drawled, some of her ire at losing her pet project fading, "I have someone waiting outside to pitch her latest idea. I thought it was pretty hot myself, and the timing couldn't be better."

"Excellent. The rest of you are dismissed."

Unspoken, his distrust hung in the close, tight air of the conference room like a discordant note. VCONN was a small but prosperous company, and he hated not being able to trust his own employees. His gut protested that his management team was solid, but at this point, he couldn't risk it. He refused to throw away their fall season, even if he must hurt a few kind souls who were innocent.

However, his resolve weakened as soon as he saw the person who'd come to pitch the new show idea.

Shiloh Holmes shook Mal's hand and with a bright smile, turned to him. He felt the impact like a quarterback sacked from his blind spot. She was one of those people who managed to brighten up the room as soon as she entered. Literally, it felt as though someone had yanked open the blinds and let the Texas sun come pouring into the darkened, cavernous room.

From her very first interview at VCONN nearly a year ago, she'd reminded him of a purring, tawny kitten winding around his ankles. A kitten that simply begged him to pick her up by the scruff of her neck and carry her home. Meeting his gaze head on with a saucy little grin that tightened his groin, she took his hand and it was all he could do not to squeeze his fingers incrementally until she cried out.

I have a feeling it wouldn't be a whimper of pain, either—but a welcoming purr of desire.

He forced himself to release her and shot a dark gaze at Mal, who wore a particularly smug little smile. Frustrated, he reached back and jerked the ponytail holding his shoulder-length hair tighter. The CEO of the company could not come on to one of his employees without opening himself up for sexual harassment charges, let alone a boss with his particular proclivities.

Watching Shiloh set up her storyboards, he tried to pinpoint exactly what attracted him so strongly. It was more than her honey-brown hair that curled and bounced about her face, her dark chocolate eyes, and her lush, curvy body. She was attractive, yes, but he'd known or worked with many other beautiful women who'd never tempted him like she did.

No, it was the way she managed to meet his gaze directly, even with her head tilted slightly in come-hither shyness—or a position of unconscious surrender. Her bubbly personality was warm, open and charming, yet she also managed to throw down an unspoken challenge at him.

Try to break me. I can take whatever you give me.

Surrender and challenge at the same time—a dichotomy that compelled him to investigate. Clenching his jaws, he breathed deeply, forcing that thought away. She couldn't possibly know...

He read the title of her proposed show and caught himself tapping his fingers on his right thigh. Maybe she did know after all.

America's Next Top sub: Submit to the Master.

"Thank you so much for the opportunity, Mr. Connagher." Nerves made Shiloh talk faster than usual. "I've been working on this idea for months."

For you.

Standing at the head of the conference table—just inches from Victor Connagher, the man she'd been fantasizing about for months—she found herself practically babbling. From a distance, he commanded an aura of impressive power. Up close and personal, she felt his presence like a thunderstorm tearing the sky with constant lightning.

With his sleek suit and ostentatious cowboy boots, he played the part of the wealthy Texan CEO impeccably. Yet no matter how hard he tried to appear civilized and suave, there was something barbarous hidden behind his corporate shields. His hair was rebellious, falling in a glossy black mane. He kept it pulled back tightly, accentuating the harsh planes of his face, but her fingers itched to tug that hair loose and muss it up.

She wanted to muss *him* up.

Her instincts insisted that the expensive suit and business-like demeanor were merely a front. Beneath his calm, controlled façade hid the star quarterback she'd been years ago before an injury forced him to quit. That man liked to be sweaty, dirty and just a bit bloody as he battled toward the end zone.

Now if he only likes his sex the same way.

As their sexy lineup implied, everyone at VCONN was open in their sexuality. Everyone except the CEO. His incredible charisma and sex appeal screamed make-you-whimper Dominant, but she couldn't be sure. It wasn't like she could simply walk up before her boss's desk, strip off her clothes, and—

Shuddering, she pushed that favorite night-time fantasy into the back corner of her mind and concentrated on her pitch. "VCONN has already established a reputation for envelope-pushing programming about sexuality, while managing to portray alternative sexual practices in a positive and healthy light. It's a fine line between edgy sex and porn, but VCONN has succeeded." Deliberately, she paused and met his hooded gaze. "For the most part."

His left eyebrow shot up but otherwise he remained implacable.

She'd used the past months to study Victor Connagher with the single-minded dedication of the most besotted submissive. It only took one glance at the trophy case in the lobby displaying all his awards and championships to realize that he hated to lose. She needed to bait him into accepting her challenge—without squashing her like a bug.

"One area where VCONN could stand to improve is education. Obviously, no one wants to watch a sex ed class, but with some high-interest reality TV and titillating challenges to balance the educational information about BDSM, I think *America's Next Top sub* could take VCONN to the next level."

"Reality TV's been done to death." He dusted invisible lint off his trousers in a careless, slapping swipe of his palm that made every muscle in her body go on high alert. He had big, powerful hands that would torture—or please—exquisitely. With those magnificent hands, he could break her into little pieces like kindling and she'd go with a smile on her face.

"Not a *BDSM* reality show. Nobody's risked it."

"It's a hot idea." Ms. Kannes's rich, smooth-as-chocolate voice matched her dark skin perfectly.

Shiloh hadn't needed to see Malinda's pictures all over the local bondage club to recognize a formidable Mistress. With her unusual amber eyes that pierced to the bone, she could make anyone, man or woman, scurry to do her will. Anyone but Victor Connagher, the Master himself.

"My worry is getting contestants in quickly enough," Ms. Kannes continued. "And what about the set? We're on an extremely tight timeframe. To be frank, the only reason you're getting a shot at this season at all is because we had a last-minute cancellation."

"I've already worked through the contestant angle," Shiloh replied. "Part of my research and planning stage was to meet with the local BDSM club's director. We could easily make use of Silken's facilities and their more experienced staff, as well as ours."

Mr. Connagher's eyebrow climbed even higher, at odds with the subtle rumble of intensity building in his voice. "Do you mean we should ask VCONN employees to participate as contestants?"

"*Reality* show is a misnomer," Shiloh replied calmly, even though every nerve in her body was humming. She had his attention. The hook was baited and he was nibbling. She couldn't haul him in too quickly or she'd lose him entirely. "Even long-running reality shows control their settings and select their contestants very carefully. We know our goal is positive education combined with the entertainment factor of a reality show, so we pick contestants we already know portray the right attitudes and knowledge about BDSM. It'll be much easier if we take volunteers from your staff."

"You're suggesting we stack the deck." Ms. Kannes was unable to hide the gleam of interest in her eyes, but Mr. Connagher was impossible to read. His eyes were too dark, solemn and intent—the better to see her every weakness. "I'm assuming you'll have some sort of prize for the winning contestant. How do we keep everyone happy when only one person wins?"

"It's a BDSM show." Shiloh let a sultry smile curve her lips, but she didn't look directly at him. She didn't trust herself not to plop down into his lap. "If we set up the correct challenges, everyone will go home extremely happy regardless of who wins."

He checked his watch, warning that his patience was almost gone. "Either this is a reality show or it's not. There has to be a winner, and I won't stand for cheating among my own employees."

"It's a dual competition." Shiloh fought not to blurt out her response in a desperation plea. "We'll have submissives competing to win the Dominants' favor, but also a single Dominant could win the title of Master, if he selects the correct submissive to win it all."

Ms. Kannes laughed. "By God, Victor, it's brilliant. I could compete as one of the Dominants, with my submissive as one of the contestants. Patrick could compete too, and that would give us another two or three submissives, depending on who's in his stable right now. If we can get another couple from Silken, then we'd have an interesting mix of newbies and experienced players. The experienced ones would be teaching the rest, as well as having a little friendly competition among us all."

Frowning, Mr. Connagher shook his head. "There's not going to be much drama between you and Patrick. You're too evenly matched and know each other too well."

Shiloh let out her breath and took a step closer to him, waiting until his gaze swung to her. "That's why you should compete, sir."

His eyes narrowed to slits, his mouth flattened into a hard slant, and his shoulders squared, chest broad and muscular in a universal signal of male dominance that his suit couldn't conceal.

Her heart froze a moment and then exploded into a rapid, thunderous pace that made her ears roar. He didn't refuse outright, though, which gave her the courage to continue. "The show needs a Master with a capital M. Someone who'll really bring the competition to a peak. Based on our demographics, it should be a male, and preferably, his submissive should be female. It will be even more exciting if he's unattached, so the unowned submissives all feel like they have a chance of winning his attention. The ultimate prize, then, will be the Master's collar, not money like the typical reality show."

Evidently he didn't like that idea at all. Silence stretched out, painful and heavy, his midnight eyes locked on her. Her mouth went dry and her heart hammered, but she stood her ground without blinking or flinching in the wake of his intensity. She didn't even dare breathe.

"You presume, then, that I'm not only a Dominant, but also a man who'd be interested in a giggling, immature submissive who's incapable of any sort of serious play." He blew out his breath in a low snort and turned to the other woman. "As though I'd give my collar to someone just because they thought they'd won a show that we set up from the very beginning."

Sucking in a deep breath, Shiloh squeezed her hands together so hard she felt her nails digging into her skin. She fought to hide the fierce elation burning through her. He might be dismissive, but she'd been right all along. He did have a collar, he was Dominant, and if she played this right, it'd be impossible for him to back out. The competitor in him demanded excellence in all things, even a reality show.

Feigning indifference, she shrugged and turned away from the table. "Then perhaps you can recommend another Master."

Shuffling through her carefully researched boards, she

moved the most important one to the front. Her best friend and roommate—who just happened to be a graphic design artist—had helped with the artwork. A masked man stood on a dais, dressed like an English riding master with a wicked-looking whip in his right hand. Despite the costume, the man bore a marked resemblance to VCONN's CEO.

Contestants knelt in an arc before him, all in submissive positions, head down, some stretched out prostrate before him. Two others stood on the steps to the dais but lower than him, a man and woman, also in Victorian riding wear. Despite their higher position than the contestants, they inclined their heads to the man above.

In bold letters across the top, the board read: *One Master to rule them all.*

"V," Ms. Kannes breathed out, her eyes bright. "You're perfect!"

"I don't want to do it." Yet he stared at the board, his right hand opening and closing into a fist, as though he ached to reach out and grab that whip. "There's no way in hell I'm unleashing that side of me on a bunch of—"

Shiloh pulled out the next storyboard and his voice fell off. In this sketch, a woman knelt at the Master's feet and leaned against his legs. One hand was wrapped around his thigh; her other fisted in his shirt as though she was trying to climb his body. Her face was pressed against him with her hair pulled aside to bare her back. Long red stripes marked her skin and the Master's whip curled around her vulnerable body with the heading: *One sub to please the Master—in any way he wishes.*

He ground out, "It's all wrong."

Shiloh's heart plummeted and her shoulders slumped with defeat. She'd gambled everything on this show. If he didn't like it, then she'd totally misunderstood every single signal she'd picked up from him. She'd even had her friend stylize the winner after her, a deliberate message to him, if only he were paying attention.

She'd planned this show down to the smallest detail, dreaming about winning it all. Wrapping herself around him. Learning to please him in every single possible way he'd ever dreamed. Winning *him*.

Her eyes felt hot and dry, and her bottom lip trembled. It was ridiculous to be heartbroken over a man who'd never touched her. Never looked into her eyes and burned with need. Never taken her on a long, hard ride to a sweetly painful submission they'd never forget.

"You came very close, Ms. Holmes."

She whipped her head up.

Victor Connagher gave her a hard smile of teeth and dominance that wound her heart into knots and sent icy chills dripping down her spine. "I can live with the English riding style." He kicked back in his chair and propped his limited-edition Lucchese boots on the edge of the conference table. "But this Master only uses a riding crop."

Chapter Two

Mal waited until the other woman left the room as asked, carefully pulling the door shut behind her. "Did you see the look on her face when you said you prefer the crop?"

Victor took a moment to respond. He'd definitely seen the flare of darkness in Shiloh's eyes, the softening of her luscious mouth, and the pink flash of her tongue across those tempting lips. She hadn't been repulsed by his admission, not at all. When he'd regained control of his voice, he answered, "Yes."

"And did you notice her likeness in the—"

"Of course I did," he snapped, jerking his legs down off the table so he could pace.

"So what's the problem?"

"It's complicated."

"She wasn't on my staff for *Internet Secrets*, so it's highly unlikely that she's your spy. Her entire body screams submission when she looks at you. She's perky, creative and well liked by everyone on her team. Her instincts are dead on and she's developed an incredible show that's perfect for you and VCONN. If you snapped your fingers and ordered her to heel, she'd be at your feet in a heartbeat."

He made himself halt in front of the window and jerked the blinds open. Blindly, he stared out at downtown Dallas, blinking his eyes against the light. "That's not what I want."

"I'm worried about you." Mal joined him at the window but he couldn't bear to see the sympathy in her gaze, so he pretended extreme interest in the skyline. "You haven't been serious about anyone in years."

Since Kimberly, echoed in the silence. Despite his best friend's care not to mention his ex-fiancée's name, he still winced. "I've dated."

"You've taken women to charity events," Mal said in a flat, careful voice. "You may have even taken them to your bed. But you haven't taken a woman who knows your true needs and makes damned sure you're satisfied."

He couldn't help the twitch of his mouth into a grim, sad smile that matched the emotions he kept buried in his heart. "No one can satisfy me."

With a growl, she thumped him on the back. "Don't give me that crap. You and I share many of those darker urges and you know I'm more than happy with Andy. He needs me as much as I need him. He likes me mean and nasty with a flail in my hands."

"Kimberly knew what kind of man I am." Each word sliced Victor's throat like razorblades. "We met at Silken. She still couldn't deal with the truth."

"She liked you well enough to accept your engagement ring and enjoy your money for months." Mal didn't bother keeping the disdain out of her voice. "She used you. She wanted a top who would tie her up and dedicate hours to her enjoyment, without demanding anything from her in return. She acted like it was a privilege for you to devote hours to *her* pleasure. She never took care of *you*. She never loved you."

"That's unfair. I know she loved me." Victor closed his eyes. Kimberly's delicate face blazed in his mind, an image from the night she'd left him. Tears streaked her face, her eyes wide, white, rolling with terror while she babbled her safeword over and over, a litany to save her from the nightmare. She'd sobbed in his arms for an hour before leaving for good, and he'd never forget her parting accusation. *You hurt me.* "She couldn't handle heavy edge play."

And I'm always on the edge. He shook his head ruefully. The sad fact was that the longer he denied himself, the sharper and more vicious that edge became.

"She couldn't have loved you, not the way you deserve," Mal insisted. "Not if she couldn't handle your kink. You're punishing yourself, V, and I hate it. I hate seeing you close yourself behind prison bars just because one sub couldn't deal with the full Master."

"It's not just one and you know it. I've trained dozens of bottoms over the years, introduced them to the scene, and time after time, they leave me and move on to another top. Someone safer. And I can't say that I blame them."

He finally met his friend's gaze and let all the disappointments and failures of his thirty-six years weigh in his gaze. "I'm tired, Mal. I'm tired of breaking in the young ones while knowing full well that they'll never be able to handle my kind of needs. I'm too old for this shit."

"You're burned out."

"No. Far from it." Victor smiled and even the strongest, proudest Mistress in Dallas flinched and dropped her gaze. It took constant control to keep that vicious clawing need buried deeply enough for him to function like a normal human being. "I'm a sadist in the truest sense of the word. Why do you think I didn't make a play for Shiloh months ago? My brief meet-and-greet interview with her after she was hired almost set my desk on fire. It's been pure hell to know she's been under my power here at VCONN this entire time, close, available, as attracted to me as I am to her, but there's absolutely nothing I can do about it. All it takes is one phone call to the police, one trip to the hospital, and I won't have to worry about this season's ratings. I'll be in prison."

"I know the risks all too well, but that's why it's important not to shut yourself off from the people who understand. You quit going to Silken—"

"For good reason," Victor said dryly. "My ex-fiancée married the owner."

"Which is why I started hosting my own parties, but you always refuse to come. You can't just turn off being a Master no matter how much you want to. Why else do you think Shiloh picked up on your vibe? You can't help broadcasting your power, and she's not afraid of you."

"Yet." He destroyed the small hope that threatened to sprout. "The green ones always start out interested, but a little bondage and spanking are typically all they want. Anything heavier sends them running for the hills. I can't do the light stuff anymore and pretend that's enough. I just can't. I need..."

He jerked his ponytail tight enough his eyes watered. He relished the small pain. It sharpened him, woke him up, made him feel alive and in control. He needed pain, and if he couldn't give it to somebody else, then he'd at least give it to himself.

"In her storyboards, did that whip in your hand look like a toy? What about those stripes on her back? She knows, V. She's offering you a blatant invitation to try her out under the guise of this show. This is your chance to approach her in a safe, controlled environment."

"If she freaks out, the show is ruined and the season goes down the shitter."

"We can do nothing and the season still goes down the

shitter. Or," Mal drawled out, "Master V and his new sub melt everyone's socks off and the show is the biggest hit in Dallas history."

He took a deep breath and let the big picture form in his mind. He'd always had the ability to scan the field of play in an instant, evaluate the defense and guess which receiver was most likely going to break free for the big play. His competitive senses vibrated with excitement. Win it all and go home with the trophy, or lose and cry in the mud, at least he'd never been afraid to play the game.

He'd been *The* Victor, the leader who took his team to victory, no matter the cost.

This was the biggest game he'd ever played in his life. This game was for his heart, and he always played to win. If Shiloh Holmes had wanted the Master's attention, she had him brutally focused. *On her.*

"Well then. I guess we have ourselves a new show."

Victor schooled his face back to the stern CEO mask, took his seat and nodded to Mal at the door. She opened it and gestured for Shiloh to return to the room, then took her seat across the table from him.

Head high, eyes bright, Shiloh stood at the front of the room, her nerves betrayed only by the tight clenching of her hands together at her waist. She wasn't afraid but excited, her eyes sparkling with energy. She might be a submissive in the bedroom, but she displayed no cowering wallflower tendencies, even though she stood before the two most powerful executives of the company whom she knew were both Dominants.

Victor tried to remember her exact age from her file, but when he'd first met her, he'd been too entranced by her personality. She was older than he'd first thought, closer to thirty than twenty, not so much younger than him that he'd feel like a dirty old pervert.

Is she experienced—or is she going to need slow, careful hand-holding?

He glanced at the storyboard with the woman wrapped around the Master's legs, her back striped red from his attentions. No, she wasn't going to need hand-holding. She just needed a strong, skilled hand when it came to the whip, or in his case, the crop.

He shifted slightly, working down the desire threatening to burst free. "Why don't you tell us what you envision for the pilot?"

He'd thought it impossible for her to light up any more, but she flashed a bright smile, her eyes as warm as molten chocolate, and turned to her storyboards.

"Typically, a reality show begins with tryouts." She shuffled forward a board that showed three Dominants seated at a table with a hopeful contestant standing before them. This time, the bottom was a man with spiky red hair and slim shoulders and hips who looked exactly like Andy, Mal's current live-in submissive, dressed in normal street clothes. "People who can't carry a note in a bucket try out for *American Idol*; people who have two left feet try out for *So You Think You Can Dance*; so we need a few people who absolutely freak out or become hysterical when the judges begin their evaluation. Tryouts are all about the drama."

"So we should test them in some way," Mal said, her voice huskier than usual.

Victor hid a smile. Even a simple storyboard image of her boyfriend affected her. He watched Shiloh and noted the tiny quirk of her mouth. She'd noticed too, and was pleased by the Mistress's reaction. More, he guessed Shiloh had deliberately started with Andy's image to ensure Mal was interested. *Just as she deliberately challenged me to win the title of the Master.*

"Absolutely," Shiloh continued. "It can be something small or more meaningful. An order to remove an item of clothing or to serve one of the judges in some small way. We should show both sides: rude, desperate bottoms who cling and make nuisances of themselves, as well as the polite, trained ones who know exactly what to do when approaching a Dominant for the first time, trying to garner interest on the scene."

Shiloh pulled another board forward. In this one, a contestant sat in a comfortable chair with another woman. The contestant wore a simple white shift and corset, while the other lady was dressed in a vintage—but not riding—gown. They were faceless behind elaborate masks.

"We need a host for the show whose main job is to interview the contestants and talk the audience through the judges' expectations. This scene should highlight the importance of the questionnaire about what the sub wants to do, is willing to try, and the absolutely-do-not-want-to-do list. Since our underlying concern is education, we should also touch on the contestant's medical history and make it very clear that the scene should always be safe, sane and consensual. To keep it interesting, we should highlight the emotions, making it arousing or even comedic, depending on the final contestants. The host should be unafraid to touch on the emotional or sensitive topics but still have a great sense of humor."

"I think Georgia would be perfect for this," Mal said. "That would certainly take some of the sting out of losing her star role on *Internet Secrets*. Her Southern charm will appeal to the audience."

"Agreed." Victor had to admit he was impressed with the way Shiloh had managed to weave basic, solid good sense of the scene with interesting, dramatic show content. "One question, though. Why the Victorian wear?"

"I thought the corsets and strict morality of the era made a nice contrast to the openly sexual tone of the show." Shiloh gave a little shrug, her cheeks touched with an endearing blush. For the first time, her gaze slipped away, giving him the cue that she was personally affected by such clothing. "Plus we had all the costumes on hand thanks to the Victorian Country House Party spoof VCONN did three years ago."

"Creativity *and* frugality," he drawled out, letting his voice heat. "I like it. Plus, corsets are damned hot. Don't you agree, Mal?"

"Oh, absolutely," Mal purred out a laugh that had been known to send male submissives into a helpless squirming heap at her feet. "It might be fun to give it a modern twist, though, so it's not obvious that we're recycling old costumes. How about we mix in some steampunk elements? Something a bit futuristic with wings, goggles and weird machines. I bet Andy could concoct a fantastic steampunk contraption that will blow the subs' minds."

Smiling, Victor stood and reached out to take Shiloh's hand. "You've sold us, Ms. Holmes. Mal and I will co-produce the show, but I'd like for you to be the show runner."

Her eyes gleamed, shimmering with unshed tears. "Thank you so much, Mr. Connagher. It's an honor to work with you."

He didn't release her hand and she made no move to pull away. "Mal, get to work on the contracts for our in-house people. For sure, lock Georgia into the host position if she's interested. We need to be taping by the end of the week. Preferably tomorrow if we can swing the set. Make sure every single person down to the lowest gaffer on set signs the confidentiality agreement. I don't want a single word of this leaking before we're ready."

"I'm on it." Mal gave Shiloh a knowing smile and headed for the door. "Welcome to the team, Ms. Holmes."

"Just Shiloh, please," she said, smiling.

The door shut. Victor watched the emotions flaring in her eyes and across her face: pure, sunny excitement, lip-biting anticipation, growing warmth in her eyes the longer she stared back at him. Slowly, he tightened his fingers. Her breathing caught, quickened, and her eyes turned smoky and heavy-lidded without a single hint of fear.

"If I must be one of the judges competing for the title of Master, then you must be a," barely, he managed to avoid saying *my*, "submissive for the show."

She rolled her bottom lip between her teeth and it was all he could do not to lean down and place his own teeth on that tender flesh. "I hope it's not too presumptuous of me to admit that's exactly what I planned."

He squeezed harder, waiting for that little gasp of pain that said he'd gone far enough...so he could go just a little bit further. "There were easier ways to approach me than to devise an entire show to lure yourself into my clutches."

She laughed, a low groan that was music to his ears. God, it had been entirely too long since he'd worked a responsive sub over and enjoyed that symphony of pain and pleasure. "It wouldn't have been very professional of me to prance into your office stark naked."

"Not professional," he agreed, drawing her closer. "But a damned pretty sight. Are you going to be able to handle show runner duties as well as putting up with me on set?"

"Of course." She blinked away some of the haze darkening her eyes. "I've dreamed of nothing else for months. I can do it, Mr. Connagher."

He squeezed harder, his grip brutal, he knew, crushing her delicate hand in his big palm that could still throw a football in a perfect spiral at fifty yards. Greedy, starved, he felt as crazed as an addict who'd fallen off the wagon after years of abstinence.

She whimpered, a cry that sliced his heart into ribbons even while lighting a fire in his blood that wanted her writhing and screaming, begging him to stop.

It's better to know now, he tried to console himself, waiting for her to jerk away. Maybe she'd slap him and stomp out of VCONN entirely. It would be the best for both of them. Certainly safer than putting herself into his hands, hoping he'd have the mercy and decency to control himself without committing serious harm.

Knees crumpling, she fell against him, sliding down his legs so she knelt at his feet. Rubbing her cheek against his stomach, she twisted her head so she could look up at him. "What may I call you, sir?"

Hauled up and tossed into a chair, Shiloh sat shaken and confused, staring at Mr. Connagher as he paced back and forth. She cradled her throbbing hand in her lap. Each thud of her heart spread that pain like a pulse through her body, melting her bones and priming her for his full attention.

What did I do wrong?

"When we're alone, then you can call me Victor, a mean sonofabitch, or a low-down dirty bastard, anything you want." He jerked to a halt and whirled to face her, his eyes blazing. "But we need to take care that you're alone with me as little as possible."

"I don't understand," she said carefully. "Are you not...available?"

He jerked his hair tighter, and she winced in sympathy for his tortured scalp. He must have one hell of a headache. "I'm so available I'm about to tear the seams in my pants."

Studying his hair kept her gaze from wandering lower to see just how *available* he might be. He hadn't made any outright claims on her, so she didn't feel like she had the right to ogle him. Yet.

"It will be safer for us both if we limit our interaction to the show, at least until I've been able to take some of the edge off."

He looked so glum, that she started to rise so she could wrap her arms around him. Throwing up his hand to ward her off, he resumed his furious pacing while he slapped his right thigh. Her skin heated, tingling with longing. She wanted those slaps on her body, not his.

The longer he paced, the more he began to favor his left knee, until his limp was pronounced. Victor Connagher had been a college football star on the verge of the NFL when he'd blown his knee in a championship game. Pictures from his glory days were in the case downstairs. By all accounts, he would have been a star for any professional team.

Tears burned her eyes. Until now, she'd never seen him display any weakness, any hint that the old injury still pained him.

Finally he growled out, "I don't want to go too fast for you."

"Too fast?" She laughed, but it came out harsh to her ears. "I've been planning this show for months, hoping, praying you might..."

That you might need me as badly as I need you.

Although she'd often seen him around VCONN Tower, she didn't know how to approach him while at work. It was just too sleazy for her to come on to him as she'd joked. She'd even gone to a mixer hosted by the bondage club to get an introduction, but the frenzied feeding-ground atmosphere just wasn't her style. Besides, he hadn't even been there. During her research, she'd scanned Silken's current membership roster, but it hadn't included his name, which didn't really surprise her. Many prominent members would rather keep their names secret or at least low key, which was one of the reasons she'd devised a show where everyone could wear masks.

Fantasizing about him had only made her attraction worse. Nothing could touch the aching black hole that expanded day by day deep in her belly. Nothing but him. The pain in her hand only served to wake up that miserable, ravenous monster. She wanted him with that riding crop he'd mentioned in his hand, wicked and hard and wild. After he'd put that image in her mind, nothing else would do.

"How else was I supposed to introduce myself as an interested submissive? A f—" self-censoring in mid-word, she changed to, "freaking letter?"

He gripped her chin and tilted her face back up to him. A smile softened his face, but not his grip. "I'd much rather have this show than a letter. I'm pleased, Shiloh, more than I can say." Shadowed desire flickered in his eyes despite his encouragement and his fingers dug into her cheeks. Even in trying to comfort her, he wasn't—couldn't be—gentle. "I am available, I promise you, and so attracted that I don't trust myself right now. It's been a long time since I did a scene, and I never..."

His jaws worked back and forth as though it took all his concentration to soften his grip on her face. Sighing, he released her and turned away. "I don't want to seriously hurt you."

Incredulous, she stared at him, her mind whirling in a frenzy.

Victor Connagher, the fiercest, most incredible Master she'd ever hoped to meet in her life...was afraid.

Chapter Three

"Um, you do know that I would love for you to hurt me, right?"

Victor sucked in his breath and demanded his body remain calm and controlled like the Dominant he was, not a rampant horny puppy.

"Do you want proof?"

"Absolutely not." Her voice was so sultry he was afraid the windows of the conference room might fog over. Just the thought of sliding his hand beneath her proper business skirt to see how wet she was made him shudder. Maybe he'd strip those dampened panties off and slip them into his pocket. Then he'd make her walk around the set bare, needy, ready for him...

He deliberately shifted his weight to his bad knee, enduring the ache until his mind cleared.

"I would if you told me to," she said in a solemn, gentle voice that made his blood pump harder. "Just tell me what you want, and I'll do it without question."

"What I want," he growled out, turning to face her with his most intimidating glare, "is for you to quit playing with me."

He cursed his poor word choice as soon as they left his lips.

Laughing softly, she stood and began to gather up her presentation. "I haven't even begun playing with you yet."

Damn it all to hell, she gave him her back. To him! Uncaring, unafraid, with a little flirty glance over her shoulder, she walked toward the door with her storyboards tucked under her arm.

He pounced, seized her in unforgiving hands, and slammed her against the wall. He pinned her with his body, using every inch of his taller, stronger, muscled frame to punish her for such audacity, grinding her against the wall. Storyboards tumbled to the floor.

And the little saucy wench arched into him with a welcoming sigh.

Dropping his forehead against hers, he sucked in a breath and held it for a count of ten, tightening the reins of his control. "Save it for the show or I'm going to drag you off to my dungeon and torture you to my heart's content."

"Promises, promises."

He couldn't help but laugh then. God, her spirit was unflappable. "You don't know what kind of player I am. I'm on the edge, baby, and as heavy as you can take it. And then, since I'm a selfish, cruel bastard, I'm going to take you even further." He swallowed hard and forced the words out. "I want to hurt you real bad."

"Good," she purred.

"Damn it, don't you know the difference between sensual pain and downright injured? Give me some space and time to—"

"Yes, sir."

He pulled back enough to look into her eyes. Had he been away from serious play for so long that he'd forgotten the most basic elements of a scene? Of course she'd rather have his orders. "On the show, I'm Master V." She nodded, staring at him intently. "*Your* Master."

Her body sagged against him and she buried her face against his neck. "Thank you, sir."

"Off the show, I'm Victor, your boss and the producer of our show. No playing, no taunting, all business."

"And after the show?"

Reluctantly, he backed away, keeping his hands on her until he was sure she was steady on her feet. She looked up at him with such hope and longing in her eyes that his throat closed and for a moment, he couldn't breathe. It'd been so long since a woman had looked at him like that, as though he were her entire world. As though she'd die if she failed to please him.

"If I haven't scared you away yet," he replied, his voice gruff with emotion, "then, God help you, you're mine."

Bending down to pick up her scattered boards, she flashed a smile that melted his heart. The curve of her slim spine and the rounded swell of her buttocks outlined by her skirt made his hand clench in longing for his crop. "I don't scare easily, Mr. Connagher."

"You don't know me yet, Ms. Holmes. Now make your escape before I change my mind."

"If nothing else, you've certainly given me incentive to make sure we're taping as soon as possible. Don't be surprised if you get a call to begin this afternoon."

"Tomorrow is soon enough for taping. Use Mal to help you get the resources you need, and if either of you have problems, call me. A few scenes at Silken will be fine, but see if Mal can get creative with a set here. I'd prefer to spend as little time at the club as possible."

"All right. Anything else?"

"Stop by this evening around seven o'clock and fill me in on where everything is. I live here in the penthouse, and I'll tell

Léon to let you in."

He could see the conflicting thoughts flickering in her eyes: a rush of raw lust that she might get him alone in his home warred against uncertainty about another man. He didn't fault her for being wary—she couldn't possibly know his sexual preferences. Something he hoped to correct very, very soon. "Léon is my personal assistant and chef. He's a friend and employee, nothing more."

"Sorry, I don't have any right to question you."

"Yes, you do. I have no intention of sharing you, Shiloh, not with another man, not with another Dominant, no one. I warned you I was a selfish bastard."

Relaxing, she laughed. "That kind of selfishness I approve of."

She paused at the door, her teasing laughter fading to something much more serious. In a slow, sensuous perusal, she ran her gaze over him. He could feel the passing of her chocolate eyes like a flaming physical touch, lingering on his throat, shoulders, biceps, and hands. He knew exactly what she was doing: assessing the strength of his arm, his ability to deliver a blow exactly where he wanted it, and the formidable might of his will. He squared his shoulders, widening his stance and shifting his weight back on his heels so the heavy bulge in his pants was prominent and obvious.

With her eyes locked on his groin, she asked in a husky voice, "What if I don't win top sub for you?"

"You will, or I'm no Master."

She jerked her gaze up to his face, her eyes smoldering, her lips as soft and full as though she'd been kissed thoroughly—or had put her mouth to good use. "To the Victor belong the spoils."

Chapter Four

Do you know what it's like to be a young, attractive, single woman who walks into a BDSM club looking for a new male Dominant? It reminds me of those shark specials on channels like Animal Planet where the scientists toss bloody, chunky soup into the ocean and the water simply roils with the Great White's feeding frenzy.

I guess some women think that kind of attention is flattering, but there are too many weirdos in this world for me to risk it. Of course, there's that little quirk of mine I mentioned that makes my situation even more complicated. I want a man to hurt me, sure—but I also want to walk away.

So I can ask him to do it again.

People never understand how a seemingly normal woman could be so fucked up. How can I possibly explain this need hiding inside me? It's like a massive beast curled up in the pit of my stomach. Day by day, it sinks its claws deeper into my spine, twisting and burning hotter, more desperate.

I need a man who's not afraid of that need. He needs to stand toe-to-toe with this horrible starved creature and beat it into submission. Take everything I've got and demand even more. Wring every emotion, hatred and rage, fear and need, and yes, love, until finally the relief is complete and utter surrender takes me.

I look at Master V and I see His strength and incredible body, and yes, I feel pure physical attraction. I want Him. Badly.

But I also see the strength in His arms, His wide shoulders, His large hands, and all I can think about is what it would be like to have that strength turned against me.

Could He whip me into surrender? For once in my life, could He force me into complete submission? My body says yes every single time I look at Him.

Yes!

Please, Master V. Use Your whip, Your flail, whatever Your weapon of choice may be, and conquer me. Force me into submission, and I'll be Yours forevermore.

At first glance, Silken looked like a normal dance club, especially in daylight hours. But then Shiloh started to note the mirrors on the ceilings and the small alcoves tucked in the shadows. Heavy velvet curtains could be dropped down for privacy, or left wide open for the voyeuristic patrons. In each alcove, a large black-and-white picture hung on the wall, all depicting a common bondage or torture scene. Her co-worker was in many of them.

Mal photographed beautifully, her high cheekbones and large eyes a striking combination with her voluptuous figure. In one picture, her black hair had been pulled back tightly, accentuating her long, graceful neck and the sharp planes of her face. Her eyes screamed at the camera, wild and ferocious and hungry, magnificent with her booted foot propped on a kneeling sub's back.

The first time Shiloh had come to the club, she'd scanned

each picture, hoping against hope to find Victor Connagher's distinctive face, but if he'd ever participated in the club, she hadn't found any proof. Although she'd never seen the rooms upstairs or the basement, the club boasted a full-fledged dungeon containing every sort of torture device, spanking bench, or even a plain old bed, outfitted, of course, with chains.

Mal led the way toward the office off the bar. "I've known the owner, Ryan, for a long time. I bet he jumped at the chance to get some publicity for his club."

"He was very cooperative when I spoke to him."

"Did you meet his wife?"

"Kimberly, right? She was in both of my meetings with him."

"What'd you think of her?"

Shiloh studied the other woman, trying to decide how honest she ought to be. Mal was one of Victor's best friends and most trusted partners at VCONN. She certainly didn't want to get a reputation of lying to his friends and associates, and Mal must have some sort of agenda behind such a question.

Lowering her voice, Shiloh replied, "Beautiful woman, but she seemed...fragile, like a delicate china angel. Her husband obviously dotes on her."

Mal nodded. "She wanted someone to treasure her, to take care of her every need. I always thought she was too weak and timid for Victor, but they were engaged for a few months."

Shiloh felt like someone had just slammed a sledgehammer against her skull. Unbidden, she pictured Kimberly standing beside Victor, her hand on his arm, his ring on her finger. They would have made a beautiful couple with Victor's tall, dark good looks and her slender, ethereal grace.

He'd given her a fucking engagement ring. Had he given her

his collar too?

Ruefully, Mal patted Shiloh on the back. "Sorry, but I thought you should know before you come to any sort of understanding with V. If you ever figure out what he saw in her, fill me in, because for the life of me, I never got it."

Shiloh ground her teeth together and thought really hard about marching back into VCONN and punching the smug bastard square on the nose. He had to have known she'd end up coming over to Silken today, and he'd never once thought to warn her about his past relationship. Okay, so that was pretty immature. She knew she had no claim on him. *Yet.* But knowing he'd been engaged to this woman put her in an entirely different and highly uncomfortable light. "Are my eyes green right now?"

Mal laughed and gave her an admiring smile. "Why yes they are, girlfriend, and your fingernails are positively claws. Do you want me to handle this?"

"No." She took a deep breath, held it until her chest hurt, and then let it out in a slow, controlled exhale. "For all I know, this is one of his tests."

"I'd certainly do something low and dirty like that," Mal admitted, "but not V. He's not into mind games. Honestly, he probably thought nothing of it, because she doesn't mean anything to him any longer. He might be too proud to admit it to you up front, but Kimberly broke up with him. I doubt he could have gone through with the wedding, but I know he took it hard when she dumped him."

Shiloh's mouth fell open and she laughed more easily. "Thanks, Ms. Kannes, seriously. I'm not jealous at all now, not after hearing about such blatant stupidity."

"Call me Mal. Everyone does."

Ryan came down the stairs with a huge grin on his face, his

wife behind him. "Mal! I haven't seen you in ages!"

They made the casual small talk of acquaintances that hadn't seen each other in quite some time as they settled into comfortable chairs in the office. To avoid glaring too hard at Victor's old girlfriend, Shiloh looked about the large room. They sat in a cozy conversational area with a large stone fireplace dominating the wall. On the opposite side of the room was the true office area, complete with desk, bookshelves, and filing cabinets.

Along with a massive picture of Master V.

He wore jeans with the pant legs tucked into his trademark boots and a simple light-colored shirt unbuttoned to his waist so it hung open, baring the bulge of his pectorals sprinkled with dark hair. Long sleeves were rolled up to his elbows, giving her a good look at his muscled forearms. Even from ten feet away, she could see the lines of tendons and veins beneath his skin, the promise of strength and skill with the long crop in his right hand. Oh, God, his hands, those broad palms, long, graceful fingers, explosive power in every inch—they drew her eyes like magnets.

He stood with his right foot up in a chair, his right elbow braced on his knee, the crop held casually—but prominently— in his hand. He wore a black hat with a silver band. An old-fashioned gun belt rode low on his hips with ornate pistols holstered on each side. In his left hand, he held a coiled lasso. He was prepared to wrestle a steer into submission, hang a horse rustler...or whip a sub within an inch of her life.

Dark hollows beneath his eyes carved out the harsh planes of his face, giving him a wicked, grim look that made her tummy quiver. His eyes burned with hunger, an unquenchable need that would never be satisfied. That look promised harsh punishment, no tenderness, no softness whatsoever.

Why did I ever picture him dressed as an English lord?

If she'd seen this photograph before devising the show, she would have done the whole damned thing as a Western so he could keep his boots.

"Ah, you've noticed our most prized possession," Ryan said. "Isn't it fantastic?"

Not trusting herself to speak, Shiloh nodded. She couldn't tear her gaze away from that picture. Her heart raced, her throat tight with tears. That look on his face made her want to throw herself at his feet and beg. Not for him to stop, not for mercy, but to use that vicious crop on her until that hunger blazing in his eyes was finally satisfied.

"Without V's help, I wouldn't have been able to open Silken, let alone keep it open all these years. He used his resources at VCONN to give us good press and educate the general public. He hosted company parties here and made sure he recommended us when anyone contacted him with questions."

"We owe him a lot," Kimberly said in a bedroom-soft voice that jerked Shiloh's head around. Ryan took his wife's hand and kissed the back of her knuckles. "If there's anything we can do to help with this new show, we want to do it. Gladly."

Mal gave Shiloh a searching gaze, asking one more time if she wanted her to take over. She shook her head slightly and forced a smile as she pulled out the storyboards for *America's Next Top sub.* "We're going to do a mock reality show, and we're under a severe time crunch. We need to be taping tomorrow, so we don't have time for extensive casting. If you can recommend some skilled practitioners who'd be willing to help us out under such tight dates, we'll be grateful.

"We're looking for submissives who fit a certain stereotype. It can be their true personalities, or an act, we don't care, as long as it's believable. You're familiar with the tone and quality of VCONN programming, so you know we're going to make the show as sexy as possible while remaining tasteful."

She showed them a storyboard with an aloof Dominant and a clinging, crying young woman on her knees. "The first one we need is a contestant who may be submissive but doesn't know or simply doesn't follow the correct way to express interest in a Dominant. They're the ones who make a general nuisance of themselves, can't accept no, and try to insinuate themselves into a group or party with an invitation."

"Ruby," Ryan and Kimberly both said at the same time. They looked at each other and laughed. Ryan continued, "She'd be perfect for it, and she has gorgeous flaming hair. She'd look great on TV and I'm pretty sure she'd leap at the chance."

Mal groaned out a laugh. "I knew you'd throw her into the mix. She even came on to me the last time I made an appearance here. You're right, though, she'll look fabulous on TV."

"Great." Shiloh pulled out the next storyboard. This one showed a man with his hands fisted at his sides and a scowl on his face. He hovered between a proud stance and softened knees, as though he wanted to kneel but couldn't quite bring himself to do it. "We'd like another submissive, male or female but I think a male would be more believable, who fails the most basic submissive tasks. Wounded pride, ego, or maybe he wants to play but just doesn't know how. Maybe he's not quite dominant enough to be a fierce player, but he's not submissive either."

"Honey, that sounds like you to a T," Kimberly said.

Surprised, Shiloh watched the woman's husband, but he wasn't insulted. Laughing good-naturedly, he dropped his arm around Kimberly's shoulders and gave her a squeeze.

"I love the scene, obviously, or I wouldn't own this club, but

I'm far from a formidable Dominant. I could easily play a man who was desperate to join the scene, but just didn't have what it takes to be a submissive."

"You're Dominant enough for me," his wife whispered, dropping her head to his shoulder.

It was touchingly sweet—and sickeningly irritating at the same time. Shiloh averted her gaze. How had that woman ever looked into Victor's smoldering eyes, felt the crippling power in his big hands, and ever thought she belonged with him?

"Who's next?" Mal asked in a sharp, impatient voice.

Grateful for the prodding, Shiloh brought out the last storyboard. "We need a submissive who's well trained and knowledgeable. She knows her limits and is solid in her ability to stop the scene when the play is getting too heavy. This sub needs to be able to participate in several shows, but when it comes down to the final competition, she must bow out. The level of punishment at this point of the competition will just be too much for her."

"And that sounds like you to a T," Ryan said to his wife.

"I would love to be on the show with you," Kimberly cooed in that sweet fragile voice. "We'll have so much fun!"

An avalanche crashed through Shiloh, stifling her. The last thing she wanted was Victor's old girlfriend on her show. Ironically, Kimberly was right. She'd be absolutely perfect for the part.

"That's a horrible idea," Mal retorted. "Victor is playing the Master of the show."

Kimberly blanched—or at least Shiloh thought she paled a little. It was hard to tell with her porcelain complexion. "Then it's even more appropriate that I fail to win the show."

"Why would you even think he'd want you anywhere near

his set?"

"I owe him." Kimberly bowed her head, her lips quivering. Tears dripped on her hand clasped in her husband's. "He's too much the gentleman to be offended, and I can help. You need me."

Fighting to keep her face smooth, Shiloh rubbed her palms on her skirt. Her stomach roiled. She'd planned this show every waking moment, and then dreamed about it every single night. Not once had she ever imagined having Victor's ex-fiancée competing for his affections. How would he feel to see her again?

If both his past and his hopeful future girlfriends were kneeling before him, who would he choose?

Mal said something about getting Victor's approval first, with polite goodbyes and excitement from club's owners at the thought of being on the show. Numbly, Shiloh shook the couple's hands, unable to stop comparing herself to the other woman.

Her competition. Literally.

Mal was blind if she couldn't see why Victor had wanted the elegant, fragile woman. With her pale, translucent skin, delicate bone structure and willowy figure, he would have been badly tempted to try and break her. A harsh word would make her beauty crumple like a trampled flower; his crop would mar her perfect skin.

She was just too fragile for a man like him to resist.

Shiloh had never had a poor body image or lacked for self-confidence, but standing face to face with Kimberly, she knew she was the woman's opposite in many ways. If Victor had once planned to marry this woman, how could he ever feel the same way about her?

Victor broke the water's surface and settled in for a long swim, but his mind was occupied elsewhere.

On Shiloh.

He'd already worked out on the weights, pushing harder than his physical therapist liked, but he needed to wear himself out, even if his knee hurt like a bitch later. If he wasn't handicapped by his knee, then he'd be out pounding the pavement for miles, or better yet, letting a defensive end pound him into the turf. Swimming in his infinity pool was about all the aerobic activity he could manage and still walk unassisted the next day.

His cell phone began ringing. With a frustrated sigh, he levered himself out of the pool. He couldn't concentrate anyway. If it were a work call, he'd ignore it, but his brother—

"Conn! I haven't talked to you in ages."

"What's up, big brother?"

"Nothing much." Victor tried to laugh, but it sounded forced to his ears. "Working non-stop as usual since the fall season is just around the corner."

"No, I'm serious," Conn said, concern echoing in his voice. "Is something wrong?"

"Why do you ask?"

"Miss Belle insisted that you needed me to call, now, before I even got home. I'm driving up and down the hills so might lose you."

Miss Belle was their eccentric—some may say crazy—grandmother who insisted that she could talk to ghosts, or at least their dead grandfather.

"I'm fine, really," Victor replied, shaking his head. He'd never been able to get anything past Miss Belle—even though she now lived six hundred miles away. God help him if Mama got wind of anything unusual; she could be knocking on his door in thirty minutes.

"Miss Belle said that if you didn't want to talk to me, she'd be calling Mama next."

"Can't I meet someone without my entire family sticking their noses in my business?" Setting his phone to speaker so he could scowl at his brother, Victor toweled off. There'd be no more swimming today. "Next Vicki will just happen to stop by too."

"So you met someone. That's wonderful." Silence stretched out for several seconds. "Isn't it?"

"Yes and no." Victor blew out his breath, trying to find the way to get some of the turmoil off his chest. "Do you remember when you visited a certain club with me?"

"Ah, I certainly do remember. You and your friend Mal taught me everything I know there. Did you meet her at Silken?"

"No, but she knows, Conn. She knows what I am."

"So what's the problem?"

Victor sat down on the bench and stared down at the phone in his hand. Absently, he rubbed his bad knee, stretching his leg out before him to take some of the pressure off the strained tendons that never seemed to heal completely. "Mama said you're dating someone. That it's serious."

"If you can keep a secret, I'll admit that we're engaged, although I don't plan to announce it formally until everyone comes up for Thanksgiving. You are coming, aren't you?"

"Congratulations! Yeah, I'll keep it secret, but you know I'm tempted to tell Mama just so she'll get off my back about grandbabies. I can't wait to meet your girlfriend, but I'll have to see how the season is going before I can commit." Victor sighed and leaned his head back against the wall. "Does your fiancée know what you are?"

"Of course. She's my old student I told you about. I finally found her again. It took us a while to work through all our issues, but we're happy, V, in large part thanks to you. If you and Mal hadn't taught me so much, I might have..."

Victor heard the lump in his brother's throat. "You might have hurt her."

His brother made a low sound of regret.

"That's the difference between you and me, bro." He tried to keep his voice light despite the heaviness pressing on his chest. "You're reluctant to hurt the woman you love. Me, I can't wait. And that's why I've got a problem."

"Hold on a minute. I'm going to pull off the freeway. This talk is too serious for me to concentrate on driving."

Victor waited, contemplating just hanging up. His little brother might be Dominant, but he didn't have the same kind of single-minded aggression. If someone Victor wanted to talk to hung up on him, he wouldn't call back; he'd be sitting in their living room before they got home. Even if Conn did leave him alone, Miss Belle would certainly uphold her threat, and hands down, he'd rather talk to his brother than his mother about sadomasochism.

"Still there?"

Mouth quirked, he replied, "Yep."

"I was afraid you'd hang up on me."

"I thought about it."

His brother laughed, but then turned serious. "I have to admit that I don't get the pain aspect. I mean, I know it hurts when I spank Rae, but I don't start out with the intention of causing pain. I don't *try* to hurt her, and by the time it does start to hurt, she's feeling too good to care."

Victor caught himself nodding even though his brother couldn't see him. "You're both into sensual spanking. You don't spank her to hurt her; you spank to get her off and you work off some of your aggression in the process."

"If I ever hurt her, I mean, really hurt her..." Conn growled out a curse beneath his breath. "It'd tear me up inside."

"It tears me up too," Victor admitted softly, remembering the suffocating guilt he'd felt when he'd frightened Kimberly so badly that she dumped him. "I don't want to like it, but I do. Nothing gets me off like pain, even if I feel bad about it later."

"Pain you feel, or someone else?"

"Both. I like the feel of pain myself—it makes me appreciate what I'm doing for my partner. I know exactly what it feels like. I used the crop on myself long before I ever thought to use it on someone else."

"I thought you were a sadist," Conn said carefully.

"I am. I like to think of myself as a connoisseur of pain. I just like pain, even my own."

"If your new girlfriend likes pain..."

"She does."

"Then...are you worried you'll go too far?"

Victor closed his eyes. "I know I will. I can't help but go too far."

"You've been with subs before. I saw you do a scene at Silken and you were completely in control. Your partner was happy as far as I could see."

"She was," Victor agreed, shame churning in his stomach. That woman had been Kimberly. He'd worked so very hard at controlling himself for her, denying that darkness that

49

threatened to bubble up every single time he stepped into a scene. She didn't want the Master in him, let alone his crop. "But I wasn't."

"It looked to me like you were having a good time."

Victor ground out a harsh laugh. "That's because I'm a damned good actor." He pulled the ponytail holder out and rubbed his hand through his wet hair. He'd had his hair pulled back so long that his scalp was tender. "That was kindergarten shit for me. It wasn't serious. It sure as hell didn't get me off."

Not until he'd gone home and jacked off while hitting his thighs so hard with his crop that he'd been bruised the next day. He hadn't had a choice. The only way he could come to Kimberly and love her the way she wanted was if he punished himself first.

"Sorry if this is too personal, but can you get off without pain?"

"Sure. It's just not as good. It hasn't been good in a long, long time."

"The first time Rae and I were finally together, I was damned close to losing control, but I made it through by the skin of my teeth. After that, I trusted myself more."

"I'm not worried about losing my control during sex. Not exactly." Victor kneaded his scalp. The soreness didn't do much for his erection that hadn't faded since Shiloh's presentation. "It's the scene where I'll go too far."

"So don't do a scene with her, not until you can control it."

Victor shook his head. "Won't help, bro. I've already established what I want from her, and it's not just sex. She's not a submissive who's going to be happy with a little light bondage or pleasant sex, not for long, and neither am I. Pain *is* sex for us, the best kind of all, and I'm afraid..."

He closed his eyes and forced himself to admit the truth. "If it's just me, I can control myself, but she's not just a submissive. She's a masochist, and she's far from afraid of me, which is dangerous. She's going to push and taunt me into crossing the line, and I've barely even touched her. She'll let me go too far."

"If she knows how to stop you..."

"She'll know how to tell me to stop, definitely. But I'm afraid she won't. She wants me to hurt her as badly as I want to hurt her. I tried to scare her today and she laughed and deliberately antagonized me. What if I can't control us both? What if I get lost in the pain and take her too far? Once it's done, what kind of damage will I have caused her? Will she hate me, then? God, Conn, I don't want to seriously hurt her!"

"'Tragedy delights by affording a shadow of the pleasure that exists in pain.'"

"Don't quote poetry at me," Victor groaned. "You know I never understand it."

"You'll understand this one: 'Ah, me! Alas, pain, pain ever, forever!'"

Yeah, he certainly did. Pain was always with him, and something he couldn't help but seek. "What happened to us, Conn? I mean, seriously, I'm more messed up than you, but neither of us is exactly normal."

"I don't know, V. I wish I could help more than just listen to you."

"Miss Belle was right to have you call me, but don't tell her so. It helped just to talk about it."

"Do you think we got these urges from her? Or maybe—"

Victor let out a laughing groan. "Don't even go there. I can't even begin to wonder if Mama or Daddy gave us these needs.

Are you trying to give me nightmares?"

"So what are you going to do?"

"Hell if I know." Victor sighed. "What makes this all even more hilarious is both Shiloh and I are going to be doing a reality BDSM show for VCONN's new season."

His brother blew out his breath in a low whistle. "You're coming out of the closet, so to speak?"

He hadn't thought of that. How many Dallas citizens would recognize him? "We'll be wearing masks and costumes."

"You know Mama wouldn't miss a single show from your station, right?"

Great, that was exactly what he wanted to hear. Not only did he have to worry about protecting Shiloh from himself, but now he'd have to deal with his mother's fury if she witnessed him seriously hurting a woman. It'd been one thing to know he ran a sexy cable show; how would she feel to know he was *participating?* As the Master?

"I didn't think about that," he admitted. "I guess I should warn her."

"Too busy thinking about getting into your new woman's pants, huh," Conn joked.

But Victor didn't laugh as they said goodbye. He'd been too busy thinking about how long she'd go before giving her safeword and fleeing him for good.

Chapter Five

Freshly showered, Victor limped back to the poolside bench to fetch his phone. He was going to have to ice his knee tonight if he had any hope of skipping the brace for tomorrow's taping, assuming Shiloh and Mal had made enough progress. He checked his watch. He ought to know within the next hour how the day had gone.

His phone rang, and his stomach tightened with the irrational fear that it might be Shiloh calling to say she'd changed her mind. That she didn't want to see him at all, let alone risk coming into his home. Stupid, he knew, because he'd been too careless to make sure she had his personal number so she could reach him. He'd told her to call if she had problems, but like an arrogant ass, hadn't provided her with his line.

"Hey, Mal. How'd the day go?"

"We made amazing progress. Shiloh's a fireball of boundless energy, and she had most of the details already thought out. She even has sketches for the hosted segments, including interview questions, which Georgia is eating up. It was just a matter of making a few final decisions now that Shiloh has our backing to proceed. You've made quite an acquisition in her, V, for yourself and VCONN."

He knew Mal too well not to recognize the tightness in her voice. "But?"

。

"You should have warned her about Kimberly before we went to Silken."

He ran his hand through his damp hair and muttered a curse. "You're right. I never thought about it. How'd that go over?"

"Shiloh handled herself with class," Mal admitted. "But there's been a development that affects the show, and I'm not sure what you'll think about it." She hesitated, and Victor bit back the urge to reach through the phone and throttle her. "Kimberly wants a role on the show as a contestant."

Silently, he let possible outcomes play through his mind. He didn't care one way or the other. After two years and the hope he'd found in Shiloh, he didn't give a damn whether he saw Kimberly again, married or not. But how would Shiloh feel to have his ex on *her* show, competing for his affections? "This is a mess."

"You're going to have to be very careful. On the surface, Shiloh is unsinkable and as gracious as a lady, but I saw the turmoil and doubt on her face when she looked at Kimberly. She sees her as competition, your not-too-distant past, and how can she possibly measure up?"

"Shiloh is night and day different from her."

"Exactly," Mal said. "So if you wanted to marry Kimberly, how can you possibly have serious affections for Shiloh?"

"Fuck."

"That's exactly what she's going to think. That you only want her for the scene and what she can give you."

"What can I do to make sure she knows I'm serious?"

Mal snorted. "You're asking me? I don't have any patience for hysterics and drama that some women seem to relish. Shiloh may be different, but I never understood why you wanted Kimberly, so I honestly can't tell what you think about this new girl."

What did he feel for Shiloh? Temptation, certainly, and hope that she might not be afraid of his darker sides, but he hadn't allowed himself to think beyond the possible scene they might play. Despite the initial attraction months ago, he'd only let himself contemplate claiming her today. He'd refused to even let the thought enter his mind, because once he decided that he wanted her, he'd be driven to win her at any cost by his competitive nature and his own damned pride.

Deep down, he knew he'd spoken the truth when he'd told her she was his after the show, assuming she hadn't bailed on him. It was too late for Shiloh to back out now; the Master had his entire will focused on her.

"I might have given Kimberly a ring, but I never gave her my heart. I couldn't risk letting her in that far without her seeing all my darkest most horrible secrets at the same time. She never knew the monstrosity I carry in me, Mal. I pretended for her."

"Why?" The shocked softness in his friend's voice told him she was bewildered. "Why her?"

His chest felt heavy and constricted. "I wanted to try and be the kind of man she wanted. Someone safer, gentler, kinder. I thought it would make me a better man to control and eliminate my darker urges. But I was wrong, so wrong. I'm worse now than I ever thought I could be. I want..." He growled out a curse and swiped his hand through his hair, deliberately tugging it hard. "The things I want to do... Shiloh ought to run like hell."

The door slammed behind him. He whirled around, forgetting about his bad knee. Pain shot up his thigh and the knee gave, throwing him off balance.

Shiloh glared at him, her mouth tight with fury, her

55

shoulders stiff. She marched close and shoved him hard enough in the chest that he collapsed to the bench behind him. "You're an incredible man, Victor Connagher, and you're sure as hell not getting rid of me that easily."

Shiloh didn't stop to think about what she was doing. While he was off balance—mentally and physically—she knelt and pulled his foot into her lap so she could exam his knee. He only wore a pair of black sport shorts and his hair was still wet. Shirtless, hair loose about his shoulders, and his muscular body practically bare, he didn't seem as intimidating...just drop dead gorgeous.

It was much easier to concentrate on the surgical scars than soak in his bare chest. Gently, she probed his knee with her fingers, noting the swelling and soreness each time he tensed. She risked a glance up at his face.

A muscle ticked in his jaw. "Mal, I'll talk to you later." He hung up and set the phone on the bench beside him.

Before he could interrogate her, she asked in her most professional voice, "ACL and MCL tears, right? How many surgeries did you have?"

"Two, with a third on the horizon if things don't improve."

She wrapped her hands around his upper thigh and firmly drew his leg through her fingers, over his knee and down his calf.

On a low groan, he dropped his head back against the wall.

"Too much?"

"Hell, no. I can stand it harder if your hands are up to it."

She repeated the long strokes, concentrating on the deep tissues above and below his knee to work out all the knots that had built up over time. *Think of him as a patient, not as a man you've dreamed about for months.*

After a good fifteen minutes, he asked, "Where did you learn how to do this?"

His voice sounded thick and mellow, his muscles melting beneath her hands. What she wouldn't give to give him a full body massage. "I took a sports injury class at a highly recommended massage school."

"My knee has never hurt this good before. You've got magic hands, baby. I don't remember anything on your resume about certification."

She felt her cheeks heating, so she concentrated on her work. "I never worked as a massage therapist. Just a hobby, I guess."

He leaned forward and grabbed her chin, tilting her face up to his. His fingers were gentler than when he'd touched earlier. Even his eyes were softer, and hot enough to melt her into a puddle. "You took that class for me."

"A hunch," she admitted. "If you lie down I can do a better job."

He studied her for long seconds while her heart lodged somewhere in her throat. With a wide, startling smile, he set his phone on the floor and stretched out on the bench, shifting to get his long frame comfortable. She didn't fail to note that he kept the towel he'd used on his hair strategically placed across his lap. "Well, then, I'd better think real hard about the best way to thank you."

Swallowing the lump in her throat, she stood and moved to the foot of the bench. "Getting my hands on your body is reward enough, sir."

"V," he replied in an easy voice. "Or Victor, I don't care which. I might be a Master, but I really don't care for all the formalities. I'm not interested in a slave relationship."

With firm, deep strokes, she rubbed her thumbs down the top of his knee to the back on both sides, using cross friction against those sore tendons. "What are you interested in?"

"You, whatever that means."

Ducking her head a little, she concentrated on his knee. After meeting his ex-girlfriend, she had her doubts.

As though he read her mind, he said, "I apologize for not telling you about Kimberly. She means nothing to me."

She worked her hands up higher, kneading his quadriceps. "She wants to be on the show with us, along with Ryan."

"I couldn't care less. If you don't want her there, tell them both to forget it with my blessing."

"Why me?" She bit her lip and flicked her gaze up to his face to check his reaction. He had closed his eyes and his mouth was soft, his lips barely parted. She'd never seen his face so fully relaxed before. He could almost be asleep. *Good, maybe he didn't hear my insecurities blurted out like a teenager.*

"Did you see my picture at Silken?"

She shuddered at the memory. Not asleep, then. "Yes."

"I should have demanded they give it to me instead of letting them keep it in their office like some sort of holy display." He blew out a disgusted breath that made her lips twitch. "Which Victor was in that picture: the CEO of a sexy cable channel or the sadist?"

His thigh was heavily muscled from the years of physical therapy he'd invested to rehabilitate his knee. Dark hair sprinkled across his skin, matching the thin line of hair that led up his ridged abs to the darker patch on his chest. She licked her lips and thought about pressing her face between his pectorals. Would he allow her to breathe in his scent and rub her face on him? "You were all Master V."

Softly, he whispered, "What did you see in my eyes?"

She clenched her thighs, trying to calm the need burning through her body. She ached, desire humming in her so loudly she was surprised he didn't hear it like a siren call luring a ship to its doom. "Hunger."

"That's why you're here with me now. Ryan and Kimberly think that picture is just a sexy photograph done as an old-time Western. They don't see the real me in that picture." He paused, waiting until she looked back into his face. His eyes bored into her. Even lying flat on his back with a swelling knee, he possessed the commanding presence of an emperor. "They don't see the man who aches to use that crop on you until you beg me to stop."

"I won't," she choked.

His eyes narrowed and he tensed beneath her hands. His breathing rasped loud in the silence. Blistering coldness flooded over her, along with a sense of his withdrawal.

Quickly, she explained. "I won't beg you to stop."

The tension bled out of him, but he closed his eyes, and his voice was gruff. "You will, baby. You will."

"You don't know me well enough to make that judgment." Leaving his knee, she moved to the opposite end of the bench. She sank trembling fingers into his hair, seeking his scalp. He made a low purring sound and tipped his head back into her caress, so she swirled her fingertips along his temples. She drew her fingers back in firm strokes, as though she could pull out every last bit of tension and pain that lingered in his magnificent body.

"Every time I go home, Mama threatens to have my brother hogtie me so they can give me a proper hair cut."

"Don't you dare," she growled out.

He arched a brow at her but didn't open his eyes. Afraid she'd overstepped her bounds with him, she changed the subject. "You should ice your knee tonight to keep the swelling down."

"Hand me my cell. I'm lucky I didn't fumble it when you tackled me."

Blushing furiously, she handed him his phone. "I did not tackle you. I pushed you to get you off your knee. You'd already strained it enough."

He leaned up on his right elbow and typed in a text message. "I'll ask Léon to bring up some ice packs and bandages, if you'll be so kind as to help me wrap it."

"Of course."

He set the phone aside and stretched back out on the bench. His eyes smoldered, but a faint smile played about his lips. "Now you have approximately five minutes to kiss me before we're interrupted. This is your chance to taste me without me trying to bite a hunk out of you."

If she thought it amusingly fair to keep him off balance, then the least he could do was surprise her in return. Unbelievably mellow after her strong, deep massage, he hadn't felt this relaxed in years.

Shiloh Holmes had accomplished the unthinkable: she'd wrung lighthearted teasing out of the sadist.

She eased around to his side and trailed her fingers across his face to lightly stroke his lips. "Maybe I'd like for you to bite a hunk out of me."

"Promises, promises." He quirked his lips into a wide smile the likes of which his face hadn't seen in years. He'd forgotten how much fun sensual teasing could be. He was usually too aggressive to even think about a joke. "Time's a ticking. Léon is most efficient in his duties. The only thing that may delay him is whatever concoction he has bubbling on the stove for dinner."

She leaned down to hover over his mouth. Her warm breath sighed out against his face. He smelled the sweetness of her scent, no heavy cloying perfume but a hint of sage that made her smell as green and fresh as the outdoors. Their lips just inches apart, his heartbeat thudding like a bass drum inside his skull, he waited for her to close the distance.

He knew she expected the Master to reach out and take control. He was curious how she'd react if he made her close the distance between them. Would she suspect him of some trick? Or would she be too shy to take what she wanted from him? Too hesitant because of her natural submissive inclinations?

She locked her mouth over his. She inhaled his lips, her hunger as great as his own. He felt her desperation, the endless ache swelling within her. Emptiness, loneliness, and yes, the deep, raw need to wallow in pain, to let its molten heat blaze through her.

A need that would lure him to the dark side.

He opened his lips and she surged deeper, groaning against him. Her thumbs tugged at the corners of his mouth, urging him wider, trying to prod him into taking control. Fisting his hands, he fought down the urge to do exactly that. He wanted to give her a nice, safe kiss while he was able. They'd never have another first kiss, and he didn't want her memory of it to be pain and darkness.

Sucking on her tongue, he drew her deeper. God, he could drink her down, drain her dry, and still crave her taste. He raked his teeth over her tongue, reminding her of his threat, and it took every ounce of control not to sink his teeth harder

61

and punish that tongue for daring to invade his mouth—so he could suck her deep again.

Sliding her hands down his neck, she gripped his shoulders and pulled him closer, silently begging him. She made a little sound that sounded suspiciously like a sob. And then her teeth sank into his bottom lip.

Growling, he clamped his left hand on the back of her neck and jerked her down so she fell against his chest. Yet she didn't let go of his lip. Splinters of pain fired through his veins, pumping blood harder, faster through his body. She knew exactly what she was doing to him, too, because she gnawed harder, rubbing her teeth against that tender flesh while her tongue teased from the other side.

He shifted his head and used his tongue to trap her upper lip in his own teeth. Now they were like two snarling dogs fighting over a bone, only to realize they'd latched on to each other instead. He rolled to his side and jerked her down, forcing her head lower than his, her body low to the floor.

A knock at the door froze him. Breathing hard, he released her lip, and she let him pull his free. He tucked her face up against his shoulder, holding her close. "Thank you, Léon. Just leave them there. Shiloh will assist me."

"Certainly, sir. Dinner is ready when you are. I need to leave by seven thirty tonight."

"Understood." Disappointment warred with relief. He'd planned to ask Shiloh to stay and eat with him, but if his assistant needed to leave, he didn't want her here alone with him tonight. Not after that kiss. He didn't trust himself not to chain her to his bed, the world—his cable channel's season and her show—be damned. He joked to keep the mood light, "Watch out Dallas, Léon has a hot date."

"I wish." His assistant laughed, his voice fading as he

returned down the hallway. "Feel free to send a hot young man my way!"

She clutched Victor's neck, shaking against him. "I'm sorry," she whispered. "I know you meant to be careful, but it wasn't enough."

"You're not going to make this easy on me, are you?"

She shook her head and burrowed lower, sliding her nose deeper into his chest. "I can't."

He laughed ruefully and sat up, drawing her with him. "I wouldn't want you nearly as badly if you did. You're quite the challenge, Shiloh."

Sitting back on her heels, she regarded him intently. "Is that a good or bad thing?"

He smiled again to let her know how very much he appreciated the challenge. "It's a terrible thing for my sanity. It's going to give me very little sleep, lots of cold showers and long, exhausting workouts. Otherwise, it's an excellent thing. I wouldn't have you any other way."

She dipped her head and peeked up through her lashes in a very submissive posture that still managed to convey audacity. Evidently she'd seen through his thin attempt to politely screen his erection because she eyed the towel with interest. "I could help you with some of that."

Groaning, he averted his gaze from her tempting mouth. "Gather up the supplies outside the door so I can get you out of here intact."

Immediately she stood, went to the door and returned with a stack of ice packs and elastic bandages. "And then what?"

"You're going to ice my knee and allow Léon to escort you to your car or whatever transportation you use to go home." She opened her mouth to object so he gave her the Master's look that silenced her. "If he could stay awhile, I'd let him act as your chaperone so we could eat together, if you were free."

Her tongue flickered up to touch her upper lip that still bore red indentations from his teeth. "For you, I'm free."

Chapter Six

Call me crazy, but I think I finally have an answer to my dilemma.

After months of my boss treating me exactly like every other employee, I've decided that I need a way to approach Him and express my interest—without Him calling security or having me committed to the insane asylum.

Finally, it came to me. Without giving away too many details—after all, this is an anonymous blog—His company deals with television shows. So...what better way to approach Him than through television?

Think about it. Reality shows are all the rage. Why not have a BDSM reality show? Surely in this big wide sexy world there are other similar shows so I could still hide behind my anonymity. It would be the perfect way for me to say, "Are you interested in playing with me?" Of course, I'm hoping He'll say something like, "That depends, baby, on how hard you like to be whipped."

I don't know if He uses a whip or a crop, chains or latex or other dungeon shit. I don't care. I'll try anything He's into. This show would give me the perfect opportunity to not only advance my career but approach Him in a safe and non-threatening way.

There's just one problem: I'll have to devise a show that He'll actually want to participate in. No, that He feels compelled to win, and I intend to be His prize. After all, I'm V's Gift.

On their brand-new set for *America's Next Top sub,* Shiloh had never felt sexier. The outfit wasn't exactly historically accurate, but from the darkness burning in Victor's eyes, she'd accomplished her purpose. She wore a short muslin shift barely more than a tank top with a white corset over the top, lifting her breasts and pushing out her booty. To make the scene as sexy as possible, she wore white lacy high-cut panties that disappeared beneath the corset. Without any skirt or petticoat, her ass was barely covered enough for cable TV.

Delicate pink stockings encased her legs to mid-thigh, tied with white ribbons, and she wore heels elaborately covered in sparkling crystals. Sweeping white feathers formed her mask, swan wings to frame her face and conceal most of her hair. She didn't think her own mother would recognize her.

Victor wore tall gleaming riding boots and black jodhpurs that concealed the protective brace on his knee. His shirt was plain white linen, loose and open at the neck with billowing sleeves tied at his wrists. She hadn't dared ask, but he'd opted to leave his hair loose, glossy black and tousled about his shoulders. Black wings covered his face except for his mouth and eyes, sweeping tight to his head and down to his shoulders.

Of course, the Master's look was completed with his crop.

She stared at that crop and her stomach turned to cold, hard lead, even while a rush of liquid warmth flooded her veins.

"What's the set up?"

The distant, reserved tone of his voice helped her focus on the show, and not the Master. "This is the opening shot that will play at the beginning of every single episode. We didn't want to associate our show with Silken every single time, so we chose a basic neutral shot here."

"Good." He gave a curt nod, barely meeting her gaze. "Where do you want me?"

It felt strange to give *him* orders, but he'd made her show runner. This was her idea. She wanted it to succeed on multiple levels, not the least of which was her career.

She directed him to sit in a simple wooden chair with the crop in his lap. "The scene opens with you cleaning and preparing your equipment. The light will be focused on you, casting the rest of the area in shadows. When you're satisfied with the gleam on the leather, stand up. The lighting will slowly brighten to show me at your feet, waiting for your attention. We need a few minutes of Master/slave play." Her throat tightened, making her voice gruff. "Your choice."

"Excellent." He smiled, and it was far from the mellow ease last night as he groaned beneath her hands. This man couldn't wait to bring that crop down on her flesh. "I always thought we should eroticize the cleaning and care of our tools."

Mal snorted. "I think your tool gets plenty of care, V."

Chuckling, he spread his knees wider and picked up an oiled cloth. "Not yet."

He met Shiloh's gaze and her nerves zinged as though she'd been electrocuted. He pointed the crop at the floor to his right. He didn't have to say a word. From the tip of his smallest finger to the soles of his boots, the Master commanded her to kneel at his feet.

That quickly, she slipped fully into the role of his submissive. The show meant nothing. This was their first scene, her chance to give him exactly what she'd been dreaming about. As gracefully as possible, she knelt where indicated and pressed her face to the floor six inches from his boot.

Cameras rolled, lights blazed into his eyes, but Victor had one thought only: the woman waiting at his feet. He'd never enacted a scene for one of his shows before, although he was no stranger to performances. Sometimes it was hard to ignore the crowd; other times, the audience fed off the scene's energy and multiplied it, frenzied as though they could feel his lust and power. That's exactly what he wanted this scene, this entire show, to bring to Dallas.

With slow, deliberate intent, he stroked the cloth over the leather, lovingly caring for the weapon that could bring so much pain. He'd carried it for years, and although he'd tried various other tools of the trade, he always came back to this crop. It fit his hand perfectly, flexible but stout with a wide tip that combined to make a wickedly vicious *whoosh.*

"That's good, V," Mal called from the side. "It looks like you're making love to the crop. Prepare for the lights to brighten."

He gripped the crop in both hands at either end and stood, letting the camera focus solely on the Master's weapon. He wanted the viewers to lean toward the screen, breathless with anticipation about what he intended to do with it. Light flooded the floor, and someone off to the left gasped, even though they'd all known Shiloh was there.

He raised both arms overhead and turned his body slightly, giving his profile to the camera. Poised, he waited what seemed like an eternity, and then he jerked his left hand down toward his thigh. The crop whistled through the air. Leather smacked against his thigh in a satisfying crack. The stinging cut of the crop heightened his senses, focusing his mind and body on one thing only.

Dominion.

Shiloh's hand crept out to touch his boot, begging for the next blow.

He waited until she wrapped her hand around his ankle, and then he reached down, seized a handful of her hair at her nape, and hauled her up to her knees. Bending down, he glared into her eyes. "Why are you here?"

He chose to say those words because that's how he always opened a serious scene, and while this scene might be taped for a show, it was real, serious, heavy shit, to him at least. He wanted to make sure she had committed to it as much as he did. Unscripted, her responses would reveal her true intentions. What did she expect to get out of a scene with him?

"To submit to you, Master."

He straightened slightly, widening his stance, his left arm held out and back to the side, keeping the crop visible for the shot. "What may I do to you?"

"Anything you want, Master."

Ah, yes, she couldn't have given him a more perfect response.

He drew her closer, deliberately lifting her face toward his crotch. She made it look pretty instead of vulgar, her back arched, her gorgeous ass lifted to tempt him. Even if they were alone, he wouldn't have let her touch him. He merely wanted to torment her with what she couldn't have. Not until she'd satisfied his other urges.

Her lips were soft, open, her face hauntingly beautiful with the stark lights blaring down on her and feathers curled about her cheeks. She resisted his grip, pulling her own hair in order to lean closer, trying to get her mouth on him.

The lights dimmed, breaking the moment.

"Hold on just a minute," Mal said to him, then louder,

"Bring up the backlights. This next part we want only their silhouette. Okay, good. When you're ready, V."

"Ready for what?" Someone asked in a loud whisper.

He whipped the crop over his head and brought it crashing down on Shiloh's buttocks.

She let out a low, throaty moan that tore at his control. He knew the blistering fire that had exploded on her skin, the deep throbbing pain despite his care to control his arm. He never started as heavy as he would end. Even as a sadist, he took care to begin with a sensual blow and not a cutting one backed by his full strength.

However, after denying his darker urges for so long, he was close to coming from that blissful sound of her cry alone. To reward her, he let her rub her face high on his thigh.

Shocked silence hung over the set for several long seconds, and then his crew erupted into cheers.

"Bring the lights up," Mal said. "Let's see the whole thing from the beginning and see if we need to re-shoot."

Victor clenched his fist on the crop, grinding his teeth with fury. He did not want to stop. He did not want to sit down and watch the tape. He wanted—

Shiloh stared up at him, her eyes wide, glistening with tears, pleading. "Please."

Don't stop.

People talked and moved about the room, babbling words she couldn't seem to understand. The lights hurt her eyes. Her ass stung, the sweet burn of his single blow a mere taste to whet her appetite for more.

But I'm not getting more any time soon.

The thought made her eyes fill up with tears.

Victor loosened his grip on her hair and straightened, breaking the fierce bond he'd formed as the Master. Cut free so suddenly, she wavered, dizzy and sick, too deep into the mental zone he'd already created.

She ducked her head and gripped her thighs, digging her fingers into her flesh as hard as possible. She couldn't function for the show like this.

"Come here, baby." Hands gentler than she expected, he gripped her upper arms and pulled her up to sit in his lap. She clung to him, hiding her face against his throat. His skin was hot, his pulse thudding as hard as hers. "Give us a minute. She's all right," he said to someone. "She's still deep in the scene. It's hard to shift her mind back from the game and focus on business."

His left hand stroked her buttock, unerringly locating the stripe he'd given her. His fingers danced along the welt and her breath caught in her throat.

"What's your safeword, Shiloh? That might help bring you back to the present a little quicker."

"I don't know," she mumbled against his neck.

His fingers stilled, and she felt his sudden intensity in the tensing of his thighs beneath her. "How can you not have a safeword?"

Talking helped return her clarity. She sat up straighter, curious to see why he was so annoyed—or alarmed?—by her answer. "I haven't needed one."

His eyes were smoldering midnight coals in the harsh planes of his face. "You've done a scene before. You're too well trained and comfortable with play to not know the basics. Every sub has a safeword, Shiloh, or they shouldn't play. No Dominant who gives a damn would even consider playing with a sub who couldn't tell them when to stop."

"I know the rules," she replied defensively, stiffening her shoulders. "I was taught by a very caring Dominant years ago."

"And he never gave you a word to stop him?" Victor made a disgusted sound. "Then he wasn't so very caring."

Her cheeks heated. She glanced about to ensure most of the crew had stepped aside, giving them a little space as he'd requested. "I had a word with him but we never used it. There was no need. Besides, I don't want to use the same word with you. It'd be like wearing another woman's engagement ring."

A muscle ticked in his jaw at her deliberate jibe. "Why did you have no need for the most basic beginning rule of the scene?"

"He couldn't hurt me enough to make me use it."

His fingers prodded the sore spot on her buttock. "Couldn't, or wouldn't?"

"Couldn't. That's why we mutually agreed to part ways. Besides, he was much older. We never planned to have a future together. He was merely teaching me what I needed to know to protect myself."

Victor muttered beneath his breath. "From men like me."

She jerked away and stood up, staring him in the eye proudly. "I don't need protection from you, Victor Connagher. I can take whatever you dish out."

With menacing grace, he stood, towering over her with a fierce scowl on his face. "You *will* have a safeword."

"Fine," she snapped, whirling away only to jerk to a halt.

Sweet and pure like an angel, Kimberly stared, her perfect bow mouth falling open into a delicate O.

Tears clogged Shiloh's throat, but she kept her head high. If he wanted to hear her whining and crying out a safeword like the white flag of surrender, then maybe he really would prefer to have the fragile woman. She'd certainly beg and sob prettily.

Deliberately cocking her hips in a blatant dare, Shiloh paused and glanced back over her shoulder at him. She reached back to lightly stroke the fading welt he'd given her. Her eyes burned and her lips trembled, because the pain was already gone. His mark was fading, and now he wanted something that she feared she wouldn't be able to give.

With a little jerk of her chin, she marched off set. "My safeword is chutzpah."

Chapter Seven

Changing into her jeans, Shiloh struggled to regain her balance. Even though Victor was obviously interested, she hadn't expected it to be easy. No Master of his ilk would ever make it easy to win his heart.

She could scream and plead with the best of them once the whipping began. That she was begging for more, harder, faster...well, she'd have to see what he thought. As soon as she stepped out of the dressing room, however, her hard-won confidence was immediately rattled.

"Hi," Kimberly said in that sweet voice that grated on Shiloh's nerves. "Could we talk a moment?"

The last thing she wanted to do was talk to Victor's ex-fiancée, but her mother had raised her to be more than a bitch. Mostly. "Sure."

"When we talked yesterday at Silken, I had no idea that you were dating Victor."

"I'm not exactly dating him." Shiloh fought to keep her face smooth and not bare her teeth at the woman. "I didn't know you'd been engaged to him, either."

"That makes us even, then."

Barely, Shiloh bit back her frustration and jealousy. Hell no, that didn't make them even, not by a long shot. He'd planned to give her his *name.*

The woman stepped closer and lowered her voice. "We don't know each other yet, so I'm sorry to ask such a personal question, but I really need to know. May I?"

Whatever her past with Victor, Kimberly was polite and gracious. The least Shiloh could do was talk to her. Maybe she'd learn something that would help her figure out his hang-ups about her safeword. "As long as it stays between you and me."

Kimberly's eyes were big and dark in her creamy face, her voice serious. "When he used his crop just now, did it hurt?"

Shiloh shrugged. "Of course."

"And that didn't bother you?"

"I liked it."

Kimberly's lips curved into a startlingly beautiful smile. "I'm glad, then. I'm so happy for you."

Shiloh shut her mouth and tried not to gulp like a fish. "What?"

The other woman linked arms with her and laughed softly. "I felt horrible when I learned the truth." She lowered her voice, so Shiloh leaned closer, listening intently. "I had no idea he struggled to keep that side of him hidden from me, not until we were already engaged. I just couldn't take it, Shiloh. I couldn't take his crop." Her voice caught, breaking with emotion. "I hated the pain, but more, I hated failing him."

Shiloh wasn't surprised to see tears in the woman's eyes. What did surprise her was the compassion she felt. Her own lips wobbled in sympathy. She knew exactly how wretched it felt to fail to please the Master, especially when she wanted to so very badly. "You didn't do a scene with him beforehand?"

"Of course we did. Before we were a couple, I even saw him with other women. But he was always so calm and controlled.

Even when he did a heavier scene, I always assumed he was only acting out what the sub wanted. It never occurred to me that's what *he* wanted. What he needed. And I couldn't give him that. I know it hurt him when I broke up with him, but I couldn't have made him happy. Not like he deserved."

"You really did love him."

Wiping her tears away, Kimberly nodded and tried to laugh, but it came out more like a hiccupped sob. "I did. But he deserves more than a half-life with someone who can't meet his needs. He deserves you."

"Now that's got to be a sight that makes your blood run cold." Mal nodded her head toward the two women returning to the set. Shiloh walked arm in arm with his ex-fiancée and they had their heads very close together. "At least they're not clawing each other's eyes out."

It did indeed. Victor's heart weighed heavy as though the blood had pooled and frozen there, unable to flow. He could only imagine the horror stories Kimberly was sharing with her.

Watching Shiloh, he heard the madness whispering again in the back of his mind: *No safeword. She has no safeword. No limit. No need for protection and safety. Until me.*

He knew he should be worried, if not downright terrified, but lust had unfurled sharp claws deep in his stomach. He ached to test her. He burned to find her limit and stake his territory there as brutally as only a sadist could.

His fucked-up pride insisted that he find a way to force her into surrendering her safeword. *Only to me.*

He averted his gaze. "Shiloh wouldn't stoop to that."

"The hell she wouldn't." Mal arched a brow at him. "If she thought she could win you that way, she'd shred that woman

into ribbons. But if she thinks you'd rather have Kimberly..."
His friend shook her head as though she couldn't bring herself
to believe he'd be that stupid and blind. "Well, Shiloh certainly
has the class to walk away."

He gritted his teeth and fisted his hand tighter on his crop.
"I won't let her go."

"Does *she* know that?" Mal asked. "Because I didn't get the
impression she was too happy with you when she walked away
earlier."

He breathed in deeply and concentrated on relaxing each
muscle in his body until he stood loose and comfortable instead
of vibrating on the edge of violence. "She challenged me."

Laughing with not nearly enough sympathy in his opinion,
Mal took her seat at the end of the plain office table they'd set
up for judging. "The worst thing a sub can do is dangle a
challenge before a Dominant, let alone Master V."

The man on the opposite end of the table joined in the
amusement at his expense. "That's like waltzing into the bull's
pen and whacking him on the nose."

"I'm reminded why I never liked you much." Victor had to
take the middle chair, which only served to irritate him more.
"You're too dainty to be a Dominant."

Although Patrick was shorter than Mal, the female
submissives at Silken had always flocked to his Hollywood good
looks. They took one look at Victor with the crop in his
hand...and fled in the opposite direction.

"If you didn't snort fire, blast thunderbolts from your eyes
and trample anyone who even thinks about approaching you for
a scene, then maybe I wouldn't call you a bull."

"At least bulls are well hung."

"Now, now, we don't need to get into a measuring contest,"

Mal broke in. "We've got a show to tape."

Patrick slapped him on the back good-naturedly. Victor thought really hard about breaking his arm. "Let's get this show going. I could use another pony or two in my stable."

"You guys are off to a great start."

Mal's smirk sent Victor's suspicions to high alert. He glanced over at the cameras. Hell, red light. Tape was rolling. Grudgingly, he had to admit that was well done of her. The bantering between him and Patrick—half friendly, half serious—wouldn't have happened if they knew they were being filmed, and it was personal elements like that which would make or break the show.

"Let's see the first contestant before the Dominants begin pounding each other to relieve some of their aggression."

Two hours of head-bashing frustration and laugh-out-loud hilarity followed. Victor had no idea where Mal and Shiloh had scrounged up so many contestants. They covered the range of everything from "I want to be on TV—wait, what if Mom sees this?"—with which Victor certainly sympathized—to "Oh my God, this guy's crazy—call the police."

If the contestant had even a somewhat sane personality, the judges took turns giving them little commands. Patrick asked one woman to remove her panties. She did so...and tossed them in his face. He tilted his head back, dangling the scrap of silk from his nose. "She's a keeper."

Mal tried the same thing, only to have the male contestant moon the panel and stomp off set indignantly.

Victor had to admit that he hadn't had such fun in years. Dallas viewers were going to eat this up and beg for more. So far, they'd managed to include the best and worst of reality TV, yet Shiloh still managed to convey the more somber realities of alternative lifestyles.

A young man in his early twenties walked in and went to his knees before the table with no prompting from the judges. His identity was masked by a metal helmet that made him look like some kind of alien bug, emphasized by skintight lime green pants and matching shirt. Despite the contestant's costume, Victor had no trouble recognizing Brandon, VCONN's most talented computer effects programmer.

In her best Mistress voice, Mal asked, "Why do you want to be *America's Next Top sub*?"

"I've been trying to find a Master for years." Really getting into his part, Brandon wrung his hands with desperation and his eyes glistened in the stage lights. "I'm tired of hanging out in bars trying to find a man who knows exactly what I like. Without..." The young man bowed his head and sobbed loudly.

Victor didn't need him to complete his sentence. *Without injuring me.*

Gay male submissives abounded with few trained Dominants available to take care of them. All too often, they went home with someone a little too edgy without a steady Dominant's control, and they ended up hurt. Or dead.

Victor knew Brandon was gay, but he'd never seen him at Silken before he quit going. He hoped the young man was merely acting, because he hated to hear about this kind of story, especially from one of his employees.

"I'm sorry," Patrick said gently. "I'm not homosexual."

The young man peered up at Victor and gulped, his Adam's apple bobbing nervously.

"Nor I," he said, and before asked, "and no, we can't pretend just to help you get off. Domination and submission are sex for us."

Brandon's blush rushed down his neck, clearly visible despite the helmet mask covering his head. "I know, sir. That's why I need it." He looked to Mal and his shoulders slumped with defeat. "You neither I suppose."

"Next round, we'll have a homosexual Dominant," Victor promised, meeting Shiloh's gaze to make sure she heard. She gave him a little nod and jotted a note in her planner. "Try back then." He made a mental note to ask her and Mal privately if Brandon was a plant—or if he seriously needed help. Victor would make sure he got it.

The next contestant was Ryan. He stood before the judges, eyes lowered like a proper submissive, but any Mistress worth her salt would recognize the defiance in him. His shoulders were tight, and he kept wiping his palms on his pants. Mal asked him a few questions, and he kept licking his lips and tugging on his ear, both signs of nervousness. If a woman gave Victor those signals, she'd be a definite no, no matter how physically attractive he found her.

"Kneel," Mal ordered in a deceptively pleasant voice.

Ryan did so immediately and kept his gaze down, good, typical submissive behavior, but his shoulders were still too stiff.

Mal left her chair and walked around him in a circle, casually looking him over like he was a horse for sale at the fairgrounds. "On your face."

His shoulders vibrated briefly and then he leaned forward to do as she ordered. That slight hesitation was a failing grade. Victor would have struck him a sharp blow across the shoulders with the crop if this were his scene, and then walked off in disgust.

"Kiss my feet."

Ryan jerked his head forward and gave a quick peck to the toe of her Jimmy Choo's.

Turning away smoothly, Mal returned to her seat and

didn't spare him another glance. "No."

Ryan stumbled to his feet. "What? Why? What'd I do wrong?"

"Everything. I wouldn't let you rub my feet, let alone warm my bed." Mal planted both hands on the table and glared at the trembling man. "If a Mistress tells you to kiss her feet, you make love to her feet. You shine her shoes with your breath and wash them with your saliva. If she's barefoot, you lick each toe until she tells you to stop. You'd never survive as my submissive, and you're certainly not fit to be on this show."

Clenching his hands at his side, Ryan trembled, his face red but sincere. "Please, Mistress, let me try again. I can do better. I didn't know what you wanted. Train me! I'd be perfect! Give me another chance!"

With a small jerk of her head toward Victor, she silently asked him to make a statement. Letting his cruelest Master smile twist his mouth, he slammed the crop down on the table in a loud crash. The other man paled, gulped, and raced for the door.

Another contestant stepped forward, and his amusement at Ryan's retreat faded. Kimberly stood before the table, demure and pretty in a baby blue dress that displayed her figure to perfection.

Sitting back down, Mal gave him her sweetest—and most alarming, for anyone who truly knew her—smile. "This one's all yours, V."

Chapter Eight

From the sidelines, Shiloh willed herself to view the scene as the show runner and not as a competitor for Master V's affections. They needed a woman who was a terrific sub but had a very low tolerance for pain. Beautiful, graceful and well trained, Kimberly was perfect.

However, watching him rise from his chair and approach his ex-fiancée with that small smile flickering on his lips was like a knife in the heart.

"Why do you want to be on *America's Next Top sub*?"

Jealousy burned in Shiloh's gut. Had he ever used that silky voice for her? Even when he called her baby it came out with barbs and hooks to dig into her psyche.

"I want to serve," Kimberly whispered. God, she even made trembling look fantastic.

"Do you want to serve *me*?"

"If that is your will, sir."

He walked around her, lightly tapping the tip of his crop on his boot. Arching his brow, he released a pleased little sound at her rear view.

For the camera's sake, Shiloh retorted silently. *He's putting on a good show. Nothing else. Right?*

He sauntered back around to stand in front of Kimberly.

Leaning down, he whispered in her ear, but loudly enough for the cameras to pick it up. "I think you're afraid of me."

"A little," she replied in a tremulous voice.

Staring over her shoulder directly into Shiloh's eyes, he smirked. "More than a little, I'd say. I can hear your teeth chattering."

"I'm sorry, sir. I can't help it."

"I didn't say it was a problem." He straightened and winked at the camera. "I *like* my sub to be afraid of me and worry about what I might do with this crop. How hard will I strike? Where? For how long? Will my arm tire? Will my will fade? How long can you endure the pain simply because I want you to? Or will you crumple at the first blow and give me your safeword? You do have a safeword, right?"

Shiloh fisted her hands and clenched her jaws, fighting to remain calm and unmoved by his taunting. So much of what he was saying to Kimberly, he was also saying to her. Warning her.

"Yes, sir, of course."

"You're afraid of my crop." Lightly, he stroked the tip over Kimberly's bare arm, his voice gentle and sure. "You already hate it."

She flinched and hung her head. "Yes, sir."

"Good. You should always fear the Master." Victor returned to his seat. "You may remain until you fail me."

Keeping her head down and avoiding the camera, Kimberly rushed off the set. She saw Shiloh watching and hesitated. Her mascara had run in black pools down her lovely face. Her nose was red, her eyes accusing, *See what kind of man he is?* Averting her face, she pushed by the remaining contestants, bumping them out of her way to make her escape.

In that moment, Shiloh hated him, just a little.

He knew full well how much Kimberly had cared for him. She'd been shocked and scared when the darker side of the Master had been revealed after he'd taken such pains to conceal the sadist for so long. After their talk earlier, Shiloh couldn't help but like the woman, even though the thought of her with Victor—making love to him, his tenderness, his exquisite care not to alarm her for months—drove her insane with jealousy.

He hurt Kimberly deliberately, and not just for the sake of the show. Those harsh words from the man she'd once loved had devastated her gentle soul. She knew she'd failed him, and nothing hurt a submissive as much as disappointing her Dominant, especially when in a committed relationship.

He locked gazes with Shiloh again, his mouth still twisted with brutal intent. Shadows had swallowed his blue eyes, clouding them over like a thunderstorm. He stroked the crop, running his fingers over it lovingly, and she knew what he was thinking. Despite—or rather, because of—Kimberly's fear, he yearned to bring that leather down on her tender flesh just so she would scream out her safeword and quit.

Pitiless, he radiated his need to raze and ravage and punish.

He hurt her because he enjoyed it. And he's going to hurt me too.

Impatient, Victor checked his watch for the hundredth time. They'd been taping for hours with very few breaks. A thirty minute lunch of cold cuts ordered in from the deli down the street had come and gone ages ago. Sitting here watching Mal coo and torment her sub like she hadn't played with every single part of his body a thousand times and more made Victor want to throw up.

His frustration simmered hotter, flashing toward ignition.

Shiloh hadn't even looked at him for at least an hour. He knew, because he could sense her attention like a quarterback blitz from his blind side, and he hadn't felt that tingle since Kimberly had raced off the set in tears.

Damn it all to hell, what did Shiloh want from him? If he'd been nice to his ex-girlfriend, she would have been even more pissed at him. So he'd been mean, all sadist, getting a few digs in to help salve his wounded pride—*she* had dumped *him*, remember?—and now Shiloh refused to look at him.

At the last break, he'd jerked his hair back into a ponytail. He hadn't intended to leave it loose for so long anyway. When he'd seen that the morning's taping order listed a scene with just the two of them, he'd tried to send her a subtle message. Evidently a fucking waste of time.

God, he ached so badly he wanted to toss the table aside and beat the shit out of anybody who stood between him and Shiloh. Maybe he'd just throw her across the table and give her his crop for the camera. She wanted it. He knew she'd enjoyed the single stroke he'd given her this morning. *She* sure as hell wouldn't flinch away when he touched her with it. She'd arch her back and beg him for more.

Merciless hunger gnawed in the pit of his stomach until his fingers ached on the crop's handle and his breathing rasped too loud. "Enough," he broke in. "Tell him to stay or get the hell out of here, I don't care. How many more contestants remain?"

Mal managed to look a bit guilty as she returned to her seat. Andy swaggered off the set with a knowing little smirk that made Victor grind his teeth together. There was something about that young man that jarred his instincts. He definitely liked Mal's type of scene; he gleefully took whatever his Mistress saw fit to give him. But for a sub, he seemed to hold something back.

It wasn't his body. He displayed none of the hesitations that Ryan had so skillfully demonstrated as the prideful sub. Andy had secrets, and Victor was fairly certain that his friend was too besotted with her young man to care. Perhaps it was no coincidence that it had been Mal's show that was leaked to KDSX.

"Only one," Mal replied.

One. That meant Shiloh. He closed his eyes and pulled his hair tighter, giving himself a mental shake. *Control, V. You can do this without crossing the line. Remember the cameras. Remember the show. Focus on the end zone.*

Patrick stood. "I'll handle this one."

Victor's eyes flew open. He planted his palms on the table and started to rise. Fury pulsed in him, so ugly and vicious that he made himself stop. Sit down. Release his death grip on the crop.

Shiloh halted a few feet from the table and gave him a pleading, panicked look that made him feel a bit better. He managed to give her a little nod of encouragement, and then narrowed his gaze on the other Dominant.

Nobody was going to lay a finger on her. Nobody was going to hurt her. Nobody but him.

The Master had given her the nod. He wanted her to do this scene. Whatever that entailed.

She shouldn't feel betrayed. After all, Victor hadn't laid formal claim to her. She wasn't truly his sub. She wasn't really dating him. The most she could say was that she worked for his company, and now they were doing a reality show together.

Absently, she rubbed at her breastbone and tried to slow her frantic pulse.

"You don't look like top sub material to me." The Dominant named Patrick made the same lazy circle about her that they others had done around their interested subs. "Are you sure you're in the right place, honey?"

"If this is *America's Next Top sub*, then yes, I'm in the right place."

Patrick tsked and paused off to the side, gripping his chin in contemplation. His fingers were long and graceful, an artist's, or perhaps a pianist's. She couldn't see him lifting a weapon with any real force. "That's what I mean, honey. You don't have the right attitude. The other contestants have all been smart enough to say sir, ma'am, or even Master or Mistress. They've ducked their heads and shown the proper respect."

"I haven't agreed to play with any of you, so why should I kneel?" Shiloh kept her voice pleasant and made direct eye contact. "Until we come to some sort of agreement, I'm a person, not a submissive."

"Very good," Patrick purred, giving her an appreciative nod. "Smart and spirited, a formidable combination. The spirited fillies are always the most fun to break, wouldn't you agree, V?"

"Ponies aren't my kink, Pat."

Evidently Master V didn't need his crop to land a perfectly placed blow, because the other man's face reddened. "Oh, I don't know. I think this little filly would look quite fetching in a bridle. Would you like to play with me, honey? I'll teach you to whinny real pretty."

Shiloh didn't try to stop the laughter that burst out of her lips. "Um, no thanks. That's not my kink, neither."

Still and coiled like a poisonous viper, Patrick stared at her much too intently for her liking. "What is your kink?"

Stupid, she knew, to irritate a Dominant, especially on this show. She'd have to interact with him and Mal to succeed in the challenges, but she just couldn't help herself. "I don't feel inclined to share that information with you at this time."

"Would you be *inclined* to share with Master V?"

She couldn't help but look at Victor. He gripped his crop, his eyes heavy lidded and snapping with fire. Her knees went weak. "Yes."

She was too absorbed in staring at him to notice that Patrick had circled behind her, until he whispered in her ear. "So fierce. So mean and cruel and hard. Aren't you afraid of that crop, honey?"

Swallowing her saliva, she shook her head, not trusting her voice.

"Ah," Patrick breathed out, making her shudder. His breath on her made her skin crawl. "So pain is your kink. I neglected to tell you that I can do things with a long-tailed whip that my friend here can only dream about. Would you like me to bring out my favorite toy, honey?"

Before she'd met Victor, she might have been tempted. She didn't feel any attraction whatsoever when she looked at Patrick. He didn't turn her on. His whip might have...before she'd seen the crop in Victor's hand.

"My whip can kiss your body as gently as an angel's wings." Patrick leaned in and nibbled on her ear. "Or I can split your back wide open. How do you like it, honey?"

She jerked her head away but didn't back down or lower her gaze in surrender. She had nothing to fear from him. She owed him nothing. "Not interested. Sorry."

Laughing softly, Patrick bowed deeply to her. "Don't cry later and claim that I didn't try to save you." He returned to his seat, oblivious to the daggers stabbing out of the other Dominant's eyes. "Who do you want to play with, honey?"

"I want the Master," she rasped out, "with the riding crop."

"This ought to be good," Mal said with a laugh. "Test her thoroughly, V."

Focused entirely on Shiloh, Victor barely heard her. He controlled each movement, forcing himself to move with slow, deliberate care. He even managed a friendly pat to Patrick's back that didn't knock the man unconscious.

He halted in front of Shiloh and simply looked at her, unblinking and intent.

Bowing her head, she whispered, "Master."

"Do you want to play with *me*?"

"Very much, Master."

After endless hours of taping, this is what he'd been waiting for. He'd been waiting for this since yesterday when she'd first looked into his eyes and let him squeeze her hand until her knees gave out.

No. He'd been waiting for this moment his whole life.

He stepped off to her side, keeping the camera in sight. Landing a single, teasingly light tap to her outer thigh, he asked, "Are you sure?"

He was sure the camera had zoomed in to catch the moan that escaped her lips, the heaving of her breasts as she struggled to breathe. "Yes, Master, please!"

He flicked the crop out again. She sucked in her breath and quivered, but she didn't cry out. There was no need. Even Kimberly could have borne that much pain, if she wasn't so terrified of him.

"Are you into punishment?"

"No, sir."

That surprised him. "You haven't been a very naughty girl? You haven't had any dirty thoughts you want to be spanked for?"

"No, sir." Although she arched a brow back at him and gave him that saucy grin that made him want to crush her mouth beneath his. "I admit that I've certainly had dirty thoughts ever since I came onto this set, but would you rather play silly games to decide that I needed punishing? Or simply have your sub come on out and ask you for what she wanted?"

"That depends." He smiled, all punishing teeth and domination. "On what you want."

"I want you to whip me until you can't lift your arm."

Drums reverberated in his head. *The show. Make it hot for the show. Don't scare her away. Not yet.*

"As a sadist, I admit that I don't hear that request very often." Somehow, he managed to laugh instead of drag her upstairs to do exactly that. He assumed she'd come up with some pseudonym for the show to hide her identity. "What may I call you other than mine?"

"Gift."

"Gift," he drawled out thoughtfully. He stepped closer so they were face to face, well into her personal space. Reaching behind her, he gave her a harder blow to the back of her leg. "That's a nice name. Why do you think you should be V's Gift?"

She swayed slightly but didn't press closer or fall against him. "I can take whatever you give me, Master."

"Despite the generosity of your name, you've got this all wrong, Gift. You're not *taking* anything." He brought the crop down slightly harder, but if she enjoyed pain as much as she said, this was nothing but teasing for her. "You're going to *give* me everything."

Staring up into his eyes, she whispered fervently, "Take everything I've got, Master."

"Cut," Mal called out. "Whew, V, I was right about you two. I'm surprised you haven't melted the cameras yet."

Staring down into Shiloh's eyes, he fought for control. Her crisp, fresh scent of sage filled his nose, so much better than the cloyingly sweet powder scent that Kimberly wore. Shiloh's eyes were dilated and dark with arousal. Her breathing came in soft, frantic pants. Sweat dampened her upper lip, and it was all he could do not to lick and bite that lip as he'd done last night.

He dropped a hand to her waist to steady her, but stepped back out of her space. She took a deep breath and smiled tremulously, but she hadn't gone as deep as their first scene.

Because I gave her a sharper blow this morning.

God help him, she might really be a full-blown masochist, the rare breed of submissive who relished all the punishment a top could dish out. The kind of sub he could injure dreadfully and not realize it until later.

Shame pulsed in him, as dark and raw as the need to lay her down across his bed and use his crop on her until they both came. He buried that need, chaining away the beast that snarled and clawed, ravenous for her pain, her cries and the unmistakable sound of leather striking her lush body.

He turned away and slapped the CEO mask back onto his face. Another lock, another barrier to hide the wretched lust blazing inside him. "That's a wrap for taping today, but I want our editors burning the midnight oil and ready to show me the first cut for the premiere at eight o'clock tomorrow morning. Taping begins at nine."

Shiloh moved to exit with the rest of the crew, but he caught her arm and smiled as softly as he could manage, drawing her back to stand beside him. "Mal, can you join us for dinner? I'd like to talk through what the next episode will entail."

"For Léon's masterpieces, absolutely." Mal couldn't hide the incredulity flashing in her eyes. "I was going to be alone for dinner tonight anyway."

He knew his friend must be busting at the seams with questions. Sure, he hated the idea of company during his first semi-date with Shiloh off the set. However, he needed someone present to make sure he didn't do something unforgivable, both for her sake and the show's. If he damaged her too badly to continue taping, or frightened her so badly she quit, then VCONN's season would truly end up in the shitter.

He leaned down and brushed his mouth against her ear. "Are you free?"

"I already told you," she said in an even, flat voice. "For you, I'm free."

He regretted the disappointment flattening her mouth and dulling the fire in her eyes. Tightening his fingers on her arm, he tried to put some of that molten heat back into her gaze. "Then consider yourself claimed."

Her eyes narrowed. "Do I get to spend the night?"

A rush of lust hammered him to the ground and threatened to tear down every single control he'd managed to lock into place. "No," he growled out. "I'll drive you home."

Why did it sound like he was trying to convince himself?

Chapter Nine

Standing outside the penthouse entry, Shiloh thought really hard about turning around and heading back downstairs. Yesterday, Léon had directed her back down one level to the fitness area, so she hadn't glimpsed much of Victor's home. From the expensive, tasteful décor of VCONN Tower, she could only assume his private apartment would be as sumptuous as the man himself.

And here I am dressed in jeans and a T-shirt.

He wanted to see storyboards for tomorrow's taping, so she hadn't had time to run home and change into something less comfortable and sexier to tempt the Master. Why bother if they were going to have company and then he was going to drive her straight home? It wouldn't matter that she was exhausted, less than fresh and gritty-eyed from long hours at work.

Within seconds of ringing the doorbell, Léon welcomed her inside. "Come in, Ms. Holmes, welcome. It's so good to see you again."

After meeting him, she'd known her original assumption that he might have a sexual relationship with Victor was highly unlikely. Trim and wiry with a wide, easy smile, Léon might be gay, but he gave off a very obvious Dominant vibe to anyone used to paying attention. Nothing menacing like Victor, but Léon was definitely a man who would be in control of the relationship. "Thank you, Léon. Is Mr. Connagher home?"

"He's waiting for you with Ms. Kannes. Right this way."

The two biggest executives of the company were waiting for her. Not the Master and the Mistress. Nervous, she followed Léon down the hallway, running every detail of the show through her mind. However, the room where they waited was relaxed and comfortable. Victor lounged on red silk cushions at a low Japanese-style teak table with Mal across from him. The wine bottle had been open long enough for Mal to have a little extra smoke in her voice, while Victor...

Eyes blazing like molten sapphires, he reached up to lay claim to her arm and drew her down to sit beside him. "Thank you, Léon. Give us a half hour before serving. She needs to catch us up on what tomorrow holds."

With a knowing wink, the young man bowed and shut the door.

"What's your pleasure, red or white? Or Léon can bring you something from the bar."

Her pleasure would be red, all red, her ass on fire. Somehow she managed to say, "Whatever you're having," around the tightness in her throat.

A muscle ticked in Victor's cheek as though he'd heard her thoughts. He poured her a glass from the open bottle and then leaned back and dropped his arm around her.

His heat and scent enveloped her. He'd showered and changed, so unfair, and he smelled like soap and cotton hot from the dryer. Dressed in loose black drawstring pants and a matching tunic, he could almost be wearing pajamas. The Master almost managed to be as relaxed as he'd been after her massage last night.

"So are you heading down to Texas A&M for the big game this year?" Mal asked.

Casually, he rubbed the pads of his fingers over Shiloh's bare arm. "I doubt it. Mama's heading north for Thanksgiving this year with her mother, Miss Belle, to meet my little brother's new girlfriend. She's already nagging me to come with her." He brushed his mouth against her cheek and she could barely keep back the sigh that threatened to escape. "What are you doing for Thanksgiving?"

"My mom remarried and lives in California. She always invites me, and I always refuse to go."

Mal swirled her glass. "Family issues, or simply the long travel time?" Shiloh hesitated, and the other woman smiled apologetically. "Sorry, didn't mean to get too personal. Although Mama despises my choice in men and V bitches and moans about how much his Mama nags him to get married and churn out those grandbabies, we're both very close to our mothers. It saddens me when my friends are having family issues."

She might have only really known these two for a few days, but the demands of running the show and its intense subject matter made Shiloh feel like they had the beginnings of friendship. Real friendship—the kind where people talked about old hurts that shadowed the soul. "My Dad passed away about fifteen years ago and he left a huge void in Mom's life. She'd never lived on her own. She had no idea what their finances were like, how to pay bills, how much life insurance he had. Luckily Dad had seen to everything for her, but she just couldn't bear to be alone. She needed a man to take care of things for her, and for her to cook and coddle.

"Randall fits the bill and he's a nice enough guy. He has a huge extended family and she adores them all. I went out a few years ago and I didn't know anybody. I felt really uncomfortable, and ever since..." Shiloh's throat suddenly closed off. Horrified, she realized she'd almost told them her darkest secret, the thing she was most ashamed of.

95

The sadist in Victor perked up, hungry for pain and embarrassment, even if he hadn't caused it. He shifted beside her and tilted her face up to his with his right hand. He didn't have to order her to tell the rest; she couldn't refuse the intensity burning in his eyes.

"The mentor I mentioned was actually one of Mom's friends before she remarried. They'd had coffee a few times, but he was more interested in me." She forced out a laugh, trying to blow off the guilt churning in her stomach. She'd never forget the look on her mother's face when she'd stopped over unexpectedly and caught her daughter bent over her friend's lap while he used his belt on her ass. "Needless to say, Mom's never been real comfortable when I'm around Randall, just in case I have designs on him too. She'd rather come see me. At least that would give us the chance to do things just the two of us. If she ever comes."

Eyes softening, Victor pulled her closer so she nestled into his side. "Do you talk often?"

She pressed her face against his chest, breathed his scent, and some of the pain that had been lodged in her heart all these years fluttered away, disappearing as though he'd truly devoured that old shame. "Oh, every month or so, sure. We're not feuding or anything."

"Sometimes I wish Mama would get remarried and move a few hours—days—away," Victor said with a rueful laugh. "Maybe our mothers can all move out to California and leave us in peace. A phone call a month would be nice, wouldn't it? At least then I wouldn't have to worry about her watching our show this season."

"At least she's not threatening to disown you for dating outside your race." Mal reached across the table and clinked her glass with Victor's. "Besides, your Mama might like to see her baby boy stepping out in style with a crop in his hand. Maybe the apple didn't fall far from the tree."

"First my little brother and now you." He shuddered. "Why don't you show us those storyboards, Shiloh. I think I need the distraction." Automatically sliding into presentation mode, she started to stand, but he said quickly, "Nothing formal. Just tell us what you're thinking about for tomorrow's session."

She leaned back to retrieve the storyboards she'd propped against the wall. "In the morning, we'll be taping interviews, covering the basic preferences questionnaire and going over medical history and blood work. Meanwhile, you three Dominants can be preparing for the first challenge."

She propped the first storyboard on the table, angling it so both Victor and Mal could see it. "This first challenge will deal with the basics of bondage. Each of you will have a small cubicle set up where you can array bondage equipment that you prefer to use. Anything from simple clothesline to exotic custom-made chain jewelry—whatever you'd like to see and you think will make an impact on the show. Each one should be slightly different and unique according to the Master or Mistress's taste."

Mal made a disgusted sound. "So Patrick is going to drag out all his pony crap. Those fake tails give me the creeps."

Shiloh agreed wholeheartedly. "There are several possibilities for the challenge itself. You could tell us to fetch the cheapest at-home bondage equipment, or the most dangerous equipment for beginners. For the final stage, you should instruct us to find the one type of bond that you specifically wished to use. Of course, we could not easily know what that was unless you give deliberate cues."

"Or we could be very devious and not give any clues at all," Mal drawled. "I like it. Then we can reward—and punish—at

97

will."

"Exactly. You each will play with your contestants and choose one to eliminate. Who goes is up to you."

Victor's fingers had stilled on her arm. She felt his muscles tensing along her side, his arm tightening across her shoulders. Unaware of his growing tension, Mal continued to expound on the many ways she'd punish her contestants.

While the most important person at the table remained ominously silent.

Léon's food was as delicious as usual, sending Mal into joyous bliss. Victor thought that Shiloh enjoyed her food, but she didn't say much. She was too keyed in to his emotions.

He ached to have a long, open talk with her. He wanted to know her preferences, but more importantly, he needed to make sure she wasn't suppressing her own needs in deference to his. If she'd developed the first challenge with him in mind, then she'd be sorely disappointed.

"Well, the food was as fabulous as ever, but I'd best be getting on home." Mal swallowed the last bite and sighed happily. "I want to be back before Andy."

Victor took Shiloh's hand and helped her up from the table. She smiled her thanks but said nothing. Her reticence tightened his gut. He couldn't bear to lose her so quickly. "Where's he at tonight?"

"Guys' night out," Mal replied. "He meets his old college buddies once a week for poker and beer."

"Isn't he too old for that shit?"

Mal laughed. "Which is why he does it, so I can punish him for making me wait."

He walked them toward the front door, but Shiloh saw the

guest restroom in the hallway. "Excuse me a moment."

"See you tomorrow, Shiloh. I can't wait for another day of fun on tape!"

At the door, Mal leaned against the wall instead of grabbing her bag. Inwardly, he groaned. She wanted to talk. Great.

"I like her, V. She's perfect for you."

"I like her too." He tried to keep the intensity out of his voice, but his friend knew him too well. "Let's see how long I can go before scaring her away."

"You're not giving her enough credit. She's made of sterner stuff than Kimberly. She's not going to fold on you."

He dropped his gaze to his hands, so big and calloused, made to punish. "I know."

"You're worried about hurting her."

She paused, waiting for his response. Deliberately, he kept his gaze away from hers and let his silence say it all.

"Don't you feel how much she wants you to do exactly that?"

He fisted his hands, fighting to keep the need from roughening his voice. "Don't you feel how much *I* want her?" Barely, he kept back that he wanted to *hurt* her as much as he wanted her in his bed, but Mal knew the truth better than anybody.

"Hell, I'd have to be blind and dumb not to feel you two. You're both walking orgasms waiting to happen. The sexual tension is only going to worsen your Master instincts. Why don't you ease a little of that desire with her tonight?"

"It's not that easy. She wants the Master." Sighing, he pulled his hair tighter, letting the pain feed the need rising within him, buying him a little control. "I don't know that she wants the man."

"Are you crazy? Of course she wants the man. It's the man who makes the Master and vice versa. She wants you, V. She needs whatever you'll give her."

Kimberly had loved the man but feared the Master. What if the man didn't satisfy Shiloh at all? She might be so into the scene that she wasn't interested if he didn't have the crop in his hand, and right now, he was too raw and ragged to even think about bringing his weapon of choice into his bed.

"Do you want to play a few scenes with her? Have a good time and then go on your merry way? Or do you want a relationship?"

Shiloh blazed in the darkness of his mind like a supernova. If he had her to brighten up his life, heat up his bed, and smile that saucy little grin, he could die a very happy man. "I want it all. I want her."

"Not even you can be a Master one hundred percent of the time. You need down time to rest and restore, and she can help you fill that well. If you're empty and dead inside, you won't have anything to give her in the scene. Give her a chance to know and love the man. Or..." Mal paused, waiting for him to meet her gaze. Challenge sparked in her eyes. "You can hide. You can keep secrets like you did with Kimberly. How'd that work out for you?"

He ground his jaws and bit back the curse. "It sucked."

"Give Shiloh the crop for the show. You already know she'll love it." Mal gave him a hug and headed out the door. "Tonight, give her the man, and I think you'll find she loves him too."

Following the music, Shiloh found him in a large, darkly lit living room, flipping through stations on his Bose. A leather sectional was arranged before a massive flat-screen television on the wall above a gas fireplace, with more seating scattered throughout the room. He could invite his entire production team over to watch the big game.

"What's your pleasure?" He glanced over his shoulder, mouth quirked. "For dancing."

Suddenly as shy and awkward as a teenager on a first date, she listened to the different songs, even while it felt like she was sinking into quicksand. Here was another facet of Victor Connagher that she'd never seen before. It wasn't the CEO of VCONN who grimaced at rap and tipped an imaginary cowboy hat at the oldie but goody Johnny Cash song on the country station. Every little element of his personality that he let peek out only made her want him all the more.

When he flipped over to Golden Rock, she said, "There, that's good."

He walked toward her. "I agree."

Flickering firelight cast shadows across his face. Her tummy flipped and whirled as he took her into his arms. This certainly wasn't the Master gliding to the music, holding her safe and warm against his heart.

Or maybe it is, she thought, sighing as his fingers rubbed the nape of her neck. The strength in his hands was still there, and he used that controlled power with deliberate intent. His other palm spread heat through her shirt in the small of her back, his fingers wide, holding her close to his body.

"For the challenge tomorrow," he murmured against her cheek, "pick whatever you like. I don't care."

She tilted her face up and searched his eyes. "For the final 'Master's choice' bondage round?"

"I don't care," he repeated, his brow furrowed. "I'd rather see what kind of bondage you're into, all right?"

She wrapped her arms tighter around his neck and laid her

head against his chest. "Even if I pick one of Patrick's bridles?"

Victor blew out his breath loudly in a snort and shook himself in a very horse-like move. "I suppose I can teach you to whinny, but I refuse to get one of those butt-plug tails anywhere near you."

Laughing, she rubbed her face deeper into his shirt. Chest hair tickled her nose. Breathing his scent made her heart tremble in her chest, her breathing catch and hunger unfurl. Her amusement faded, leaving her near tears.

She'd dreamed of being in Victor's arms, but the reality couldn't compare with those foggy, nebulous longings. She'd never thought he would joke and laugh, or that he'd hold her like this, swaying gently to mellow rock music.

"You know how I said earlier that you weren't spending the night?"

She jerked her head back even while clutching him tighter about the neck. Her heart pounded so hard with hope that she swayed. "Yeah?"

"I was wondering..." He hesitated and his fingers tightened on her back, as though he was afraid she might bolt. "If I asked you as a man and not a Master, how would you feel about that?"

Confused, she searched his face, trying to figure out what he meant. Victor, the man, the Master, the CEO, he was all the same to her, facets of the man she ached to please. If he didn't want to play out a scene first, that was fine, as long as he was willing to take care of that need eventually. *Soon, please God, soon.*

"Or we can just save it all for the show." He shrugged nonchalantly, but his brow remained creased and it felt like his body heat doubled.

"I'm not afraid of the Master or his crop," she said slowly, noting the flicker of doubt in his eyes, the tightening of his mouth. "I'm not afraid of you."

"I know, but you haven't seen the reality, baby. You haven't seen me let all that darkness and ugliness come boiling out. I haven't played Master in too long, and I don't..." His hands spasmed on her back. "I don't know how far I'll go. The crop can make you bleed. I could split your skin open, just like Patrick threatened, and God help me, I'd enjoy every moment of it."

She shivered but not with fear. "I don't need the crop to love you, Victor." She bit her lip, then, afraid she'd said too much. She didn't believe in love at first sight, and there were certainly lots of things they needed to work out yet, but she had recognized a man that she could love from the very first minute she'd been introduced to him. "You're a Master whether you have the crop in your hand or not."

"When I'm the Master, at heart, I'm a sadist." His voice lowered to a threatening growl that curled her toes and sent her heart thudding heavily with anticipation. His fingers closed on her right nipple and she trembled, her eyes falling shut. He pinched firmly, his fingers strong and sure, tugging on her mercilessly. "The sadist in me will relish hurting you while I love you. I can't do one without the other."

Heated pain bloomed in her breast—and shot straight to her core. It felt like he'd pinched her clit in his fingers, inexorably dragging her closer and closer to orgasm.

Over the years, she'd dated so many men who were tentative and too damned polite. Even her last serious boyfriend had never touched her with such assurance. As though he knew exactly what she liked, exactly how much to hurt her.

Exactly as Victor touched her.

Wet, hot, tight, she ached to fall to her knees and open his pants.

The thought pushed her over the edge. Letting out a laughing purr of pleasure, she sagged against him, nuzzling his neck as he scooped her up into his arms. "I can't do one without the other either."

"That's why you have my word that I won't bring the crop to bed, and I'm going to lock the sadist—and the Master—up as much as possible."

She bit back her protests and let him carry her through his house. She didn't need him to keep the sadist at bay. But Victor did. He thought he could lock away that side of him and pretend it didn't exist. Jailed inside prison walls of his own creation, the sadist—the Master—the *man*—would simply wither up and die.

Luckily, she was pretty sure she had the key to those prison doors.

Chapter Ten

Victor carried Shiloh to his bedroom, mentally reviewing his old college playbook to give his body time to cool off. She was like molten fire in his arms, pure and hot and unafraid. She ought to be afraid. The first intimate caress he'd given her had been too hard, punishing.

Yet she'd quivered with pleasure.

She bit at his neck, nibbled his ear, and she might as well have been tearing a hunk out of his control.

The man, he reminded himself, gritting his teeth as she pulled her shirt over her head. *Give her the man, not the Master, certainly not the sadist.*

Shimmying out of her jeans, she gave him that impish grin, her mouth lush and soft. "First one out of her clothes gets to undress you."

The thought of her hands sliding into his pants... Growling out a curse, he yanked his shirt over his head but promptly stalled. Unhooking her bra with her hair tumbled down in her face, she suddenly looked shy and vulnerable, not the confident saucy little wench daring him to undress faster.

Biting her lower lip, she peeked at him, dropped the scrap of silk, and slid her hands down toward her panties.

"Stop," he barked out. He jerked his hair tighter, giving

himself a moment to find his center. *Get a grip, V.*

She froze immediately, waiting with eyes down and demure like a good submissive. When had they switched from man and woman to Dominant and submissive? *As soon as you started yelling commands,* he reminded himself. He stepped closer and tilted her face up to his. "You're not the Master's slave tonight, remember?"

Relaxing, she laughed softly. "So when you start giving orders, I should just ignore you?"

"Absolutely." He dropped his gaze to her breasts and felt his control slipping all over again. Damn it all to hell, he never should have waited so long to date her. He shouldn't have waited for her to devise an entire show just to get close to him. Lightly, he traced the rounded outer curve of her breast with his fingers, trying to make up for the force he'd used earlier. "Tell me to fuck off. This is about you and me, not the Master."

"But what if I want the Master to fuck me?"

He shuddered, his fingers locking her breast in a vise. Breathing hard and deep, he fought to loosen his grip instead of dragging her the few steps to his bed and doing just that.

"Sorry," she whispered, hanging her head. "I have a bit of a potty mouth in the bedroom. If you don't like me to talk dirty, order me to shut up."

"I love it." He finally managed to form a coherent thought. "It's just not good for my control right now. If you have a truck driver's mouth, I want to hear it."

No, I want to kiss it. He devoured her mouth, crowding her backwards toward his bed. Too fast, too hard, his tongue deep in her mouth but he couldn't slow down. She deserved leisurely loving, a sweet and tender induction that she would remember fondly for the rest of their lives, not this hurried, frantic pawing.

The thin strip of lace about her hips tore in his urgency.

Without the Master's control, he couldn't seem to control the man, and he dared not let the Master step forward for fear the sadist would rear his ugly head too.

Somehow he found himself on the edge of the bed first. Shiloh had managed not only to whirl him around but had also discarded his pants. Her fingers searched the ponytail at the base of his neck, trying to find the holder without pulling his hair. "It's so tight. How do you stand it that way?"

"Leave it." His voice sounded raw to his own ears, as though he'd been chewing rocks for days. She planted a knee beside his hips to join him on the mattress, but he gathered his wits enough to point at the bedside table. "Condom."

She gave him a long look with her head cocked slightly, as though she saw through the thin veil of decency he managed to keep between her and the monster shrieking inside him. "I know your medical history for the show, and you have access to mine. There's no need—"

"I insist."

How could he explain that he needed the barrier? A reminder that she wasn't his to possess and ravish at will? He always used a condom during a scene. Always. Slipping a rubber on for Kimberly had helped him keep the sadist completely hidden away, the small ritual a mental reminder of control. He needed to make sure he took care of Shiloh the same way.

Her mouth quirked and a suspiciously devilish gleam sparked in her chocolate eyes that made his balls ache even more. She fished a packet out of the drawer, tore it open, and calmly went to her knees before him.

"We're not playing Master/slave tonight," he insisted.

"So this isn't the Master's cock." Wrapping her left hand around him, she leaned forward, deliberately breathing on him.

It was all he could do not to fist his hands in her hair. "I shouldn't worship it with my mouth first like a good little slave before you fuck me."

Good God Almighty, it was so fucking hot to hear those dirty words coming out of her sweet mouth, to know exactly what thoughts were tumbling around in her mind. He'd never had a woman talk dirty to him before. Breathing hard, he finally managed to get out, "There's no need."

She smiled wickedly. Dreading—and anticipating—what she might do, he groaned. "I shouldn't lick every magnificent inch? I shouldn't make sure it's nice and wet before I slide this rubber on?"

A threatening growl trickled out of his mouth. He palmed the back of her head and pulled her closer, letting her see the growing darkness in his eyes. "Do it."

"Is that an order?" She licked the head, traced the slit underneath, and then used her lips to nibble her way gently down his shaft. "Because if this isn't the Master's cock, maybe it's the sadist's."

She squeezed harder and slowly drew his full length through her fist. His legs trembled and he tightened his fingers in her hair hard enough she cried out. Finally, thank God, she took him in her mouth, swirling her tongue around his tip before pulling back.

"Definitely the sadist's," she whispered huskily. "So big, so thick, you're going to hurt me with this lovely cock, aren't you, V?"

"No, baby," he panted, even though the thought of slamming into her body as hard and deep as he could wormed through his blood-starved brain. "I won't hurt you. I swear it."

"That's too bad." With agonizing care, she rolled the condom down his length, licking and kissing before encasing his flesh. "I hoped you would jam deep into my throat, pressing so deeply that I can't breathe without your permission. I hoped you wouldn't have any mercy at all. Just the way I like it."

The words barely came out of her mouth and he had both hands in her hair with his cock buried deep in the back of her throat, just as she'd suggested. Horrified at how quickly he'd lost control, he tried to draw back. Swallowing to work those muscles on him, she pushed deeper and groaned out a pleading cry around him.

An iron fist hammered against his spine. Fire tore through his body, leaving him trembling, sweating, arching into her mouth on a ragged shout of release.

He'd thought the worst thing he would do was injure her with his darker lust, but he'd been wrong. Shame churned his gut with acid. Instead, he'd absolutely lost control. He'd performed no better than a high-school nerd in the back of his daddy's car, getting to first base for the first time in his life.

She slipped the soiled condom off and threw it in the small wastebasket. Flashing a sultry smile over her shoulder, she fished another condom out of the drawer. "Now for round two. I hope you have quite a stash in the drawer."

Round two started with her slammed flat on her back and Victor glaring down into her eyes. "Do you have any idea how long it's been since I lost control like that?"

She blinked up at him innocently. "You said you wanted to make love to me as the man, not the Master. I thought that meant you didn't want your control."

"Damn it, Shiloh, I can't lose control. Don't count on any sort of normal, moral instinct to protect the female to stop me. Don't you understand that I could hurt you? Badly?"

"Don't you understand that I *want* you to hurt me? Badly?"

Groaning and cursing beneath his breath, he dropped his forehead against hers. "What am I going to do with you?"

"Love me." When he didn't move, she pressed her mouth to his ear. "Fuck me real hard, V. You know I'll love it."

Cursing louder, he wrenched away and sat up. He jerked at his hair, over and over, while she knew what he really wanted to do was use those big hands to punish her.

Shivering with longing, she sat up and hugged him, pressing against his back. She kissed his shoulder. "I'm sorry, Victor. I'm terrible, I know. I'll be good. I won't say another dirty thing. I promise."

He gripped her arms, holding her tighter against him. Raggedly, he laughed. "Look at me, the big bad Master, afraid to lay a finger on the sexiest woman I've ever met. You are a dream come true, Shiloh Holmes, and here I sit trembling in my boots."

"You have your boots on?" She made a big show of peering over his shoulder. "I don't see any boots, but I see that someone is very eager and happy to begin round two. As eager as I am."

He turned back to her and slipped his arms around her waist. "Someday, when I'm old and gray and too decrepit to swat a fly, then you can tease me about this." He dropped his head to her shoulder and clutched her hard. "I'm such a fool, Shiloh. I wanted this night to be special for you, to make up for how vicious I'll be on the show."

Tears burned her eyes. Swallowing the lump in her throat, she opened her thighs and shifted so she could wrap her legs around his waist and her arms around his shoulders. She held him, soaking in his heat, without trying to instigate more intimate contact. "That sounds incredibly sweet, but I have to be honest. Vicious turns me on just as much as tender. Either way, I want you. I need you so much I hurt, and that, too, is turning me on."

He eased her back to the mattress, settling his weight between her thighs. "Where does it hurt, baby? I'll bite it and make it hurt better."

Payback's a bitch, she realized, for his words made her entire body stand up and scream for attention. She felt swollen and feverish, like her eyes blazed fire. "So now you're going to tease me?"

"But of course." He grinned, winking down at her. "Wherever should I start?"

She clamped her mouth shut to keep from blurting out exactly where he could start. *No more dirty talk.*

He nibbled at her lips, soft and gentle. He sucked her bottom lip into his mouth and stroked his tongue with hers, and all she could think about was getting that wicked tongue to head a bit further south.

The sharp sting of his teeth on her bottom lip made her jolt. "Does that hurt better?"

She wanted to beg and plead with an entire laundry list of places he could bite. Instead, she whispered, "Yes."

"That's it?" The big bad Master pouted, startling a laugh out of her. She cupped his face and sucked his bottom lip into her mouth for some teeth appreciation. All too quickly, her hunger raged out of control. She pushed at his chest, determined to roll him over so she could finish round two before he even got that condom on.

Instead, he slithered lower and snagged her left nipple in his teeth.

"Oh, yes, harder, V."

He tilted his head so he could watch her reaction, working his tongue over her captured flesh. He grated his teeth back and forth and then released her to teasingly lick just the tip.

"You would look fantastic in a custom set of nipple clamps." He gave the other breast the same treatment, until she was sure her nipples were huge and as hard as marble. "Is that the bondage you'll pick for tomorrow?"

"If you want it, it's yours."

Without answering, he wandered lower on her body, planting small, sharp bites on her tummy that had her hips arcing off the bed. "You never told me where it hurt, Shiloh. You never told me where you most wanted me to bite."

"I promised!"

He skipped her groin entirely and she ground her teeth in frustration. Opening his mouth wide, he gripped her inner thigh in his teeth, not biting, exactly, but applying pressure to the muscle underneath. He ran those powerful jaw-gripping bites down to her knee and switched to the other leg, working his way back up.

She took the opportunity to snag his ponytail, giving him a hard yank that must have hurt like a bitch because he wore it so tight. "Please!"

"Promises are made to be broken," he purred against her inner thigh.

"No, they aren't," she growled out.

"Tell me what you want."

"I want you to lick and bite me until I beg you to stop!"

He started to move back down her thigh, trailing his tongue in a wet path toward her knee. "Isn't that what I'm doing?"

With a quick twist of her wrist, she wrapped her hand in his hair and tugged him back where she wanted him.

"Oh, *here*," he whispered, letting his breath puff out against her. "Pull my hair harder, baby. I think I'm starting to understand what you want."

"Please, Victor, please." She twisted another length of his hair in her hand. Babbling, she knew she was babbling, "Oh, God, yes, there, please!"

With agonizing delicacy, he nibbled a path of fire around her sex. "I've been hungering for a taste of you, Shiloh. Dying to get my mouth on you. Burning to get inside you. Is that what you're trying to tell me? Is that what you want?"

She let out a shaking groan. *Clean, smoking hot, but not dirty.* "I want to be under your tongue."

He flattened his tongue against her and she moaned and whimpered and likely ripped a bald spot in his hair, and just when she thought she'd die, he sucked her clit into his mouth, gripping her with his teeth in such exquisite, delicate pain. No mercy, no quarter, he worked her with his tongue and teeth until she trembled from head to toe and begged him to stop.

Just as she'd asked.

When he finally settled his weight against her and slid inside, she could only cling to him and stare up into his eyes and cry at how tender and sweet the Master proved to be. He calmed her with his body, his thrusts slow and deep and druggingly tender. He slid his big palms up and down her arms, flanks and down her legs, pulling her higher against him. His fingers were strong and sure, massaging her as thoroughly as she'd done his knee the previous night.

Kissing his throat, she worked on that holder, determined to free his hair. She'd already pulled it horribly, so she didn't try to be gentle this time. She yanked the rubber band out and tossed it as far as she could. Cupping his head between her hands, she rubbed his head and combed his hair through her fingers.

He groaned, deep in his throat. For any other man, she

113

might have eased the pressure, but for Victor, she pressed her fingers harder against his scalp. She felt the subtle answering shift in his body. Instead of stroking her so carefully, he shifted to his elbows and thrust deeper, harder, grinding his pelvis against hers. He cupped her face in his big hands, stroking her cheeks with his thumbs while he took her mouth, his tongue as deep inside her as his cock.

Even tender, even sweet, he demanded her pleasure, the ultimate surrender of her will and body to his. Shuddering, she sucked on his tongue, clamped down tight on him with every muscle in her body, taking him as deep as she could until he came too.

Cradling her beneath him, he kissed her softly, still cupping her face. "Did I hurt you?"

"No," she whispered, combing his hair with her fingers.

The last bit of tension bled from his body. Shifting his weight off to the side, he drew her close so she cuddled against him. Stroking her back, he sighed heavily. "I will."

She couldn't help but shiver with anticipation.

Chapter Eleven

So it happened. The Master took me to His bed.

Why am I not jumping up and down, squealing with excitement? Because it was nothing like I expected. No crop. No punishment. No games. It was incredibly sweet. Just a man and one desperately horny woman pushing him to give me everything He needs to give.

And He refused. It was like making love to a man who wears a mask. Every time I tried to peek beneath it and see the real V, he slammed another brick wall into place.

I hate it when He holds back on me. When He hides what I most need to see.

Don't get me wrong—Master V is an incredible lover and man. He blew my mind. Even sitting here bright and early before work, remembering last night, makes me sweat and moan, squirming in my chair. I can't help but wonder what it'll be like to see Him as my boss and not my lover, my Master. Will everyone know, just by looking at me, that I'm His?

God, I hope so.

Most of all, I hope He looks at me and sees his V plastered all over me. I know it sounds crazy, but I'd let Him brand me like a steer. I want Him burned into my flesh, claiming me as His for anyone to see.

But I don't know if that's what He wants. Oh, sure, I know what the sadist needs—because I am the fuel for His fire—but I don't know that He'll ever allow that beast its freedom.

Even though my heart is howling His name, begging Him to come subdue me.

"So...?"

Victor avoided meeting Mal's gleaming gaze. Even Patrick's table of pony gear was more tolerable than his friend's curiosity. With a busy morning of going through tape and too many witnesses around to overhear, she hadn't been able to interrogate him yet. Maybe he could diffuse her interest by stroking her ego. "You were right."

"Mistress M is always right." She preened a moment, twirling a lock of hair about her finger. "I saw her this morning. She didn't bear any horrible wounds or bruises."

"No." Somehow, he managed to sound insulted, even though that had been his fear.

"You're more relaxed today, so I'm assuming..."

"Give me a break, Mal. Do you want a play by play?"

"You know that's not my kink." She brought a paper bag over to his table and dumped out its contents. She'd known without asking that he would need help; his table was glaringly bare of bondage equipment. "Are you happy with how it went?"

"Sure. It was great."

"But...?"

Sighing, he threw himself down in the folding chair. After a few more finishing touches to his worthless table of trinkets, Mal sat down beside him. She waited, calm and steady, persistent without harassing him, giving him time to find the words. "She's fantastic, sexy, daring, everything I ever wanted or hoped she would be. We had a good time, don't get me wrong. But the whole time, I felt like I was fighting her."

"Or fighting yourself?" Mal asked softly.

"You told me to take her as the man and not the Master." Even to his own ears, he sounded accusatory. He tried to take down his intensity a notch. "It was all I could do to touch her without hurting her, and she kept pushing me. Mal, you have no idea how fearless she is. She pushed every button I have, including a few I didn't even know existed."

"Sounds hot." Chuckling at his groan, Mal sat down beside him. "The best submissives are the ones who push us to our limits too. You wouldn't be as interested if she didn't challenge you."

In his mind, he heard Shiloh's sultry voice again, begging him to fuck her hard, real hard, just the way she liked it, and he had to shift into a more comfortable spot. "A smart submissive knows her Master's limits, though. She doesn't push him beyond safety or sanity. It's like she knows the absolute worst thing to say or ask for."

"Or the best." She raised her hand to halt his retort. "Name one submissive you've played with in the past five—even ten—years who truly pushed you. Who made you work at being a Master and controlling your instincts? You were bored to tears at Silken. I think that's why you hooked up with Kimberly. At least you had a new challenge then. You had to pretend like you were *normal*."

"Well, it sure as hell won't be boring with Shiloh around."

"And you're just getting started."

He couldn't help but grimace, even though his heart rate accelerated at the thought of seeing her today, working through this staged game, and then, the best part of all—taking her home with him again. "She's going to end up hurt and I'll never forgive myself."

"Sweet Baby Jesus in a manger!" Mal surged to her feet and leaned down into his face. Her index finger suddenly became a dangerous weapon and her New Orleans accent—that she'd worked so hard all these years to smooth—slurred her words. "I'm tired of hearing how bad you got it, you mean, miserable Master with a brand new submissive panting at your feet who wants exactly the kind of punishment you deal out. Get over yourself. You would never plow your fist into her face for disrespecting you, uncaring whether you broke her nose or jaw. You would never beat the shit out of her just because you felt like it. You wouldn't sell her on the street just to see the humiliation on her face, or carve her up because she's too pretty and some other man might look at her, or get her hooked on drugs so she's trapped and completely under your control. *You are not a bad man!*"

"No," he said, keeping his voice cool. "I would simply take my crop to her back, buttocks and thighs until she bore the scars for the rest of her life."

Calmer, Mal refused to back down. "If she got off while you did it, more power to the both of you."

Shaken, he stared up at his friend, his throat as raw as though he'd swallowed a belly-full of gravel. "Bruises won't stop me."

"In our world, bruises are badges of honor when given lovingly during a scene," she replied gently, dropping her hand on his shoulder.

His stomach churned with bile. "Blood won't stop me."

"Blood's a bitch to get off leather." She squeezed his shoulder, refusing to leave him wallowing in self-hatred. "I think you've got more control than you give yourself credit for. I know you, V. If you care about this woman and she's not enjoying what you're doing, you will stop."

"How do you know?" But what rang in his head was *How can I know?*

"You stopped for Kimberly, didn't you? And don't tell me that she moved you like Shiloh moves you."

"No one has ever moved me like Shiloh. That's why..." He swallowed to clear the rasp out of his throat. "I don't want to lose her. If I hurt her, really injured her badly, Mal, I don't know what I'd do."

"She trusts you."

He couldn't help but wince then, as though his friend had stabbed him through the heart.

"She's going to love you, if not already. If you don't trust yourself, you will either lose her or kill that spirit that compels you to lay claim to her body and soul. You'll force her to pretend, as you pretended for Kimberly. Is that what you want? Fake, safe sex that hides what you both really need, no matter how violent and dirty you think it may be?"

"No," he ground out. "I felt like I was dying inside a little more each day. I don't want that for Shiloh. She's too bright, too free and happy to die that way."

"Go slow, trust your instincts, and give it time. You've found the rare combination we all dream about. You've found someone who needs your kink as much as you need to give it, and will love and honor you at the same time. She's a treasure, V. Don't push her away."

Now it was Victor's turn to narrow his gaze on his friend's face, searching for telltale signs of unhappiness. "You don't think you've found the same treasure in Andy?"

"He loves my kink." Mal forced a laugh, and yes, it was forced. Straightening, she averted her face. "I never fooled myself into thinking he loves me too. Enjoy it while it lasts, V, because there are no guarantees. Besides, you know my Mama will never forgive me if I marry a white boy five years younger than me."

Victor stood and wrapped his arm around her waist. "Tell me again—why are we both so screwed up?"

"Because normal is boring." She slipped her arm around his waist too. Together, they walked down the hall to current taping session. "We have to be screwed up to get along with each other. God only knows why I've put up with you so long."

"You're fired."

Mal laughed. "You can't fire me. I own a quarter of your company and sit on your Board of Directors. You're stuck with me like a shrew of a wife you can't divorce."

On set, the host of the show was interviewing Shiloh. Victor felt his hunger blaze to life just looking at her. She wore the corset and stockings again from their very first taping, but this time she wore layers of white petticoats and a more proper shift that covered her shoulders. The vintage underclothing made her look vulnerable and delicate. Beneath the garish mask of large bug-eyed brass goggles and jumbled gears that formed a helmet, her lips were full and soft and pink.

It seemed impossible that such a sweet mouth had whispered raw, dirty words to him last night.

He listened in.

"So have you always dated within the scene?" Georgia asked.

Shiloh shook her head. "No, far from it. Public display isn't really my thing."

Silently, Victor had to agree with her. He could do the performance to a point. Onlookers certainly helped him remain fully in control, fully the Master. But for her, he didn't want public. He wanted private, dark, secure. Where the only person to witness what came out of him might not run screaming.

"So this show's going to be a blast for you." Georgia laughed. "How many Dominants have you dated, then?"

"Only one before this show."

How many years ago had she dated that mentor she'd mentioned? Victor had the impression of years. Maybe it'd been a long time since she'd done a scene too. No wonder they were both shaking and needy like an addict desperate for a hit.

"Only one!" Georgia gasped and swirled a ridiculous peacock and ivory fan before her face like she might swoon. "Have you dated men who weren't into the scene, or are you practically a virgin?"

Shiloh's mouth tightened but her voice remained calm. "I've dated for years."

Georgia leaned closer and lowered her voice, letting the fan flutter up by their faces as though they were alone in an intimate conversation. "Vanilla sex can be so boring. Did you ever try to get a boyfriend to cross over to the Kinky Side with you?"

"I tried."

Sensing the juicy details just below the surface, Georgia made a low, encouraging coo and raised the fan higher, giving Shiloh a modicum of fake privacy. Victor willed his muscles to relax and shook out his cramped fingers. She'd known the interview would get personal. It was those raw, painful elements that would make the show believable and keep people watching. But by the way his proud, confident submissive stared down at her fingers clenched desperately in the white linen, he didn't think he was going to like what he heard.

"With who?" Georgia purred.

"My college boyfriend. We'd dated through our last two years of college and were close to graduating." Shiloh shrugged, forcing a half smile. "We'd talked marriage after we both had jobs, but we weren't actually engaged."

"How did you tell him?"

"I just came right out and asked him."

"For what?" Georgia's sultry voice was perfect for this deep, intimate conversation, purring on the camera. Victor had known she'd sound luscious. Dallas viewers would be enthralled with this tiny glimpse into someone's personal pain, but damn it, he didn't like Shiloh bearing her pain. Not for anyone but him. "What did you ask him for?"

"I wanted him to hurt me," Shiloh whispered. "At first, he was horrified. He thought I hadn't been enjoying our sex life at all. I told him no, it was fine. I just needed...more."

"You needed pain."

Victor could hear his own loud, deep pants, as though he'd just run a mile at top speed back in the day. In so many ways, they were polar opposites and yet cut from exactly the same warped cloth. She'd pretended to be vanilla for her boyfriend; he'd pretended for Kimberly. *Am I going to force her to pretend for me, too, just to keep her safe?*

"Yes," Shiloh breathed out. "I asked him to use his belt on me."

"Did he do it?"

Silently, she nodded and a tremor shook her shoulders.

Georgia reached over to clasp the other woman's hand. "What happened?"

"It wasn't enough." A tear trickled down beneath Shiloh's

mask and Victor had to rip his hair tighter to keep from charging in there and hauling her off stage. "He tried, he really did, but he couldn't bear to hurt me. My dad had spanked me harder than that as a kid. It certainly wasn't enough to..."

She paused and took a deep breath, calming herself. "It hurt him, in a bad way that I absolutely hated. I couldn't ask him to do that. I like pain, yes, but I want to enjoy it, and know that the man giving me that pain enjoys it too. If he's not getting off on it, then I won't either. My boyfriend hated it. He hated hurting me. I knew he was going to end up hating me too."

"So what happened?"

"We tried to go back to just loving each other. Normal, vanilla sex, you know? But it was too late. He couldn't forget I had this need inside of me he could never meet. He knew he wasn't enough for me, and no amount of caring and respect and love could overcome that lack."

Shiloh raised her gaze from her hands and saw Victor in the shadows. She stared at him a moment, her eyes wild, her body trembling as though she'd flee.

"Did she make that shit up as a message to you?" Mal whispered at his side. "A threat?"

He considered the thought and dismissed it as impossible with a slight shake of his head. The emotion shimmering in Shiloh's eyes was real heartache. Real terror, that resonated inside him too. It took a horrendous amount of courage to bare one's soul like that, even to a lover. Especially to a lover. Because it left one open, vulnerable, naked of any sort of protection.

With a word, he could shred her wide open. With a cold glance—or a cold shoulder—he could strip her of any affection she may have stored up for him. He could hurt her more by rejecting her now than he'd ever dreamed to do with his crop.

"It's obvious from your tryout that you've set your cap for Master V." Georgia, too, had noticed who watched on the sidelines. "What happens if you don't win the title of *America's Next Top sub*?"

Lifting her chin, Shiloh turned back to the woman interviewing her. "I don't care about the show. If Master V chooses me to compete for the title, I'll endure whatever he asks of me to ensure he wins."

"What if he dismisses you from the show?"

Shiloh's hands trembled in her lap but she met Victor's gaze unflinchingly. "Then I will walk away from him, this show, everything. He won't have to tell me twice to leave."

Chapter Twelve

Standing in line with the other eleven contestants, Shiloh gripped her petticoats, hiding her trembling hands in frothy linen. Her stomach churned with anxiety. She didn't want to see Victor's reaction to her interview. It'd been hard enough to bare her soul like that, without looking up to find him watching and listening to every word.

If he thought she was dropping hints about last night...

I don't have to have the pain to love him, as long as he takes that fucking mask off!

Ironically, sitting on the set grim and silent in his black mask with the crop on the judging table before him, he was more familiar to her than the man who'd made love to her last night.

Georgia stood before the Dominants' table, putting on the show for the cameras. "Contestants, let's begin our first challenge. This challenge has three phases. After each phase, the Dominants will judge how well you responded to the task. At least one contestant will be eliminated who didn't quite make the mark. For the last phase, each Dominant will select his or her top contestant and pit them against the others to determine today's overall challenge winner. At the end of this challenge, each Dominant will dismiss one contestant from the competition. Contestants, Master P will provide your first task."

Patrick stood and gave his thousand-watt smile to the camera. "Each Dominant has prepared a table of possible bondage equipment. Fetch an everyday item that can be found in most people's homes that is also safe for beginning bondage play."

"On your mark," Georgia drawled, her eyes sparking with excitement. "Go!"

Shiloh rushed toward Victor's table, jostling shoulders with Kimberly. The other three women quickly grabbed their items— a roll of duct tape, a silken scarf, and a length of chain—leaving Shiloh still scanning the contents on the table. None of this looked like *him*, the man who was afraid he'd hurt her too much. The items were bland and boring, the same old thing any bondage kit might contain. Somehow, she'd expected more of the sadist.

Or perhaps *less*, she decided, as she snagged a length of clothesline.

She rushed back to her place in line just before Georgia called time. "Contestants, present to your Masters!"

Shiloh dropped to her knees, lowered her head, and raised her hands up as high as possible. Eyes down, arms burning with effort, she waited, barely breathing. Chairs scooted out from the table and footfalls announced the Dominants' approach. One Master, though, made his presence known with a light tapping of leather against leather.

The crop.

Sweat trickled between her breasts, her breathing short and frantic thanks to the ridiculous corset. No wonder women had been considered so helpless centuries ago—this contraption would suffocate her!

Further down the line, she could hear Mistress Mal quizzing her contestants. Then Patrick. Thank God, her arms were trembling with strain, her neck and shoulders aching. Finally, Victor spoke, and Shiloh heard the disgust in his voice. "Chains are never a good choice. You're out." He moved further down the line, addressing the red-haired woman. "What is your name, submissive?"

"Ruby." Perhaps the eager submissive wasn't so eager when the Master carried a crop, because her voice sounded as timid as Kimberly's. She hurriedly tacked on, "Master!"

"Why would you think a silk scarf would be ideal for bondage?"

"They're pretty and soft," the woman babbled. "I have dozens in my drawer at home. Everybody does. I—"

Victor slapped the crop loudly on his thigh and she clamped her mouth shut. "Gift and Willow, you may lower your selections to the floor. They are acceptable. Hold out your arms, Ruby, and I'll show you the problem with your choice."

The stage name *Willow* fit slender and graceful Kimberly perfectly. Shiloh stole a glance at Victor's ex-fiancée to see how she fared. Kimberly smiled at her shakily, her hands balled into fists on her thighs. Every time Victor tapped the crop on his boot, a tremor shook her shoulders and her eyes flared.

She'll never make it through the punishment round.

Shiloh felt no glee at that prospect. In fact, she felt guilty. She'd purposely designed the punishment round to show Victor what she could tolerate, without any consideration for a non-masochist submissive. Few of the contestants would endure much punishment, let alone a showdown deliberately centered on Victor's sadistic side.

Would he dare let her see beneath that mask even while wearing the Master's mask for the show?

Ruby cried out, jerking Shiloh's attention back. Victor had wound the silk tightly around her wrists and gave a firm tug on

127

the ends. "Twist your hands like you're trying to free yourself."

Ruby did as ordered, twisting her wrists back and forth. The camera man eased closer, zooming in on her hands.

"See how the silk is twisting over on itself? It will get tighter and tighter, until it's impossible to untie and begin to cut into your flesh. If you don't have extremely sharp scissors handy, you might experience loss of circulation and damage your fingers."

He snapped his fingers and a bare-chested male attendant with an impressive six-pack—for the female viewers' appreciation—snipped the silk scarf off her hands. "You, too, are dismissed from this challenge."

Mal walked up and down the line, eying the remaining contestants like they were at a slave market. "Use the bondage equipment you retrieved to show us an incorrect and unsafe bondage position as a lesson of what not to do for our viewers at home."

Shiloh didn't have to think very hard: She wrapped the clothesline around her throat. Victor walked behind her, sending her nerves screeching with delicious alarm. He held his hand over her shoulder expectantly, so she gave him the ends of her rope.

Again, the Dominants went down the line, explaining why wrists should never be tied flat against each other or else risk tendon damage, why nothing like rags or tape should cover the mouth in case of aspiration, until the camera homed in on Shiloh, kneeling at her Master's feet with a noose about her neck.

"This is very bad for obvious reasons." Victor tightened the rope on her throat. She didn't fight him; panic would only make the strangulation worse. Besides, he only tightened the rope a moment for dramatic effect, and then loosened the clothesline with his fingers. "Never put ropes or scarves around even the most willing submissive's neck. Air deprivation is serious on-the-edge play and reserved only for experts."

She hauled in as deep a breath as the corset allowed and studied his face. His eyes were narrowed on her, watching her for trouble or panic, but he didn't seem affected by her reaction. His eyes weren't blazing with heat, his nostrils didn't flare, and the crop was still against his thigh. Nothing told her that he was aroused by this kink, even though he'd warned her he was on the edge. She could endure a demonstration for the show, but she'd not care for such risky play in the bedroom. Hopefully he didn't care for it either.

Still gripping the rope in his hands—but not drawing it tight—Victor gave a dismissive jerk of his head to Kimberly. Relieved, the other woman quickly joined the other disqualified submissives, leaving Shiloh at his feet, Andy at Mal's feet, and a very cute and bubbling blonde at Patrick's.

The camera zoomed back to Georgia, who began prattling about the final "Master's Choice" phase of the bondage round. Leaning down, Victor pulled the rope off Shiloh's throat and whispered, "Remember, this one's for you."

Then he gave her a sharp blow on her hip.

Eyes dark, mouth soft and open, her breathing rapid and much too shallow because of her clothing, Shiloh gazed up at him. Victor read hope and confusion both in her eyes, a wild tumult of longing that she tried to hold back. She didn't want him to see how much the blow affected her...for fear he would feel pressured to give her more.

When that's exactly what he longed to do.

With her eyes locked on him, she stood with the other two submissives. Georgia gave the go, and the two submissives raced for the table, but Shiloh stayed before him.

"Go!" Georgia rushed over, a tense smile on her face for the camera. "Gift, this is it! The final challenge!"

"I know."

"But you're supposed to pick the Master's Choice!"

Shiloh smiled. "I am. I hope."

Deliberately, he kept his face smooth and hoped the fires were banked in his eyes. He felt a quickening in his heart, a leap of joy and excitement that he hadn't felt in...forever. He'd punished a lot of subs over the years, but never one who truly relished every blow he dealt. Who stared back at him with such naked eagerness.

This woman is going to be the death of me...but what a way to go.

The other submissives raced back into line with Shiloh and the alarm ended the challenge. Flustered, Georgia turned to the other two submissives and asked them about their choices first. Naturally, Andy had brought back a cock cage, while Patrick's bubbly blonde had brought back a pony tail.

Victor grimaced and shook his head. How could they possibly expect to display such equipment on TV?

Evidently, that had been the point, because both Dominants ordered their submissives to prepare for punishment. Eager attendants rushed onto set and bound the protesting—but pantingly aroused—submissives for their Dominants' pleasure. While Shiloh stared at him, waiting for his reaction.

He let his meanest, most dreadful smile twist his mouth. "Nearly every scene will include punishment at the Master's discretion. A top submissive will accept such punishment as a reward, willingly enduring discomfort, pain, and humiliation simply because her Master wishes it."

He walked a slow circle about Shiloh, tapping the crop against his boot ominously. "Would you like an attendant to bind you for your punishment and reward, Gift?"

"If that is your desire, Master."

To the camera, he said, "Most submissives like bondage during discipline. As odd as it may sound to you, being bound can make one feel very safe. A sub can simply lie back into her bonds and absorb the pain, instead of tensing her own muscles to hold position and remain upright. Accepting punishment without any restraints at all can actually be quite difficult. Are you sure you can endure, Gift?"

"For you, Master, I'll endure anything."

"Remove your corset."

"Cut!" Mal stalked toward them with a scowl on her face. "Are you sure about this?"

Ignoring the Mistress's concerns, Shiloh turned to Kimberly and asked her to untie the strings in the back.

"Sure," Victor replied easily. "Why not?"

"Can you keep it clean enough for TV?"

He studied his crop, flexing it between his hands. "Can you keep cock cages and pony tails clean for TV?"

Mal snorted. "Point taken."

He snapped the crop hard against his thigh, priming himself and letting the sound of it prime Shiloh too. Unfortunately, Kimberly's hands began shaking so much that she couldn't get the strings untied. Curtly, he jerked his head at her and attended Shiloh himself. He pulled the strings free and stepped closer, pressing his body against her back and thighs. Into her ear, he whispered, "Are you up for this?"

She hauled in a deep breath without the corset and pushed

back harder against him, her breath catching on a low moan at the feel of his erection digging into her. "I've been up for this for months."

"So is *chutzpah* really what you want to use for your safeword?"

"I don't—"

He dropped his chin to her shoulder and hugged her. "Humor me."

She sighed. "How about Christmas?"

Laughing, he released her and gestured for her to join the bound and waiting submissives. "My Christmas Gift. Now that is perfect indeed."

It took half an hour for Mal to direct the lighting and camera crew for the next part of the show. They needed enough light to titillate the audience, but still allow the submissives a modicum of privacy. Sweaty and unable to stand still, Shiloh tried not to think about how far the scene might go.

Dominance and discipline were sex for both of them. Could she actually go through with a live taping of what would basically be sex? Knowing that all of Dallas would see it?

"Darker," Victor ordered, pacing the set. "We need more privacy for this or no one's going to relax enough to enjoy it. Mal, Patrick, get your subs ready with their *equipment.* We want to spare the audience all the gory details."

"I beg your pardon," Patrick sniffed dramatically. "If anyone's going to be gory, it'll be you and that vicious crop."

Shiloh clutched the linen shift closer, feeling exposed and more vulnerable than if she were naked. Both the shift and the petticoats were practically see-through, and *someone* had gotten a bright idea of not wearing any pantaloons beneath.

What made her feel ever more vulnerable, though, was the need pounding in her veins. She knew she was soaking wet and so tight and achy with need that Victor would barely have to touch her to make her explode. Could she do it with the cameras and lights and people all around? But what choice did she have?

She could bail right now. Call the whole thing off. Victor would probably understand as far as their relationship went, but what about her job? The entire show was her idea. She'd known full well what she was getting into; hell, she'd deliberately planned it this way. She'd planned to get Victor in the spotlight, punishing her for the camera.

I can do this...for him.

On her right, Andy was down on the floor, and if she weren't mistaken, he was completely naked, although he'd drawn one knee up to strategically conceal the cage of metal about his penis. Decked out in a black velvet riding habit and a stylish hat with a long black veil floating over her face, Mal stood behind him with a flail, chatting easily while an attendant bound Andy's hands.

On her left, the pony girl wore a corset with plenty of room for her tail to show to advantage. She, too, was on her hands and knees, hobbled with leather and wearing a fake bridle on her head. Patrick warmed up with several long, easy strokes of the whip. The sound of the leather snaking over the floor made Shiloh's breath catch in her throat. He cracked the whip above his girl's head, and it was Shiloh who let out a shaking moan.

"You haven't changed your mind, have you?" Victor stepped closer, his voice low. "Surely you're not thinking about his whip instead of my crop."

"Of course not!"

He untied the neck of her shift. "Are you nervous?"

Her skin felt cold and clammy and her heart rate galloped about ninety miles an hour, but she simply said, "A little."

His mouth twitched. He knew very well how she was feeling, but he didn't call her on the small lie. "Have you ever performed a scene with an audience before?"

"No."

He turned her away from him so he stood at her back. "I am your Master for this scene. I am your whole world. If you look away from me or lose your concentration, I will bring you back into the headspace I want the quickest way I know how, so you know what that means." He punctuated his promise by stroking the crop along her bare arm. "Perform for *me* and me alone. Can you do that for me?"

Her pulse throbbed in her neck and her teeth chattered with nerves, but her skin felt alive and achy, more than ready for his strokes. "Yes, Master V."

"That's my girl," he purred against her ear. "I'm going to let Patrick and Mal go first. Listen to them, baby, and know that I'm going to make you scream louder and come harder."

Standing there with the cameras rolling, she shivered and burned, sweat freezing on her skin. Her sex felt swollen and tight. Each snap of leather and gasp of pain only worsened her rising need.

Mal and Patrick worked in tandem as though they'd been doing shows like this for years. Maybe they had performed something like this at Silken, because they had their swings down to a perfect back-and-forth rhythm that made Shiloh's blood pound and dance with longing. Each crack of the whip and duller thud of the flail winched her muscles tighter.

Andy cried out, groaning beneath his Mistress's flail. With a cocky grin, Mal planted a high-heeled boot on her sub's back and posed for the camera. "What a greedy boy."

Patrick pouted for the camera and gave a playful tug on his sub's tail that made her groan. "Are you top sub material or not? You know what I need from you, Peppi."

Another sharp crack of the whip brought a high keening cry from his submissive's lips and he got exactly what he was working toward. She wasn't quiet in her pleasure, either.

Cheeks hot, Shiloh stared at the floor and tried not to notice that the camera had swung toward her.

Victor strolled to her left, stopping slightly in front of her but not blocking the camera's view. The crop snapped against her thigh sharply enough that she sucked in her breath and jerked her gaze up to his face.

"That's better," he purred. "Did you hear how noisy those other subs were, Gift? I want our viewers to know precisely what you're feeling while I punish you. If you cry out, you'd better be giving your safeword or coming. Otherwise, I want you silent. Do you understand?"

Instead of answering, she nodded, careful to obey him to the letter.

He lifted the crop toward her face and someone gasped, but she instinctively knew he wouldn't strike her in such a vulnerable location. Gently, he stroked the leather beneath her chin, making sure she kept her face up, and then he passed the tip against her mouth, a caress. A promise of what was to come.

He flicked another casual blow to her left thigh, watching her carefully even though he spoke to the camera. "The crop is not for beginners. It delivers a sharp, cutting blow that can be way too much for the submissive who's not very far down the masochist scale. At home, start with something softer, either a paddle or flail, and work up to the crop if possible." To Shiloh, he asked, "Do you need me to switch down?" as he delivered a harder blow.

Gritting her teeth to keep the moan from escaping, she shook her head. The pain was sharp and intense, yes, but such a relief after all the teasing and yearning. She'd had the softer Victor last night. This side of him only made her want him more.

Heat snaked through her skin, the burn only intensifying her desire. So tight, agony, waiting for the next teasing blow to fall. Would it be her thigh? Her arm? Her back?

Everything faded into a misty haze except him, the crop kissing her skin with fire, and the blazing heat rising within her. Dimly, she heard him directing the camera around for a better shot. He pressed against her back and rubbed the crop against her neck, between her breasts, and down her stomach.

Quivering, she fought back the pleading sounds threatening to tumble out of her mouth. If he would touch her, just a stroke, she would climax so hard she'd probably break a camera lens with her yells.

"Hold the shift against your breasts," he whispered in her ear. His breath was hot, as heavy as hers, and only served to make her desire worse. He was aroused, too, and the thought made her drop her head back against his shoulder and arch harder into his arms. He rewarded her with a harsher blow across the front of her thighs, but then slipped away, leaving her trembling and blowing hard, her lips clamped tight.

Please, please, Victor, give me more. Please!

He grabbed the neckline of her shift in both hands and ripped it down the back. Shivering, she clutched the sagging linen to her breasts as he'd ordered. He'd been careful to leave a few inches above the hem intact, so she didn't think her ass was bared to Dallas. His big palm wrapped around the base of her neck and then glided down her back, hot and broad and strong enough to melt the bones in her body.

Gritting her teeth, she widened her stance, forcing her trembling thighs to hold her weight.

"Now this is where the real test begins. Now we shall see if Gift can endure without the benefit of bonds. Are you *my* submissive, Gift? Are you my top sub?"

The crop whistled through the air for what seemed like an eternity, warning her that this one was going to take her breath. Searing white blinded her, an explosion of sensation that picked her up and slammed her back to earth. She hunched her back slightly, giving him a better, wider canvas for his blows and could only hope she was still standing.

A blaze of fire curled along her shoulder blades, one then the other in quick succession. Breathing hard, it took her several blows to visualize what he was doing, and the knowledge made her knees sag.

Like the legends of Zorro, Victor was leaving his mark on her body in the form of Vs.

She must have closed her eyes, or maybe the lights had burned out. Maybe she had fallen. Because she felt disconnected, from the show, from her mind, from everything except Victor and his crop inching down her back. The tip curled slightly over her ribcage and her breath hissed between her teeth. Color blossomed in the darkness, great blobs of white, marked with red, his image cut into her back.

Wetness trickled down her thighs, liquid pain searing her body. The agony wasn't from his blows, but from the relentless ache in her sex. Her body remembered every detail of those precious hours in his bed. The way his teeth had played and teased. How he'd cupped her face in his hands and kissed her so tenderly while his body had claimed hers.

The exquisite pain blended with that sweetness, an agony of need that twisted her mind and clawed her heart to ribbons.

For the first time in her life, she thought seriously about blurting out her safeword.

Not to stop the pain...but to get him inside me.

Victor regretted giving her the order to be silent. He regretted the cameras and crew hovering on the fringes. Most of all, he regretted that he hadn't been strong enough to bring his crop into his bed last night, because this...

This was hotter and infinitely more fulfilling than the careful, deliberate lovemaking he'd given her last night. This was real, brutally honest, and the ugliest truth he'd borne alone in the darkest corners of his mind all these years.

And she accepted him without question.

Stripes glared red and lovely on her back, his trademark V welted into her flesh. He could have done this last night. He could have stretched her flat on his bed and put these slashes on the backs of her thighs, marking the path to where he most wanted to be.

Instead, he'd been a coward, and now, he had to pay for that weakness by sharing this priceless moment with half a dozen witnesses on set and God only knew how many viewers.

Maybe it was all these years of punishing himself when the need became too great to bear, but he felt the burn of his strokes on his own body. He felt the fire coursing through her skin, burning through her veins. He knew the throbbing clench of desire that waited for him to slide home and ease that vicious ache. There was a secret place outside himself that he'd only been to a handful of times when he'd taken himself to a painful climax, but he found that hazy haven now, without a single blow to his own body.

She'd taken him there, because that's where she'd flown as soon as he began giving her pain.

138

Tremors shook her shoulders and her legs trembled, making the petticoats froth about her legs. He read the tension in her body, the agony of need on her face, and decided she'd—they'd—had enough torture. At least one of them would feel a release.

He wrapped his arms around her, tucking her quivering body back against his strength. She sagged, immediately, as though her body simply couldn't hold itself upright any longer. On cue, Mal waved the lights even lower, giving them even more privacy so he could complete the scene.

He hauled Shiloh's skirts up with his left hand until he could slide his palm underneath and cup her. Hot and so wet, proof that she'd relished every moment of his punishment. She bowed in his arms, trembling on the verge of climax. His heart hammered and his lungs burned as though he'd run a marathon.

The show, he reminded himself, crawling back from the tide of lust threatening to drag him under. He buried his fingers in her wet heat, slammed the crop down in a final blow to her outer thigh, and held her through the resulting climax that scoured his mind. It wasn't his release, but she managed to wipe away all the years of grime and guilt he'd been carrying. She made him feel clean and light in a way that he hadn't felt in years.

She let out a cry of pleasure that tightened his throat and made his heart swell in his chest until he couldn't breathe. She made something he'd feared and hated suddenly so beautiful that he felt his eyes burning with emotion.

Mal ended the scene. He heard the voices rising, the cheers and comments flying about them. But he didn't want to share this moment with anyone but Shiloh. Irrational, perhaps, but he had the crazy thought that the lights might blaze away this sweet haze. It might reveal the ugliness he'd been hiding from for so long, like the sun burning away the morning fog. He swept her up into his arms and marched off set.

Alone. He had to get her alone. He had to make sure she understood what this had meant to him. What *she* meant to him.

He threw open the door to the women's dressing room, thankfully empty. He kicked the door shut behind him.

"Please," she moaned. "Victor—"

"I've got you, baby." He hadn't felt this desperate, this crazed with need, in years. He set her down, determined to slow down and find his control again, but Shiloh took matters into her own hands.

She jerked her skirts off, let the shredded shift fall to the ground, and stumbled over to the couch. When she leaned over the back and grabbed the cushions for leverage, he knew what she wanted, and he wasn't strong enough to refuse her.

Not when he wanted it as badly as she did.

He struck the sweet curves of her ass with his crop, too hard, he feared, surely too much. "Shiloh," he panted. "Tell me what you want."

"You, I want you! Please, V, as wild and hard as you want."

She arched into his blows, raising her hips, and he couldn't wait any longer. He jerked his trousers open and surged inside her. "Where's all those dirty words, baby?"

She twisted her hands, tearing at the cushions. "I'm trying not to horrify you with my potty mouth."

"Tell me exactly what you want."

"Use your crop while you fuck me so hard I can't walk back on set."

Her words sent his heart thudding so hard, so loud, he

thought his head might explode. He thrust deep, slamming her into the couch, while he brought the crop down on her outer thighs, swinging the blows from side to side in a whistling arc.

She screamed, and guilt tore through his pleasure. Too much, he'd hurt her too much...

No, she clamped down on him in another orgasm. Shifting his grip, he brought the crop down on his own thigh and let the release take him too.

Sweaty and curiously relaxed, fully replete and at ease within himself for the first time in countless years, he laid his head against her back and kissed every single lingering mark he'd left. Only then did he realize that he hadn't used a condom.

She'd already told him he didn't need to use protection, and he'd certainly gone over her medical records. There truly hadn't been a need to use prevention, other than his own determination to keep her safe.

He'd lost control. Again.

His control was unraveling, fraying like a rope against a sharp rock. Another string broke, another link in the chain crumbled, and eventually, his cruelty would be free to ravage her to the ground.

She pushed up and turned in his arms, nuzzling against him like a kitten. "Don't start feeling guilty. You felt how much I loved that, didn't you?"

"Yes," he whispered against her hair, cradling her head tighter to his throat.

"I'm not going to break, Victor." Her words were muffled against him, but he heard the steel ringing in her voice and felt the fierce determination in her grip, her hands sliding up his back to hold him close. "You can't scare me."

He closed his eyes and held her harder, unable to say the words strangled in his throat. *Be afraid, baby, because I'm scaring the hell out of myself.*

Chapter Thirteen

V's Gift Blog:

Finally, Master V let me see beneath the mask. He gave me a taste of His crop, right there on set for our show. I swear on a stack of Bibles that I've never come so hard in my life. It was a wonderful, glorious, sweaty session, except for the camera crew, of course. I couldn't help but give Him everything, even though so many people watched.

The sad truth is, I'd do anything for Him. Anything at all. I have no pride, no modesty, no sense of shame, not when it comes to Him.

I can't even pretend to have any resistance. I don't want to shut Him down or play hard to get. I just want Him. Whatever that means, whatever He wants.

I'm His.

"What're you writing?"

Shiloh nearly jumped out of her skin. She whirled around and tried not to look guilty, but it was too late. Andy leaned over her shoulder and read the screen of her private blog.

Shit! Why did I ever start this stupid blog?

Grinning, he waggled his finger. "Oh, Shiloh, what were you

thinking? Didn't you sign a confidentiality agreement?"

"I haven't broken my agreement." *So why are my hands shaking?* She turned back to the computer and shut the browser, but the damage had been done. "I've never mentioned the show, VCONN, or anyone by name."

"Master V. Your cute little name for the show, *Gift*. Don't you think people will figure it out? I read enough to know you are talking about a BDSM reality show. How many other shows like this do you think there are?"

"I've had this blog for months, and I've never given away any particulars of the show."

"Do you think Mr. Connagher will give a shit whether you mention him by name or not?"

Her head thumped and she didn't feel like her knees would hold her if she tried to stand up. Victor would understand. Wouldn't he? What else had she had of him for all these months? She'd had to write out her emotions or go crazy.

"Are you..." She swallowed the choking lump in her throat and looked Andy in the eyes.

He flashed a wicked smile and headed for the door. "Don't worry, *Gift*. Your secret's safe with me...as long as you allow me to win top sub."

"What?"

"I don't care if you make it to the final round. That's totally cool. But you'd better bail on that final challenge and let me take the title. Mistress Mal must be the top *top*," he winked, "or I'll be having a little chat with Mr. Connagher and you, dear Gift, will be looking for a new job and a new Master."

Sick at heart, she took a deep breath and wracked her brain. She could fix this. She wasn't going to let Andy win the show, *her* show, not after everything she'd gone through to get here. She'd fight tooth and claw to win this show.

"By the way," Andy said, sticking his head back in the door. "I almost forgot the reason I stopped by. You have a crisis on your hands. Kimberly is hysterical, sobbing her eyes out, and swears she's quitting the show."

Great, just great. Not only did she face losing Victor because of her stupid tell-all-the-dirty-thoughts-I've-had-about-my-boss blog, she had to hand-hold his ex-fiancée to keep her from quitting the show.

She caught Kimberly on her way out at the large glass doors of VCONN Tower. Pale but calm after whatever hysterics Andy had witnessed, Kimberly saw Shiloh coming and kept right on walking. "I won't do it."

"Do what?" Shiloh walked with her down the sidewalk. "Nobody will make you do something you're uncomfortable with."

"I read tomorrow's sketch and I can't do it. I won't."

The next day's taping was titled "The Master's Hand." Shiloh had planned to have all the remaining contestants blindfolded and bound, while the Dominants then teased and played with them. The contestants would have to recognize their Dominant's hand, even if a different weapon was used.

"What if we only have the other two Dominants test you?"

Kimberly jerked to a halt and faced her. "You just don't get it, do you."

Taken aback, Shiloh floundered at the sudden antagonism. Despite the woman's past with Victor, Kimberly had seemed like a nice person. She'd cared about Victor's welfare. So why the sudden one-eighty?

"It's not Victor I mind. I told you, I loved him. I was devastated when I realized I couldn't be the kind of woman he needed. It's his crop that's a problem. But I'm going to have the same problem if it's Mal's flail or Patrick's whip, or a paddle, a belt, a cane... I can*not* handle pain. Not at all."

"I know," Shiloh mumbled, suddenly near tears herself. She could handle the pain, needed the pain, and was on the verge of helping Victor get over his hang-ups too, only now everything was falling apart. She'd gotten closer than ever to him, only to feel like she was falling out an airplane. "I thought just a little would be okay. Just enough for the challenge."

"It would look fake and forced," Kimberly said, relaxing back into the gentle demeanor Shiloh was more familiar with. "Just the thought of a blow, even a warm-up, makes me sick to my stomach. I'm sorry, but I learned a long time ago what my limits are. Pain is not a threshold I can play with."

"I understand." Shiloh stared across the street at the park, trying to make her brain function. Did she really have to have this challenge? Could she come up with something else at the last minute? But why bother, if Victor would be forced to fire her for breaking her confidentiality agreement?

A couple walked hand-in-hand in the park, laughing. Another family played Frisbee. She'd almost begun letting herself imagine a future like that with Victor.

"Shiloh? Are you okay?"

The marks on her back burned faintly, a reminder of what he'd done just hours ago. She'd hoped it would be a beginning, not an ending.

Her eyes burned, hot and dry.

Kimberly laced her arm with hers and led the way into a shop. Numbly, Shiloh went with her, fighting back the tears. "Sit. I'll be right back."

The dark, rich smell of coffee filled the air. Grateful, Shiloh sank into a chair in the corner. In a few minutes, Kimberly handed her a latte. Wrapping her hands around the hot cup, Shiloh breathed in and decided that the world could go to hell in a hand basket, as long as she had a cup of coffee along the way.

Kimberly sipped her drink. "Do you want to talk about it?"

"I'm afraid Victor might fire me."

Elegant, classy Kimberly snorted, an indelicate sound that made Shiloh smile at least a little. "After what I saw today, honey, Victor won't let you out of his sight. I'm surprised you managed to escape VCONN without the Master chasing after you with his crop."

Despite the joke, she shivered. Her body responded to the idea, more than willing to be run down by the Master and dragged back to his lair.

"You're serious, aren't you?" Kimberly reached over and squeezed her hand. "Is it something about the show?" Shiloh nodded, fighting back tears. "Oh, no, and here I am threatening to walk out on you! Is it something you can talk about with me?"

"I did something stupid and someone found out. Now they're trying to blackmail me into throwing the show even more than we already rigged it."

Kimberly narrowed her gaze. "Does this someone have red hair? That bastard. I never liked him. You know the best way to deal with blackmail, right?"

"Sure." Shiloh drained the rest of her coffee. Maybe the caffeine buzz would help her face the Master's fury. "Tell the one person I really don't want to tell."

"He loves you."

Startled, she thumped down her cup harder than she intended. "You don't know that."

"Not officially, maybe, but he does care for you, Shiloh. I've known him a long time, and it's obvious."

She really didn't want to think about exactly how well this other woman *knew* him. Certainly in the biblical sense, which made her grip the cup harder and contemplate bashing her over the head.

"It's as obvious to me that you are falling in love with him too."

"I'm that transparent?"

"Well, the screaming and moaning from the locked dressing room kind of clued me in."

Great, now her cheeks picked that moment to flood with color.

Laughing, Kimberly hugged her. "Oh, honey, sorry, I couldn't resist. So what are you going to do?"

"March straight back to VCONN and ask to speak to him. That's where I was headed before the same little prick who's threatening me said you were walking off the show."

Kimberly's amusement faded and her hands trembled enough that the cup clattered on the table. "I'm really sorry, Shiloh. I just can't do it."

"I understand. I'm sorry I didn't think things through better beforehand." Shiloh hugged her back and then stood. "Thanks for the coffee. I think I have the courage to face the Master in his lair now."

"Anytime. Are you going to be okay?"

My career? Sure, I can always find another job. My heart? Probably not. But Shiloh forced a smile. "Tell you what. If you want to know how everything unfolds, come back to the set tomorrow afternoon. That'll give me time to rework the challenge, or at least stage it where the non-masochists can exit gracefully and set up the next stage. I won't ask you to do anything that even begins to make you feel uncomfortable."

"Are you sure? I mean, I know the amount of work that goes into setting up the scenes and arranging the cameras. Plus, you have to write up at least a few lines for Georgia. Can you pull off a change this late in the game?"

"Worst case we delay taping until the next day." No, worst case was the show was scrapped altogether, but she refused to even consider that option. "Let me talk to Victor and Mal, but we'll go over everything after lunch tomorrow. Hopefully we can get something taped in the evening and not fall too far behind."

"Good luck, and remember, he does love you, Shiloh. Even if he doesn't know it yet."

Which only made the thought of losing him all the more painful.

"Ms. Holmes is here to see you, sir."

Victor pressed the intercom button and said, "Send her straight in," to his secretary. He'd hoped to drag her away from work early tonight, but she hadn't been in her office, and then he'd made the mistake of stopping by his own before going upstairs. If he didn't show up in the next half hour, Léon would be thoroughly insulted.

Shiloh stepped inside and the ground fell out from beneath his feet. She was pale, tense, and couldn't meet his gaze. Instead of stepping into his arms eagerly, she hesitated close to the door.

As though she's afraid of me.

His stomach felt as heavy and cold as though he'd swallowed his weight in lead. He'd seen the morning-after remorse hit a Dominant countless times, not just himself. Take a date home, show them a good time, a really good time, and then in the morning, they suddenly began thinking about exactly what happened. In the heat of the moment, the scene was hot and acceptable, but later, in the cold of the dawn, some submissives were suddenly horrified by what they'd done. Maybe they were ashamed of exactly how far they'd let the Dominant go. Or maybe they were just afraid.

He schooled his face to the calm, disinterested mask of the CEO, even while inside he panicked and thought very hard about throwing her over his shoulder and rushing her upstairs to his bed before she could escape.

It's too soon for me to feel this afraid of losing her. Isn't it?

His hand trembled as he tightened his ponytail.

"I need to speak to you as my producer and boss, not as my Master."

He breathed in deeply and held it several seconds. "All right."

She raised her gaze to his face and his heart slammed against his ribcage. Tears gleamed in her eyes, her lips trembled, and that was the end of his careful attempt as disinterest. He drew her into his arms, tucking her tightly against him. "What is it, baby?"

"I need to tell you something about the show, and I'm afraid..." His heart thudded so hard he almost groaned out loud. "You might fire me."

Cautious relief slowed his heartbeat down a bit. She didn't jerk away from him. She wasn't afraid of him in particular, and he didn't get the impression that she'd changed her mind after what had happened on the show. No, something else was bothering her, and the relief almost had him sinking to the floor on his knees and praising the Lord.

He kept his arm around her but drew her over to sit before

his desk. Sitting on the edge of his desk, he planted both hands on the arms of her chair and leaned down to kiss her. Her mouth trembled beneath his and he felt her breath hitch in her throat. "Why would I fire the one brilliant woman who brought the perfect show to me?"

Who made me face the darkness inside and showed me the light on the other side? Who isn't afraid of me—when I am?

"I have a private blog that I've been keeping for months. It's always been a habit of mine to keep a journal. It just helps me figure stuff out." She searched his eyes, begging him to understand. "I started it right after I met you. I know it was stupid to put it on the internet, but carrying around a diary made me feel like a horny teenager."

"Hmm," he murmured against her cheek. "I was feeling rather like a horny teenager myself today."

"I swear that I never mentioned you or the company by name. I never gave details that would help anyone figure out who either of us are. Mostly, it was stupid stuff, like I saw you on the way to my office one morning, so I had to stop off at the bathroom and..."

She ducked her head, her shoulders tight, so he could very well imagine what she'd done. "So you had to get yourself off before you could face me? And then you wrote about it in this blog?"

"Yes," she whispered, tightening her shoulders even more, making herself as small as possible. Out of fear, or guilt? "I'm sorry."

He dropped his mouth lower to her ear. "Dare I hope that you occasionally used the same dirty words that you whispered in my ear last night?"

A small moan escaped and goose bumps jumped up on her arms. "Yes. Sometimes. I just never thought anyone would find out, and what if they did? How could they know it was me or you?"

"What did you name this dirty little blog?"

"*V's Gift.*"

Ah. He'd wondered how she'd chosen that name for the show. "So you're afraid that with the show coming out that some very clever Dallas viewer may track it down? And then somehow figure out who you are, or who I am?"

"Someone has." She lifted her chin, her eyes hard. "Someone threatened to tell you and ensure I was fired for breaking my confidentiality agreement, unless I let him win top sub."

Victor knew exactly who'd threatened her. He sat back and blew out his breath. "Damn. Mal is going to be heartbroken. She loves that scrawny little runt."

Shiloh made a small noise, and he smiled at the disgruntled look on her face. "Here I thought you might not believe me, but you don't sound surprised."

"I suspected that Andy was my mole that caused us to scrap *Internet Secrets*. I just didn't have any proof." Scowling, he leaned back down close. "And I will always believe you, baby."

"You don't think I'm capable of lying to you? Not that I will, but—"

"You're capable," he agreed, nibbling at her lips. "And I'm more than capable of making you tell me the truth, no matter how awful you think it might be."

The last of the tension eased from her shoulders. Leaning into his embrace, she wrapped her arms around his neck. "I swear on your crop that I will never lie to you. I never mentioned you, VCONN, my real name or the name of our show on the blog. Just all sorts of inappropriate fantasies I've been having about my boss and an unnamed reality show I created to...how did you put it? Lure myself into your clutches."

"I should still punish you."

She hummed out a low sigh against his cheek. "Yes, please do."

"You're incorrigible. I thought I would punish you by having you read some of these inappropriate fantasies to me out loud."

"I can do that." Her arms tightened around his neck. "Andy might be a prick but I don't know that he was leaking show details. What are you going to do?"

Gently, he stood, removing himself from her embrace. "Let's continue this conversation upstairs, if you're free for dinner?"

She stood, too, one hip cocked daringly, her chin up and high, her eyes bright and confident. "I already told you, if you're asking, I'm free."

Turning back to his desk, he made himself keep the tone of the conversation light. "Then I'm asking you to spend the night with me." What he really wanted to do was clamp his collar on her neck, his ring on her finger, his name on hers and drag her away somewhere just the two of them.

Before she can change her mind like Kimberly did.

"Let me run home and get a change of clothes for tomorrow so I don't have to rush off like I did this morning."

He nodded and forced a smile. "I'll see you in an hour, then?"

Shiloh headed for the door. "We have another issue brewing on our hands too, so I need to rethink tomorrow's taping. I'll bring all my notes and storyboards. Maybe you'll have a brilliant idea."

"The first trailers are running on VCONN tonight too."

153

"Then it's too late for your mole to leak the show's details—we're going to be baring it all ourselves." She paused, her eyes sparkling mischievously. "You did call and warn your mom, right?"

Victor groaned. "I'll call Mama right now. God help me."

Chapter Fourteen

With a glass of wine at hand, her belly full of delicious French food and the sexiest man alive ensconced beside her on a cozy leather couch, Shiloh thought she'd died and gone to heaven. He'd even flicked the switch so the gas fireplace cast a lovely intimate glow in the room.

"All we really need to do is delay the punishment round for the finale," Victor said. "Then we can eliminate Kimberly and any other submissive not interested in the pain round."

"So we need a new challenge that portrays the lifestyle in a positive manner and with which someone like Kimberly would be comfortable. In the end, most of our viewers are going to be happier with a scene like that too, right? So we've done bondage, and we're going to do punishment. What else?"

"That's obvious." She turned in his arms so she could search his face. "Service."

"Remember, this has to be clean enough for TV."

"I don't mean *sexual* service." But his arm tightened about her shoulder, pressing her tighter against the side of his body. "Some Dominants love the sight of a bound submissive fetching useless things or performing small tasks." Evidently her distaste was obvious because he chuckled. "I take it you aren't into that kind of play."

"Would you rather have me on my knees servicing you or

trying to pick up a drink in my teeth because my hands are tied behind my back?"

"Hmmm," he hummed against her hair. "Let me think about that."

She elbowed him in the ribs hard enough that he grunted. "If you have to think about it, then I guess I won't do either of them."

"You won't?" He slid his hand up her back to palm the back of her head. "Even if I tell you very nicely?"

She resisted his grip, stiffening her neck and shoulders. "I would rather you tell me meanly."

"Would you, now." His fingers tightened in her hair, making her eyes water. His arm weighed heavy on her shoulders. A simple flex of his arm forced her head into his lap. "You can use your hands to pass me my wine but from then on, all mouth, baby."

Sliding to the floor, she reached behind her toward the coffee table, blindly feeling for his glass. He hadn't released her hair, so she couldn't turn her head. In fact, he held her tighter, closer, his fingers digging into her skull, making her pull her own hair to do as he'd ordered.

Which fired her blood and made her heart pound with anticipation. Phantom marks stung down her back, her skin remembering how just hours ago he'd put his mark on her body and then claimed her so forcefully. Her fingers dipped into the glass and she almost spilled it in her haste to begin. Finally, she retrieved the glass and lifted it, slowly rotating her shoulder and lifting her elbow to avoid spilling the red wine all over the carpet.

He took the glass from her and snagged her hand so he could lick the wine from her fingers. "Give me your other hand too."

Rubbing her face against the growing bulge in his pants, she lifted her left hand. He gripped her wrists, straining her shoulders and making her work against his grip to get her mouth on him. She lipped the zipper into her teeth and tugged it down so she could feel the hard ridge of his erection encased in his silk boxers. Tugging her arms harder, he shifted beneath her, making it easier for her to work him free.

Maybe the wine had taken the edge off her need, but she thought it more likely that the scene with the crop earlier this afternoon had given her the self-control to hold him gently in her mouth. She was as tender and slow as he'd been last night, making delicious love to his cock. Even his release was a low, deep groan of pleasure. No frantic need, no sharp agony twisting their muscles into a frenzy.

She rubbed her face against his thigh, lulled by his pleasure and the steady stroking of his fingers through her hair. She watched him take a long drink, and then he lowered his glass, turning it so she could put her mouth in the same spot.

She didn't make any move to return to the couch; it felt too good to wrap herself around his thigh. "Didn't you say Léon wants to open his own restaurant?"

"Yes, and I've already convinced him to let me provide his financing for a share of the business. All he's waiting for now is to finish college and save enough to purchase his building."

"Do you think he'd be open to serving a fantastic dinner for our Dominants?"

"I'm sure he'd be thrilled. What are you thinking?"

"We set up a nice dining table and you three order complicated, fantastic food that he'll prepare. Throughout the dinner, you could give each of us small tasks to perform, service, as you said. Then at the end, you can quiz us on what you ordered."

"So I would ask you questions, or would all the Dominants quiz you?"

"It'll be better if you all quiz each of us, but I know I'll do poorly for everyone but you." She rubbed her face against his thigh. "For some reason, I just can't take my eyes off you."

He drew her up into his lap. "Me neither, baby, but are you going to be able to let someone else win?"

Especially *her*, Kimberly, his ex-fiancée, who would certainly do well in this sort of challenge and look beautiful while doing it. Shiloh swallowed her jealousy. "This is the best way to let her and the other non-masochists save face. They win, and when the Dominants offer reward—which will really be punishment—they can bow out with whatever token reward you decide to offer."

"My jeweler called today and said the prizes are ready." He paused, giving her a heavy-lidded gaze that sent chills racing down her spine. "I had some work done on my collar so it would make more of a statement for the show."

Questions whirled and shrieked in her mind like hurricane gusts. *Did you give her your collar? Did she please you like I do? Are you ever going to love me like you loved her?*

He trailed his fingers across her throat, light and soft. "It'll look fantastic on your throat."

"I know it's just for the show." The narrowing of his gaze made her bite her lip. "I mean, you don't have to—"

He surged up out of the couch, his hands brutal on her hips as he held her against him. Without a word, he strode to his bedroom, set her on her feet, and began removing her clothes. He wasn't angry, but the grim set of his mouth and his silence unnerved her. "What about Andy?"

"What about him?"

Victor shoved his pants down his thighs and her heartbeat sped into the fast lane and kept right on going. She climbed into bed and hoped that he didn't plan to simply cuddle and go to sleep. "What if he's the spy?"

"I'll give him enough rope to hang himself once and for all." Victor turned off the overhead light but left the bedside lamp on. He stretched out beside her, propped up on his elbow so he could look down into her face. "Remember today when you put that rope around your neck and handed it to me?"

She nodded, searching his face for clues to what he was thinking. Shadows chased across his eyes, darkening his face, the grim face of the Master, but he wasn't giving pain or making demands. Nor was he trying so painfully hard to be the tender, gentle lover from last night.

"You trusted me. Even with a noose around your neck."

"You wouldn't have hurt me," she protested. "Even if we were doing a real scene instead of the show, I knew you wouldn't risk my life or try to scare me like that."

"There's no way in hell Kimberly would have done that. She didn't have that trust in me, because she knew I was hiding. She knew there was darkness below the surface, and she had no way of knowing exactly how deeply it went." He wrapped his palm around her throat, letting her feel the strength in his hand even though he didn't hurt her. "Ask the question that's tearing you up inside, baby."

"You asked her to marry you. Did you give her your collar too?"

"She was a good submissive: obedient, kind, graceful, beautiful with a gentle soul. Everyone at the club liked her, except Mal, but in this, I ignored her instincts despite the ten years of friendship. I had already hit thirty and realized my life was slipping through my fingers. I wanted to get married. I wanted to give Mama the grandbabies she's been hounding me about, and Kimberly was the kind of woman I thought she'd approve of.

"I was a fool, Shiloh. I thought I was being mature and responsible, while day by day, I died a little bit more inside. I hated what I was becoming and I didn't know how to stop it. Desperate and frantic, even if I couldn't show it, I took Kimberly home with me to the family ranch, and Mama was barely civil to her. Incensed, I told Kimberly we were leaving and had the argument with Mama that Mal had been trying to tell me for months."

Shiloh stroked her fingers over his lips. "What did she say?"

"She told me if I was stupid enough to marry a dishrag, then I deserved to drown in my own misery." He let out a self-depreciating laugh that tore at her heart. She tightened her arms around his neck, trying to pull him down for a kiss, but he wasn't finished yet. "I couldn't be a Master as long as I was with her. I couldn't show her what I really was. I couldn't ask her to respect me, because I didn't respect myself. I couldn't ask her to trust me, because I didn't trust myself."

He tightened his fingers on Shiloh's throat hard enough she could feel her pulse reverberating against his palm. "How could I give her my collar when I couldn't give her the Master? You trust me even though I haven't completely found my way back to trusting myself, and that's why I'll give you my collar, if you choose to wear it."

He couldn't seem to breathe while waiting for her response. He wasn't even sure that his heart was beating. Eyes large and wet in the faint light, she drew him closer, rolling toward him and hooking her heel behind his knee. That was an invitation he could not resist, so he pushed inside her, melding their bodies together as closely as he could. He held her, skin to skin, heart to heart, breathing in perfect synchronization.

Kissing his shoulder, his neck, his ear, she finally whispered, "I'll wear your collar. Proudly."

His heart exploded into a frantic flurry of joyous determination. It was all he could do not to drag her to the jeweler's and bang on the door until he opened the shop and let Victor have his collar so he could lock it on her neck.

She pushed against his chest, and he willingly rolled to his back so she could ride him at her pace. God, she was gorgeous, her eyes shining, her heart in her eyes. "I want to be yours, V. I want to do everything you've ever dreamed about, even the darkest most secret things you've never told anybody. That's why I called the blog *V's Gift*: I wanted to gift myself to you, body and heart and soul. Own me, take me, use me. I'm yours."

Despite the warmth flooding his heart and tightening his throat, he kept his hand on her neck so she wouldn't forget the trust she'd put in him. "Tell me what you wrote in that blog. You said you saw me, and you had to go into the ladies' restroom. What did you do?"

"I went into the stall farthest from the door," she whispered, her breathing ragged. "And I looked beneath the doors to make sure no one else was in there. I thought I'd just take a few minutes to breathe and calm myself down, but I couldn't stop thinking about you."

"What did you think about, baby? All the things I wanted to do to you? All the things you'd let me do?"

"I kept thinking that maybe someday you'd just look at me, snap your fingers and order me to follow you. And I would, Victor. I'd follow you anywhere. I'd do anything you told me to do."

"What if I told you to come into my office, lock the door and remove your clothes?"

"I'll do it, as long as you let me open your pants."

If she hadn't sucked him dry earlier, he would've come right then at her words. He fought down the urge to simply throw his head back and pour into her. "So there in that bathroom stall, did you pull down your panties or simply slip your fingers inside?"

She shuddered with a soft little cry. "I pulled them down."

He drew her down closer, changing the angle so she could grind harder against him. "How wet were you?"

"Sopping," she whispered. "I couldn't stop thinking about you. I wondered if you really were as Dominant as I suspected. And I was afraid."

"Of what, baby?"

"That you wouldn't like me, because I needed too much."

He let out a laughing groan that hopefully conveyed exactly how much he was liking her. "What do you need, baby?"

"You," she whispered against his mouth. "Hard, mean, tender, gentle, you. I want all of you, but especially the horrible stuff you don't want me to see, because I have horrible stuff too."

He'd meant to embarrass her—a mild punishment—by making her tell him all the dirty things she'd written on her blog, but she turned him inside out, just as she'd done last night. Was there anything she'd ever try to hide from him? Or would she blurt out her most secret thoughts and fears without a single hesitation if he asked?

Sliding his hand down her throat, he tugged firmly on her nipple, pinching and rolling her breast. Hard, too hard, unless she truly liked pain, and damn, did she ever. She threw her head back, her neck and chest flooding with a fresh wave of color as she climaxed.

He didn't try to delay his own release. How could he, when he wanted her so badly? When he wanted to reward her for her trust, generous spirit, and her tolerance for the very pain he needed to give?

Breathing hard, he untangled from her embrace enough to turn out the light and then cuddled her close. With her face buried against his neck, she whispered, "I'm falling in love with you."

That quickly, she turned him inside out all over again. He wanted her love, he wanted her trust, but the thought scared the shit out of him. If she loved him, she might let him go further than she was comfortable with, just as Kimberly had done. Then he'd horrify her, scare her, hurt her too much, and he'd lose her. Losing Kimberly had been a blow to his pride.

Losing Shiloh would rip his heart out of his chest and leave him gasping his last breath on the floor.

He clutched her hard against him, listening to her breathe, feeling her heart beat against his chest. If he could hold her like this—and not bring out the crop—then he could keep her forever. Stomach churning, he laid there, sweating, agonizing, for hours, unable to sleep, because he knew the truth.

She wanted his crop. As much as he did. And it was inevitable that someday he'd cross the line.

Chapter Fifteen

The phones were ringing off the hook. Shiloh had Victor and Mal cornered in his office, trying to plot out the best way to attack the afternoon's taping, but his secretary kept interrupting every five minutes with another Very Important Phone Call.

The smug bastard took every single one. Kicked back in his chair with his boots propped on his desk, he listened to every shocked complaint, giggled congratulations, and lawsuit threat with a smile on his face that grew wider with every call.

Shiloh gave a disgusted sigh and set the script aside again until he was done. "Why is he so happy with all the complaints?"

"We haven't had a response like this since VCONN first opened its doors," Mal replied. "Trust me, this kind of buzz means our ratings will go through the roof. The more controversy, the better. The newspaper and the local news stations already want interviews, and all they've seen is the trailer. If the mayor calls, V will treat the entire staff to the finest steak dinner with an open bar."

"Sorry about that." Victor joined Shiloh on the loveseat, wrapping his arm around her. He leaned over and gave her a lingering, soft kiss, stroking his tongue inside her mouth until Mal made a disgusted noise. "Where were we?"

The intercombuzzed again. "Mr. Connagher, the mayor is on line one."

Chuckling, Victor stood and headed back to his desk. "Why don't you two make a list of all the filler things we can tape this afternoon, particularly the judging sessions. I want to be in a position to view the pilot from start to finish tomorrow."

Mal grimaced. "Guess I'll be stuck with the film editors all day, then."

"Suck it up." Winking, Victor sat down at his desk. "We're going live Friday night."

Walking out with Mal, Shiloh paused at the door to see if he had anything to say to her. Anything private, or at least personal after last night. Why had she told him that she loved him? Because he treated it like a matter of fact, like it was his due, and that totally pissed her off.

She'd give him anything he wanted, but damn it, she wanted him to acknowledge her gift. She wanted him to treasure her and her love. He didn't have to be so damned ecstatic about the controversy, not if that meant he was too busy to be on set, too busy to work out the measly details that would make the show a hit, too busy to play a scene again.

Too busy for me.

She knew it was silly and immature, but damn it all to hell, she'd told him that she loved him and he'd said nothing.

Nothing.

Not even a fucking thank you.

"Mayor Reynolds," Victor said into the phone in that wicked, smooth voice of his. He gave a dismissive wave in Shiloh's direction. "What can I do for you today?"

Grinding her teeth, she shut the door as firmly as she dared.

Mal arched a brow at her. "So V said we were going to switch things up with the next challenge, but he didn't give me any details. Do you know what's going on?"

"We're introducing another layer of submission." Shiloh headed down the hallway and filled her mind with the mile-long list of to-dos instead of worrying about Victor. "Some of the contestants aren't into pain and didn't want to jump right to the punishment round."

"Some contestants being Kimberly." Mal blew out her breath in disgust. "So he's bending over for her? Again?"

"It was my idea."

"Damn."

That tone made Shiloh jerk to a halt and faced the other woman. "What?"

"You already love him that much?"

Shaking her head, Shiloh resumed walking without answering.

"What does he think about that? Surely he didn't ask you to take it easy on her."

"He doesn't care one way or the other." *About me or her*, she bit back. "As long as we make a good episode and get another phone call from the mayor."

"You don't have to do this, you know."

"Do what? The whole show is my stupid idea. I'm not going to back out now."

"Love will only make it hurt more."

Shiloh laughed wryly. "You know me, I'm a glutton for punishment."

"No, I meant V," Mal replied softly. "If he knows you love him, and then he hurts you, it'll only bother him more. He'll blame himself for using that love against you."

166

Tears burned Shiloh's eyes, which only made her madder, at herself, for letting him get to her so quickly, and of course, at Victor. "Why does he hate it so much?"

"Oh, hon, I don't know. He was brought up to be a gentleman who took care of the womenfolk, though once you meet Mama Connagher, you'll wonder what kind of man would ever presume that she needed anyone to protect her."

"I don't want or need him to protect me."

"He thinks he's protecting you from himself."

Shiloh groaned out a laugh—to keep from bursting into tears. "When that's what I want most of all."

Mal gave her a quick hug. "If it's any consolation, you're scaring him to death. You're pushing his buttons and forcing him to deal with what he's been hiding for so long."

"Should I back off a little? Quit pushing him so hard?"

"Speaking with the purely selfish reason that I enjoy watching the great Master squirm, I say no. You're challenging him like he's never been challenged before. If he needs you to back off a bit, he'll tell you."

Shiloh couldn't help but wonder if maybe that was exactly what he was trying to tell her. She'd assumed that he'd be more than eager to hear her declaration of love, just as much as he'd wanted to hear her submission. She wanted to please him, whatever that meant, whatever that required.

So if he didn't want her love...did she want to keep giving him her submission? Did it really mean anything at all to him? How could she not doubt it when he refused to give her that dark, secret side of him for which she'd been made?

"If you really want to make your point..." Mal shut her mouth and shook her head. "Never mind."

"What? Come on, Mal. You know how much I care about

him."

"V is very possessive. Most of us are. If you're setting up this next round for Kimberly to win, then you're going to lose, right? What if you had yourself punished by me and Patrick?"

"What would that prove?"

"Well, for one, it'll drive him insane with jealousy. No Master likes to see another Dominant playing with his sub unless he ordered it. But if you can take what we dole out, safe and clean enough for the show, of course, then maybe he'll realize it's not just him. It'll be a risky play, though, hon. Don't enjoy what we do too much, because you know what that'll do to him. You want to show that you enjoy him more, but that you can take pain when it's not just him."

Shiloh's heartbeat quickened and her stomach tightened with dread and anticipation. He would surely be furious if another Dominant laid a hand on her; he'd told her he intended to share her with no one. But Mal had a point.

I can endure anything, for him.

"Let's do it."

Victor stared down at the platinum chain studded with diamonds. Front and center, he'd placed a large V made of more sparkling gems. Tracing his finger along his symbol, he imagined the collar lying tight on Shiloh's neck. The image of red welts slanting down her back immediately came to mind from yesterday.

She'll wear my V on her throat and on her back.

The thought sent a fierce pulse of lust through him, but his stomach churned at the same time. Despite a terrible night of sleep, he'd woken up first and had plenty of time to survey the lines of bruises down her back. She didn't seem bothered by them, but the thought niggled in the back of his mind. Would she always bear his bruises? Was that the price she'd have to pay for his love? How could he ask such a thing?

Will I always be so savagely turned on at the sight of my bruises on her flesh?

Hand trembling, he covered the jewelry stand with black velvet. Patrick and Mal each had a stand on either side of his, and a flat tray held the individual necklaces they'd give each episode. For the pilot, he'd elected to use gold chains with a simple but elegant emerald heart for the ladies and gold cuff links for Andy, although rewarding the little prick would gall him to no end.

"If the Dominants are ready, we'll start with taping the judging ceremony for the pilot." Shiloh paused with an expectant look at Victor, so he gave her a smile and a nod despite the misgivings boiling in his gut. "Then we'll tape 'Serving the Master', followed by its ceremony, and then wait until after the pilot airs before taping the rest."

The contestants knelt in an arc before a low circular riser, while Victor and the other dominants took their positions on the top level behind the velvet-draped displays. Dressed in a gorgeous blue velvet riding habit, Georgia sauntered onto the set amidst brassy music that was quickly going to give him a headache.

"Our hopeful submissives have endured the Dominants' first challenge, learning about bondage dos and don'ts in the process. Unfortunately, three submissives will be sent home tonight. But first, let's see what the contestants are playing for."

Georgia twirled around so her skirts fluttered about her and swept her arm grandly toward the Dominants. All lights suddenly went out except for a spotlight on the hostess as she gracefully took the short steps to the top. "First, we have Master

P's collar. If you would, show our viewers what your contestants are playing for."

With a flashing smile, Patrick jerked the velvet away like a magician to reveal a complicated bridle-collar combination mounted on a Styrofoam head. A blonde plume stuck up from the top and hung down the back, mimicking a horse's mane, and silver chains hung at the cheeks that the submissive would supposedly take into her mouth like a bit.

Georgia gave a delicate shudder for the camera and raised her hand up to her throat. "My, my, Master P, that looks positively frightful. Are you sure your top sub will actually want to wear it?"

"Absolutely," Patrick said with another smug smile. "Or else she won't be *my* pony girl."

Georgia skipped over to Mal's display. "Mistress M, are you hiding tack under your cover?"

"Of course not," Mal drawled out as she flicked the velvet away to reveal a spiked leather collar. "I train dogs, not horses. My top sub will heel like a good boy."

Georgia smiled for the camera and reached out to lay her fingers on Victor's velvet cloth. "Oh, folks, just wait until you see what Master V has hidden beneath this cover. It's so gorgeous! I'd almost try out his crop just to have the opportunity to wear it. May I?"

He inclined his head and let her pull the velvet aside. The camera panned in to get the full effect of the large glittering diamond V.

Georgia fluttered her hand out toward the diamonds. "How many carats?"

He smacked the crop down an inch from her hand and she snatched her fingers back, her eyes snapping with outrage. "Enough."

She drew herself up and turned a haughty smile toward the camera. "That crop is a rather steep price to pay, so hopefully your top sub will think there's enough diamonds to justify the pain."

Clenching his teeth to keep the retort back, he saluted with his crop. Nothing would justify the amount of pain he'd end up giving Shiloh. That Georgia even implied he'd give diamonds simply to buy off his sub's affections made him want to tie the woman up and give her a few sharp blows from his crop, while dangling diamonds before her.

"Contestants, these are the collars you are fighting for. These are the Dominants who may claim you." Georgia walked over to the kneeling submissives, bringing them into the shot. "If you please them enough."

Watching Victor, Shiloh knew he was angry. His jaws were tight and he reached back to yank his hair in that merciless ponytail. His eyes bored into her, waiting for her reaction to the collar displayed before him, but she couldn't take her eyes off him. When he was upset and needed to release his emotions, he would always draw her attention, not a glittering necklace collar. No matter how much she wanted everyone to see that collar on her neck and know that she belonged to him.

The music rose to a crashing crescendo, signaling the submissives to kowtow before the dais. Shiloh leaned forward and planted her face on the floor inside the diamond made by her fingers.

"First, we'll hear from Master P," Georgia said.

Four submissives on Shiloh's left rose gracefully and stepped forward to the bottom step, where they went back to their knees.

Blood pounded in Shiloh's head. The corset made such a

position difficult to breathe. She listened to Patrick's voice droning on and on, but she didn't really hear his words. She didn't care. Georgia called Mistress Mal's submissives forward, and the same judging was repeated, but Shiloh kept running last night through her mind.

One minute he was all Dominant, all Master, ordering her to his pleasure with confidence and a heavy hand, just like she'd dreamed about. But the next, he was achingly tender and filled with guilt. Tender she loved. The *guilt* she could do without. It made her feel too much like the last time she'd dated seriously. Michael had tried so very hard to learn enough of the BDSM lifestyle to satisfy her, but he'd hated every moment of it. In the end, his guilt and reluctance had killed his love for her and damaged hers beyond repair.

Will that happen with Victor? No matter how much he cares for me, will his guilt destroy our relationship?

"Lastly, we'll hear from Master V. Will the remaining submissives please come forward?"

Shiloh pushed up carefully, making sure she didn't topple over backward after kneeling for so long. It'd been a long time since she'd actually played this sort of game, so her knees and back ached with strain. Kimberly, of course, moved with that innate willowy grace that made Shiloh grind her teeth and bile churn in her stomach.

The four women knelt at the bottom step and kowtowed again, face to the floor, ass in the air, with enough room that Victor could walk among them if he so desired. Evidently he did, even though the other Dominants had made the submissives come up the dais to them. He walked down the steps, tap tap tapping that crop on his boot. Forget the stiffness and the long wait—it was all Shiloh could do not to arch her back more and lift her ass in invitation for the first blow.

In silence except for the tapping of his crop, he walked around each of them and then halted directly in front of Shiloh. She could reach out and touch his boot—if he allowed it.

"At ease."

The submissives leaned back on their knees, rising so he could see their faces. He gazed at each of them equally. Shiloh searched his eyes, hoping to see a gleam of tenderness or even a flash of irritation, but the Master mask was fully in place. He slapped his thigh hard enough with the crop that they all jumped, Shiloh with delicious anticipation, although Kimberly made a soft sound of distress.

He turned to the submissive at the end of the line. Shiloh couldn't remember her stage name off hand, but she was the one who'd brought chain in the first phase of the challenge. The grim slant to his mouth and the hardness in his eyes made even Shiloh squirm. "You failed the bondage challenge. You will not wear my collar."

The woman ducked her head, wisely shutting her mouth rather than risk his ire if she begged or pleaded.

"Ruby, you survived this challenge but I won't reward you."

The red-haired submissive inched backward out of the spotlight without lifting her face from the floor.

He moved back to stand with one foot before Shiloh and one before Kimberly. From a pocket inside his jacket, he removed a golden chain from which dangled a sweet emerald heart.

He hooked the necklace on the end of his crop and lowered it toward Kimberly's face. "Willow, you did well in the bondage challenge."

Swallowing her fear, Kimberly reached out and took the chain off his crop. "Thank you, Master V."

His eyes narrowed and his mouth tightened. Kimberly paled, ducked low and backed away from him, leaving only Shiloh in the spotlight with him.

I won't make such a mistake, Shiloh swore. She deliberately licked her lips.

He pulled out another necklace and draped it on the crop. "You won the bondage challenge, Gift, pleasing me greatly."

Her mouth was watering, which was silly. He wasn't going to let her get too crazy with the camera rolling, but she knew the best way to turn him on. A good submissive would always lick or kiss the Master's chosen tool, and Kimberly should never have used her hands to receive his gift.

Shiloh made herself wait until the crop was an inch from her mouth, and then she leaned forward slightly, turning her face so she could rub her cheek along the leather. She couldn't help but let out a small moan of appreciation, remembering how that leather had caressed—and cut—her flesh. Working her mouth up the shaft, she licked the chain into her mouth and delicately removed it from his crop.

He stroked the crop along her cheek and down her neck. Gripping the necklace in her mouth, she didn't dare beg, but he knew what she wanted. He'd always know. He fisted his hand in her hair and jerked her against his thigh. Just like the original storyboard she'd shown him, she wrapped her body around him and buried her face against his hip.

"This week, our top sub is Gift, and the top sub's reward is..."

The overhead lights dropped so they were backlit, their bodies shadowed for the camera.

She fisted her left hand in his shirt, her muscles shaking with anticipation. From the corner of her eye, she saw his arm lift. The crop whistled through the air to slice across her buttocks.

Throwing her head back in ecstasy, Shiloh whispered, "Master V."

Chapter Sixteen

Bored to tears, Shiloh blinked and made herself concentrate on Victor. The three Dominants sat at a dining table they'd set up at Silken—to take advantage of their kitchen and more elegant setting—chatting and eating like the old friends they were. Other VCONN and Silken staff handled the serving, including the young man, Brandon, who had been so desperate at the tryouts. If she'd known he was so vulnerable, she wouldn't have brought him on set, although she had to admit his breakdown was just the kind of emotional impact they needed to make it real and believable.

The episode was titled "Serving the Master," but the contestants knelt off to the side and weren't actually participating in the serving of the food at all. That would surely have been at least amusing, especially if they'd been bound as he'd teased last night. The more she thought about it, the better that idea sounded.

Maybe he'd accidentally on purpose drop his fork beneath the table and make me fetch it...which would put my mouth very close to a certain tasty part of his anatomy, which I could service while hidden beneath the tablecloth...

"Remember our deal," Andy—Beau for the show—whispered beside her.

"No deal," she hissed out beneath her breath. "He already

knows everything. I told him the truth. You can't hurt me."

By the curl of his upper lip and the wrinkle in his nose, Andy totally disagreed with her statement, but Georgia turned to them for the next segment.

"Contestants," Georgia said, "Prepare for the quizzes."

Shit. She was going to suck at this. She might not even get Victor's questions correct. She wiped her sweaty palms on the petticoat and picked up the marker and pad of paper before her.

"These questions are for all contestants, regardless of which Dominant has taken interest in you. The contestant with the most correct answers will win this challenge. At each Dominant's discretion, the contestant with the worst performance may be punished."

Uh oh. By the narrowing of Victor's eyes boring into her, he didn't like that idea at all. Shiloh tried to keep the hopeful glee off her face and turned her attention to Georgia.

"The first question: How did Master P order his steak prepared?"

They had steak? Shaking her head, Shiloh scribbled "well done". Patrick was such a fastidious dandy that he surely wouldn't eat bleeding meat.

"Contestants, show your answers."

Shiloh turned her pad around and Victor's eyes narrowed to slits. His jaws worked as though he were still eating and his right hand was clenched on the table.

The prick beside her snickered beneath his breath.

"I'm sorry, Gift, everyone got the answer correct except you. Maybe you'll have better luck with this next question. Did Mistress M drink sweet or regular iced tea?"

The sound of busy scribbling filled Shiloh's ears, winching

her anxiety higher. She had no idea. Mal was a Southern girl, so surely she'd selected sweet tea. Right? But was it a trick question?

Georgia actually tittered this time as she read Shiloh's answer. "The correct answer is regular tea."

A loud crash jerked Shiloh's attention to the Dominants' table. Victor had slammed the crop down on the top so hard that the dessert coffee cups had fallen over. Face dark and mouth a flat, grim slant, a thunderstorm brewed on his face.

She ducked her head and waited for the next question.

"What did Master V drink with his dinner?"

I know this one! She wrote down red wine and waited until Georgia gave the signal to reveal their answers.

"The correct answer is Francis Coppola's Reserve Cabernet Sauvignon."

Fuck, Shiloh growled in her mind, risking a quick peep at Victor's face to see how angry he was. He was tapping his thigh—hard—with the crop.

"Master V, will you accept Gift's answer of 'red wine'?"

He gave a short jerk of a nod, but he slapped his thigh so hard his eyes and nostrils flared with pain.

"We have a tie between Willow and Beau, so this last question is only between them to determine who is tonight's top sub. If your Dominant were to order dessert, what do you think he or she would be most likely to select?"

Although she didn't have to answer, Shiloh burned to know what Victor would select. Brownies? Crème brulee? Strawberry shortcake? She had no idea.

"Display your answers. Master V, is 'ice cream' the correct answer?"

"No."

Kimberly's shoulders sagged with dismay, while Shiloh wanted to scribble madly on her pad, flipping page after page until he finally admitted what he would have ordered.

"Is 'hazelnut chocolates' the correct answer, Mistress M?"

"Mmmmm," Mal drawled out in her sexiest voice. "I love me some Rocher."

Shiloh shared a miserable glance with the woman beside her. Victor had lost tonight because of her. She hadn't expected to do well, but she'd hoped Kimberly would be able to pull off a win for him. His competitive nature would not be pleased, not at all.

"Now for the catch to this challenge," Georgia practically purred. Damn the woman; she didn't have to sound so pleased that Shiloh was going to get punished. "Master P, do you wish to punish Peppi?" He shook his head. "Fancy?" Again, negative. By now, Shiloh's stomach felt like she'd swallowed a gallon of Pepto Bismol. "Gift?"

He gave the perfect Hollywood smile and leaned over to slap Victor on the shoulder. "Absolutely. I've been dying to get my whip on that fine little pony."

Shiloh swore she could hear Victor's teeth grinding even though he sat at least ten feet away.

Mal agreed to punish all of the losing contestants, but Shiloh wasn't fooled. She knew the formidable Mistress would save the worst for her.

"Master V, do you wish to punish Gift for failing you tonight?"

Shame burned Shiloh's cheeks. She had failed him, not deliberately, but she was goading him, and that was a serious offense worthy of punishment.

"No," he said in a cold, hard voice that made her cringe. "It sounds as though Gift has finagled enough punishment for one night."

What the fuck is she doing?

Fuming, Victor glared at Shiloh, willing her to meet his gaze and explain herself. Mal had called a filming break in order to set up the punishments. The crew bustled around, talking excitedly, but Shiloh kept her head down, refusing to look at him. Had she planned this whole thing just to get back at him for suggesting a service round? Or was she trying to make a different point? That perhaps other Dominants would be willing to give her the pain she craved if he wouldn't?

Either way, he was royally pissed.

Damn it all to hell, the last thing he wanted to endure was the sight of Patrick uncurling his whip and contemplating which luscious inch of her back to mark.

Her back is mine *to mark, mine to bruise, mine to cut with leather, and not just any leather, but my* crop.

"Put the cross here," Mal said in an entirely too bright and cheery voice. She stood directly in front of the table, ensuring he'd have a perfect view of his sub getting punished by another Dominant. "For this one, we definitely want to make sure she's bound."

Rage pulsed so dark and ugly through him that he trembled. He'd never bound her, and now another would do it and make him watch. He closed his eyes and concentrated on breathing, instead of ripping that damned contraption apart with his bare hands and dragging Shiloh upstairs where he would bind her, punish her within an inch of her life, and then make savage love to her until she never again even thought to invite another Dominant to lay a hand on her.

Something touched his knee and he flinched, his eyes

flying open. Shiloh huddled at his feet, her forehead pressed to his leg. "Forgive me, Master V. Give me the order and I'll refuse. We'll re-film the entire episode, and I'll endeavor to watch everyone's food selections instead of daydreaming about what I could do under the table with the tablecloth to hide me."

Some of the turmoil shredding his gut faded. He heard the sincerity in her voice. By the catch in her throat, she might actually be near tears. Silently, he laid his hand on her head, rubbing his fingers against her scalp.

"I'm sorry. I didn't mean to upset you."

"Yes, you did." He sighed out a long breath but kept his fingers gentle on her head. "I'm assuming Mal helped you plan this out?"

"She said it would be risky," Shiloh admitted, twisting her head so she could look up at his face. "Are you very angry?"

"Yes. And I'm going to be much angrier after I have to sit here and watch Patrick ogle my sub while he whips you."

Her eyes were dark and solemn. "Am I yours?"

He tightened his fingers on her hair slightly, a subtle signal to draw her tighter to him. "I told you I'd give you my collar, didn't I?"

"For the show."

Gripping her chin none too gently, he forced her up off his knee and leaned down to glare into her face. Her eyes glittered with unshed tears. Damn it, why would she cry about his collar? He'd already said he'd give it to her. "Is that it? You want a commitment from me off the show? You want my collar now? I'll give it to you."

"All I want is you." She kept her voice soft but she jerked out of his grip and stood, moving away to a safer distance. "You don't understand this part of the challenge at all, do you? I'm not trying to make you jealous, V, because nobody could possibly hurt me as good as you."

"You get off on pain, Gift, so you're going to have sex with another Dominant in front of me, after I told you I was a selfish bastard who refused to share you with anyone. I'd say that gives me the right to be pretty fucking jealous."

She shook her head, turned her back, and walked away. "I'm not going to feel pleasure in this, because the whip and the flail won't be in your hand. If you don't believe me, watch. See if I come. I'm telling you I won't. I'll endure it, no matter how badly they hurt me, simply because I failed you and I'm trying to make a point to you."

"What?"

She threw back over her shoulder, "Exactly what I told you last night."

Last night, she'd said she was falling in love with him. Words that had both thrilled and terrified him. Today, he'd tried to pretend he hadn't heard those words, that he didn't hope and pray for her love with every fiber of his being, because in the end, he was bound to hurt her. He was bound to scare her.

I'm bound to lose her.

They strapped Shiloh face down on a St. Andrews cross. There wasn't anything to rest her head on, and they made sure she could see Victor. So she would be forced to watch his reaction. That was the real punishment, not whatever they'd do to her back.

Mal had suggested that she strip down to the shift and pantaloons to make sure the corset didn't bite into her. Plus it would make it easier for her to breathe through the pain if she could actually expand her lungs. She knew they weren't going to spare their blows for the show.

182

They were going to punish her, for real.

There would be no sensual arousal to help balance the pain. No petting and stroking, no soft words of encouragement from a loving Dominant. No, this was pain and lots of it.

Her stomach felt curdled and tight to her spine. Her pulse beat so frantically she couldn't hear whatever Georgia was saying for the camera. It would be so much easier to bear if it were Victor dispensing the pain. Just the thought of him lifting a flail—it didn't have to be his crop—and bringing it down on her flesh was enough to turn her on. It wouldn't matter how much it hurt. The more the better. In her mind, the pain would blend with the need she felt for him and become something overwhelmingly and frighteningly orgasmic.

She closed her eyes and concentrated on breathing deeply until her panic quieted. Opening her eyes, she met his gaze. He could make this so much easier without even lifting a weapon. If he'd made a direct order that she should endure whatever they did, then she would still be able to find pleasure in the punishment. She'd have a purpose for letting them hurt her. But he was tense, his face dark, his eyes hard. She knew he didn't relish this at all.

Maybe he'll punish me himself later.

Patrick blocked her view, drawing her gaze up to his face. "How much can you take, Gift?"

"That depends, sir." She tried to be polite and not snide, but she couldn't pretend that he frightened her, let alone turned her on. "How strong is your arm?"

"Strong enough that my subs can usually only take a handful of strokes before they're crying out their safeword, and they have the benefit of play before and after. You're getting nothing but punishment, honey."

"If they can take five, then give me ten."

His eyebrows climbed. Shiloh was particularly grateful that she couldn't see Victor's reaction. "Are you sure? I don't intend to do damage, Gift, but the whip is a precision weapon with a great deal of cut. I won't allow the leather to break your skin, but I'm not going to start gently, either."

"Ten, sir." She dropped her gaze and tried to show sincere regret. Thinking about Victor's reaction to this display helped dramatically. "I deserve punishment for failing the quizzes."

Patrick stretched his arms, opening his chest and warming up his muscles as he stepped behind her.

"Her safeword," Victor said in a voice that made cold chills race down her spine, "is Christmas. I expect you to use it if you need to, Gift. That's an order."

She kept her head down for him, giving him the respect even though he wasn't participating in the scene. "Yes, Master."

"Christmas," Patrick drawled out. "Very well. Count them out, Gift, so I'm not forced to start over at the beginning."

The long leather tail snaked on the floor, rasping against the wooden planks, promising agony. He gave a trial snap that made her flinch, but the whip didn't touch her. Not yet.

He laughed softly. "Ready?"

"Yes, sir."

She heard the sharp crack of the lash before she felt the cut of his blow on her left shoulder. Her breath rushed out and she twisted her wrists in the bonds, but she didn't cry out. Damn, that hurt. He must have managed to hit one of Victor's bruises. "One."

If it'd been Victor delivering punishment in a formal scene, she would have thanked him for it, but not Patrick. Not unless her Master ordered it.

Panting, she opened her mind to the pain. She didn't fight

it or tense her muscles. In fact, she relaxed everything. Her knees sagged, but the bonds kept her upright. She fought her eyes back open and sought Victor.

Don't you understand I'm doing this for you? This is nothing compared to what I want—need—you to do.

He gave a slight nod of his head but his face remained stiff and remote. An order, or encouragement? She couldn't tell. His face was too hard, his eyes too dark.

As a consummate showman, Patrick trailed the leather across the floor, drawing out both her tension and the viewers'. When her breathing had steadied, he pulled his arm back and sent the whip whistling through the air again. Pain bloomed on her opposite shoulder.

She sucked in her breath and clenched her jaws to keep from crying out. She wouldn't make a sound for him. Screams and moans were rewards for the Master wielding the weapon, and she refused to reward anyone but Victor.

When she trusted her voice, she whispered, "Two."

"I'm impressed, Gift. I thought surely you would be whimpering by now. Maybe you'll endure ten strokes after all."

Her back burned so fiercely she did want to whimper, but she looked at Victor—his hand clenched about the crop that was laid in his lap, his other hand wrapped around his wineglass so tightly she thought it might shatter—and she clamped her mouth shut.

Blowing out a shaking exhale, she drew in another long breath, filling her lungs in a slow, controlled breath. She didn't want to hyperventilate and pass out. Patrick would be insufferable, and she couldn't bear to hear him teasing Victor about it later. He threw back his head, drained the glass and signaled Brandon to fill it again.

She'd known this would be difficult for Victor to watch. Did

185

he yearn to punish her himself? Would he see that pain didn't scare her? Could he see the difference in how she felt while Patrick did this, and how she'd react if it were Victor delivering the blows? Because just the thought of him standing and striding over to deliver a single blow with his crop was enough to make her suck in her breath and fight back arousal.

It would be so easy to let the pain melt into something else; hot, molten need coursing through her veins. But only if she had Victor at the other end of this punishment. For Patrick and Mal, it had to remain pain. She didn't trust them like she trusted Victor.

She didn't need—let alone love—them like him.

The blows continued, one by one. She had to admit that Patrick was a skilled Master. He timed each blow so that she anticipated it. She had plenty of time to think about it and know that the next blow was going to hurt more than the last. He never hit the same spot twice, so by blow seven her entire back felt blistered and charred with pain.

With her eyes clenched shut, colors burst behind her eyelids, whirling and dizzying fireworks. Pain became red and orange, the fire of the sun blazing on her unprotected flesh. The ice-blue of flame. The dark purple of a fresh bruise.

Sweat dripped in her eyes, her muscles quivered up and down her back like a twitchy horse tormented by flies. Her jaws ached from the strain, but she refused to release a single scream, even though it would make her feel better. Fuck, it hurt. It felt like he was peeling her flesh off her bones strip by strip.

If Victor were behind her, she'd know she was pleasing him. He'd be punishing her with his body, tormenting her with what she couldn't have until he decided she'd had enough. And bliss, he'd touch her. He'd speak to her. His voice alone right now could send her screaming into release.

For this Master, all she felt was the vicious strokes with no relief, no pleasure in sight.

"Ten," she gasped.

And now Mal gets to do the same thing. A soft sound escaped her lips. Not a moan, thank God, but a small crazed laugh. *This has to be the stupidest thing I've ever done.*

"Very impressive." Patrick circled her so she could see his face. "You've fully satisfied your punishment, Gift."

She'd been creeped out by him and his pony shit, and there was obvious tension between him and Victor, but for the first time, she really appreciated his skill and dedication. The whip had been like an extension of his hand, and he'd timed and placed each blow exquisitely.

She tried to smile but her muscles were jumping and trembling too much.

Georgia stepped in front of her, fluttering a fan frantically before her face. "Our viewers certainly know not to fail such a challenge when playing with one of our Masters. Well done, Master P."

"Cut." Victor pushed up from his chair, his voice as harsh as though he'd shattered that goblet and swallowed the shards of glass. "Mal."

The Mistress became producer in a heartbeat. "Let's get Shiloh out of these bonds and continue filming with Peppi on the cross while Shiloh takes a break."

As Victor approached, the other Dominant inclined his head and stepped back with a grand flourish. Without another word, Victor loosened a cuff and caught her against him effortlessly, supporting her weight while he unbuckled the other.

Now, she moaned. Yes, her back was on fire and his touch made those marks sting, but the torment came from his body, his nearness, and most of all, his control.

He locked his hands on her arms and swept her off her feet. She couldn't help but moan again. She clutched his shirt and buried her face against his neck. Just the scent of his skin and the heat of his body were enough to feed the pain blazing on her back, twisting it toward pleasure.

Yet he still didn't speak. Despite the fact that they were both dressed in period clothing, he strode out of Silken, tossed her in the front seat of a red sports car so quickly she didn't even see its make, and tore out into traffic.

"Victor—"

"No," he growled. "Don't you dare speak to me right now."

Shame flooded her face and hitched her heart in her chest. Was he that angry? Tears dripped down her cheeks, where she hadn't cried while being whipped. She'd endured that pain for him.

I would endure anything for him.

He jerked the wheel sharply and pulled into the underground parking beneath VCONN Tower. In moments, he hustled her out of the car and into the elevator, still grim and silent, his fingers locked about her arm so hard she'd have bruises tomorrow.

More bruises that would ultimately torment him with more guilt.

He dragged her down short hallway to his private penthouse, threw open the door, and marched her straight into his bedroom where he threw her flat on her stomach across the edge of his bed. Planting his forearm on her neck, he pinned her, his breath rasping in her ear.

"So you want to be punished? Let me show you what I think about your little display with *Pat*. Maybe next time you should put on a bridle for him."

The crop cracked against her ass so hard, so fast, she couldn't help but scream. All the pain she'd taken from the other Dominant's whip suddenly boiled back to life. She remembered every stroke, every whistling blow, and now Victor augmented that pain with his own. The pent up need she'd kept bottled deep inside exploded out of her. Shuddering, she came so hard she bit her lip and tasted blood.

The crop lashed her again and again, building that fire until she sobbed and moaned his name, fighting his grip. "Please, V, God, please!"

"What do you want, *Gift?*"

"Please, fuck me, Master. Fuck me so hard that I can't think, I can't breathe, I can't move without remembering you inside me."

He ripped and tore his way through her clothing and slammed inside so hard that he stole her breath. Her vision wavered and pain speared through her. He wasn't a small man, not at all, and he took no care to ensure her pleasure. This wasn't about her. This was about the Master taking what was his, imprinting himself on her psyche so deeply that she couldn't imagine ever having sex with another man ever again.

The crop came down again on her hip and outer thigh, the pain a red-hot brand to tie her to him forever.

Nobody will ever hurt me as good as Victor.

Her mind felt fuzzy, disconnected from her trembling, wracked body. She cast herself higher, giving him the screams he needed to hear, the pain he needed to know she felt and enjoyed, and yes, the pleasure that shattered her mind and left her sinking into warm, velvety darkness.

She made herself a gift and gave her heart and soul to him.

Chapter Seventeen

I've been thinking a lot about V's desk. It's a shiny black monstrosity nearly as wide and long as a king-size bed. Now if you're thinking that I'm fantasizing about stretching out on top of that desk, then you don't know me very well at all. No, my fantasy would be to hide beneath the desk.

Can't you just see some snooty high-society lady droning on and on about whatever fundraiser she wants Him to support, while I unzip His pants with my teeth?

As a Master, He'll be able to control Himself for a very, very long time, and I'm a damned good submissive. I can play for a very long time.

I love His cock, every inch of it. I'll lick it, kiss it, simply put my face on it and breathe His scent. Only when He puts His hand in my hair and shoves deep into my throat will I start to suck.

I'm terrible, I know, but it makes me laugh every time I think about it. If you're ever lucky enough to enter V's office and He doesn't rise to shake your hand, maybe my fantasy just came true.

The crop lay on the mattress, mocking him. He'd broken

his promise and brought the damned thing into his bed. Furious, he slung the crop across the room, unable to bear the sight of it.

Curled around her protectively, Victor held her in his arms, waiting for her to awaken. He listened to her breathing and watched her face for any wincing or indication of pain. Dear God above, what had he done? The great Master had so little control that he couldn't bear to see his sub play with another Dominant?

Patrick had played cleanly. He hadn't copped a feel or made any inappropriate comments, but jealousy still ate a hole in Victor's gut every time he thought about that damned whip.

Her face had twisted in pain, straining, he knew, not to cry out. Not to indicate any passion behind those blows. Had that pain been the sick, hurtful kind of pain, like pulled muscles and torn tendons? Or was it the damned good kind of pain that heated her blood and made her wet?

Damn it, he knew the answer, and that's why his belly burned with acid.

He'd never been so possessive of a sub before. Even after they'd become engaged, Kimberly had often done scenes at Silken with other Dominants, and he'd thought nothing of it. Maybe it was the pain aspect, which he himself associated with arousal and sex. The kind of pain one received in a scene was the kind that got him off. No Dominant had ever gotten Kimberly off while he watched, at least not that he knew about.

Murmuring beneath her breath, Shiloh turned in his arms and nuzzled deeper into his chest. "That was fantastic."

"I didn't hurt you?"

"Mmmmm," she nibbled and kissed his throat. "You hurt me so good."

He squeezed her tighter, fighting to keep his voice calm and even. "You weren't scared?"

She drew back so she could look up into his face. "Are you kidding? Hell no, I wasn't scared. I loved it." She bit her lip, searching his gaze, and then blurted, "I love you. I trust you. Don't you know that?"

"How..." He swallowed the ragged edge in his voice. "How can you trust me?"

Shadows flickered through her eyes that he couldn't name. Doubt? Concern? Anger? "Are you saying I shouldn't?"

Releasing her, he stretched out on his back and stared up at the ceiling. "I don't know. I don't know how far I'll go. I don't know what my limit is, and if I don't know mine, how can you trust me not to cross yours?"

"I don't know what my limits are either." She laid her head on his chest and stroked her fingers up and down in lazy swirls, teasingly giving a light pull on his chest hairs. "Are you scared of me?"

"Hell, yes, I'm scared of you. Baby, you push me so hard I'm afraid I'll drag us both off the cliff."

"Well, as long as we go together, I don't care."

She said it so lightly, as though she really didn't care, while the very thought made him ill. How could he love and protect her if *he* was the one who'd hurt her the worst?

"I suppose we ought to get back. Mal still needs to punish me."

Stiffening, he fought for a calm and reasonable tone of voice. "I really don't like another Dominant to punish you, even for the show."

She propped her elbow on his chest so she could stare down into his eyes. In a somber, gentle voice, she said, "You know you're the only one who can ever truly punish me, don't you? What Patrick did was just a show. It didn't mean anything."

"It meant a big fucking deal to me to sit there and watch him hurt you." *When I wanted to hurt you myself.*

"It hurt, sure, but it certainly wasn't as glorious as what you just did. I'd much rather have you hurt me." She shrugged, so nonchalant that he wanted to shake her. "It's sort of like prostitution."

He blinked, trying to follow her reasoning. "You're not a whore."

"That's not what I meant." Nibbling on his ear, she whispered, "But I'd be your whore, your slut, yours to take however you want. There's absolutely nothing I won't do for you."

Lust speared through him so fiercely he thought seriously about rolling her over and beginning all over again. Mal could handle the afternoon's taping. Hell, why not the whole evening?

"What I meant is that when a whore has sex for money, she might enjoy it sometimes, but it's work. It's a job. If she gets any pleasure out it, that's a bonus."

"I still don't see how that applies to what you did with Patrick today."

"It was a job. I didn't take pleasure in it. It hurt, but I didn't let it become pleasure, not like I would have if you were at the other end of that whip. Does that make sense?"

"Pain is pain, and for us, that means pleasure."

She made a disgusted noise and sat up, sliding to the side of the bed. "Don't be obtuse. You know that's not true, or else why don't you come every time your knee hurts? Patrick whipped me today. It was like your knee surgery. It was necessary. I felt no enjoyment in it."

Snagging her arm, he squeezed until she turned and looked at him. "I don't like it."

She leaned down and brushed her lips against his. "After Mal's done with me, drag me off set, slip your fingers under my petticoat, and see how much I liked it. Okay? And then, Master V, you should definitely punish me yourself."

Mal met him at the door to Silken. "All hell's breaking loose."

Sighing, Victor reached back and tightened his ponytail. *All hell's breaking loose inside me too.* "What's up?"

She gave a hard look at Shiloh that made him wrap his arm around her, instinctively drawing her closer. "You may not want her to hear the details."

"She hears everything, especially if it's about the show."

Mal flipped on the television above the bar. "Oh, it's about the show all right."

As soon as he saw KDSX sleazeball, Frank Firkuss, Victor knew it was bad news. They employed only the worst kind of backstabbing, vicious mudslingers and dirt-mongers.

"After a titillating preview of VCONN's upcoming show last night, we are thrilled to have stumbled across a blog created by one of *America's Next Top sub's* contestants. According to our information, this contestant is the exact same woman in the trailer released by VCONN."

Shiloh started to pull away, but Victor kept his arm locked about her. She wasn't getting away from him that easily.

"Even juicier, the contestant works at VCONN. Shiloh Holmes is an Associate Producer at VCONN, but reportedly began dating President and CEO, Victor Connagher, and suddenly found herself the show runner for *Top sub*." Firkuss pointed to the screen behind him to their silhouette from the trailer. He let out a slick, fake laugh. "Perhaps *dating* isn't exactly the right word. Now who does this look like to you?"

He held up a picture of Victor in profile from a recent charity event, his longer hair clearly visible. It wouldn't take much imagination for the viewers to see the resemblance.

Reeling, he felt like the rug had been jerked out from beneath his feet. He hadn't minded people within the BDSM community knowing his identity, but this... He and Shiloh had just come out of the closet in a very big way. Everyone in Dallas would know the kinky shit they were into, and the gossip and rumors would get worse with each and every episode.

Do I dare proceed with the show? If it drags Shiloh's name through the mud and airs all our dirty laundry to the entire city?

"I don't know how she got details on *Internet Secrets*," Mal said in a clipped, tight voice, "but she's been your spy all along. She's only trying to get closer to you to leak more information."

Shiloh jerked away from his arm and stepped toward Mal, her eyes flashing. "I would never do such a thing! I didn't even know about your show, so how could I have possibly leaked any of the details? Do you think I would leak my own name like that? Everybody in Dallas thinks I'm doing my boss just to get a promotion and spot on a sleazy show."

"Aren't you?"

"Enough," Victor retorted. He took Shiloh's hand and drew her back to him. "She didn't do it, Mal. I know about the blog. She told me herself."

"So? That doesn't mean she didn't call up Firkuss and tell him all about it too."

"Why would I do that? Do you have any idea what I put on that blog? How many times I wanted to approach Victor but I didn't know how, all the secret fantasies? Oh, God..." She turned and buried her face against his chest. "I'm so sorry. Everybody will read those things. They'll know it's you, won't they? It's so obvious. They'll read all the horrible language I used, see all the secret things I've thought about doing with you. I can't bear it. Why was I so stupid?"

Victor wrapped his arms around her and dropped his chin on top of her head. He'd taken the time to read several months' archives of her blog, and he suddenly found the whole situation rather amusing. He even started to chuckle. "Next time I invite someone into my office and I don't get up to shake their hand, they're going to assume you're under my desk giving me a blowjob."

She made a high-pitched wail that only made him laugh harder.

"You think this is funny?" Mal stared at him like he'd suddenly sprouted another head. "Everybody in Dallas is speculating that Victor Connagher is the meanest Master in town."

"Aren't I?"

"Well, yeah, sure, but do you want everyone to know it? Right now, we can bluster with threats of a lawsuit to shut KDSX up, but if you continue to tape the show, more and more people are going to assume Master V is you. They can't help but make that connection, no matter what kind of mask you wear."

"I know." His mind leaped ahead, imagining the fallout. After the pilot, the speculation would only get worse. *Or better*, he thought, allowing a wicked grin to twist his mouth. "Our ratings are going to shoot through the roof. Everyone will watch just to see if they can tell for sure it's me."

"And that doesn't bother you?" Mal asked incredulously. "You know what kind of Master you're showing yourself to be on the show, right? This isn't nice, safe Dominant play like what you did with Kimberly all those months. This is the real shit, V. People are going to know you're a sadist."

Despite his growing excitement for the show's success, he couldn't deny a kernel of uneasiness. "We're keeping it clean enough for TV." *As long as Shiloh doesn't push me over the line.* "We're not doing latex, ball gags or dungeon shit."

"Yet."

He arched a brow and looked down at Shiloh's head. "Are you planning a dungeon scene?"

"Not exactly." Her words were muffled against his shirt. "There is a punishment round coming up, though. I don't know how far we'll end up going. It might get rather intense."

"We can pretty it up for Dallas." He tried to keep his voice light, but Mal's eyes narrowed. She'd caught the unease in his voice. If only he could pretty himself up for Shiloh and ensure her safety. If he could keep his mind clean, his crop in control and his need for brutality under wraps...

"If she didn't leak this blog, who did?"

Victor met Mal's gaze and made his voice as soft and gentle as possible. "Andy."

She snorted and whirled away, striding rapidly in the opposite direction. He and Shiloh followed her into Silken's office. "I don't believe it."

"He's the only other person at VCONN who knew about my blog," Shiloh said. "He threatened to tell Victor if I didn't let him win *Top sub.*"

"That doesn't mean he called up KDSX and leaked the show or the blog."

"I told him earlier today that he couldn't blackmail me because Victor already knew everything. I told him all about the blog and honestly, I expected him to fire me." She peeked up at his face to judge his reaction. "I especially expect him to fire me now that his cover is blown."

"I've been hiding a long time," he said softly, leaning down to kiss her. "Maybe it's time to stop hiding Master V behind the mask of the CEO."

He didn't realize how tense she'd been until she melted against his chest. Tears glittered in her eyes. "I didn't mean for this to happen. I tried to keep everyone's identity a secret with the masks. If I hadn't started that stupid blog..."

"I love your blog. In fact, I want you to write another entry. Right now."

"What?" She spluttered as he pushed her toward Ryan's computer. "I should delete the whole damned thing before they have the chance to spread it all over Dallas."

"Don't you dare." He gave her his most intimidating glare. "I'm going to talk with Mal awhile about Andy, and I want you to write a juicy new entry. Make it as scandalous as you can imagine. Drop a hint about the leak—that you can't wait to see what happens once I get my hands on him. And then write about what we taped just now, and what happened afterward."

"You want me to say that..." Her eyes were wide, her mouth soft and so lush it was all he could do not to smash her against him for a long, deep kiss that would curl her toes.

"I was so incensed after watching another Dominant punish you that I had to drag you off set and fuck your brains out." He winked at the choked sound that escaped her mouth. "Or whatever inappropriate language you can think of. You're so much better in that arena than I am."

Victor sat with Mal before the fireplace while Shiloh typed up her blog entry. Crew came and went, cleaning up from the dinner and checking in for their next duties. When he noticed

Léon and Brandon together, he couldn't help a small, smug smile.

Sniffing and wiping her eyes, Mal stared into space. "I just can't believe it. Why would Andy do something like this?"

"I had a friend do a little digging, and it seems as though Andy has gotten himself into trouble with gambling. He and a bunch of his college buddies are playing poker pretty heavily."

"Gambling? But he never..." Mal met his gaze and he reached out to squeeze her hand. "How could he hide something like that? From me?"

He suddenly had an inkling of what Kimberly must have felt after dating him for months—and agreeing to marry him—before he'd finally shown her the real Victor beneath the calm, safe, controlled mask he'd been hiding behind. A BDSM relationship revolved around trust, and to keep such a secret from a Dominant or a submissive, broke that trust. It shattered every illusion of safety in a caring but politically incorrect relationship.

"I've whipped that boy to climax. I've tortured him with need until he begged me to come. He's licked my feet, slept on the floor, and even wore women's panties to class because I told him to. But now... It's like I don't even know who he is. I had no idea he was gambling so heavily he'd feel so desperate that he'd betray us. If he needed money, I would have helped him."

Giving Andy the benefit of doubt, Victor tried to think of something more positive to say than he was a lying dirty cheat. "Maybe he was too ashamed to ask for help."

"No." Mal shook her head. "He's asked me for help before. I've even given him an advance on his salary—out of my pocket, not VCONN's—because he said he needed to fly home to see his parents. I wonder if he ever did. Maybe that was just a lie. Maybe everything's a lie."

"What he had with you wasn't a lie."

"Wasn't it?" Mal laughed, a raw sound closer to a sob. "I've been preparing mentally for the war with Mama if I bring Andy home and introduce him as my live-in lover and possibly my someday husband, only now to find out he might have been using me all along. He's been stabbing VCONN in the back, and instead of submitting to me, he's been fucking me over this whole time."

"We don't know how deeply he's in this, Mal. I know you're hurt, and I have to admit that I think he's a prick for how he tried to blackmail Shiloh, but you're jumping to conclusions about your relationship. He might be the most committed sub—"

"No man could truly submit to me while withholding such secrets," Mal said in a flat, hard voice. "I'm done. He's getting out of my house tonight."

"I think we should play this smart. Let him dig himself deeper. If you question him, he'll only be defensive and try to lie his way out of trouble. Let him entrap himself, and, if we're very lucky and good, which you know we both are, we'll make laughingstocks of KDSX, Firkuss and Andy."

"How?"

"We let Andy leak information—but we choose what he leaks, and we play the show."

Mal released a low rumbling growl that she usually saved for the scene. "In this mood, I'm afraid I'll rip his dick off."

Smiling, Victor shrugged. "Keep it clean enough for TV."

Chapter Eighteen

Georgia resumed her hostess duties as though nothing had happened. "Mistress M, would you like to punish Gift for failing to answer your questions correctly?"

Shiloh tensed instinctively. She'd seen the emotions tearing up the other woman's face. If Mal chose to punish her while she was so angry, Victor would end up being very pissed indeed.

"Not at this time." Mal gave a hard smile for the camera, but Shiloh knew she was thinking about saving all that rage and hurt for Andy. "Although I reserve the right to punish her if she fails the next challenge."

Georgia inclined her head and turned to the camera. "Very well. Let's begin the judging."

Pressing her forehead to the cold floor, Shiloh waited in the shadows while Patrick kicked off another submissive and rewarded Peppi with her necklace. Victor had chosen rubies this time, one of Shiloh's favorite stones, which made losing this round hurt even more.

Mal went next, and she was terse with Andy even though she declared him winner. He dared to slip his hands up her thigh beneath her riding habit, giving her a cocky grin that had surely won him much favor in the past.

This time, Mistress M planted her boot on his chest and shoved him backwards to sprawl on the floor. "Remember who your Mistress is, boy."

Disgraced, Andy remained prone, face pressed to the floor.

"And now, let us hear from Master V," Georgia said.

Instead of coming toward them, Victor stayed on the dais while the contestants rocked back to their knees.

He began in a severe voice that could have blistered paint off the walls. "Gift, you failed to answer a single question correctly for both Mistress M and Master P. Service is a crucial skill for any top sub, and while you serviced me to the best of your ability, you failed to please the other Dominants. You brought shame upon your Master."

Shiloh dropped back to the formal kowtow position. Yeah, this was all a show, but his critique still stung as fiercely as any blow he could hope to deliver. She could have done better for the other Dominants, but her best would always go to Victor.

"Willow, you answered the most questions successfully tonight out of all the submissives competing for my collar, and so you win this challenge." Canned applause filled the silence, but Victor looked far from pleased with his forehead furrowed and the short, impatient taps of the crop against his hip. He walked toward Kimberly, continuing to slap his thigh repeatedly, and his face went even grimmer with each flinch she gave. "However, I have significant doubts about our compatibility."

He gave one last loud strike against his thigh, and Kimberly kowtowed before him, shaking. "I can't do it, Master. I'm so sorry. Please dismiss me instead of Ruby."

Her words melted even Shiloh's heart. His face softened and he bent down, his hand gentle as he lifted Kimberly up to stand before him. Sincere tears dripped down her cheeks, her face twisted with grief.

"I'm sorry." Gently, he latched the necklace around her

neck for her. "I cannot change who I am, and neither can you. You'll make a less edgy Dominant very happy indeed."

Taking Kimberly's hand, he bowed and kissed her knuckles, keeping with the tone of the show. Head high, she walked off set, leaving Shiloh and the other contestant before Victor. "Return to the line."

Georgia stepped forward and patted him on the arm. "I'm afraid you're not the top Master tonight."

He gave her a look that made her pale and jerk her hand back. She forced a shaking smile for the camera while the Dominants arranged themselves on the dais. Victor and Patrick stood on the lower ring and Mal took the top, although she looked none too happy about it.

"Tonight, our top Dominant is Mistress M, with her submissive, Beau, at her feet."

Victor's jaws were tight and his fingers white on the crop. Shiloh swallowed a heavy lump of guilt in her throat. It stung his pride to lose a single game. In the end, though, this loss would give the show more drama. He couldn't win every single challenge effortlessly, or their Dallas viewers would cry foul.

In her opinion, of course, he'd already won top Dominant.

After the earlier refresher course on humility, Andy crawled up the steps and pressed his face against Mal's boots. If she hadn't been so upset about his likely betrayal, she might have stretched out the performance for the camera, but she merely called, "Cut!"

The lights came up and the crew milled about, a little surprised at how quickly she'd ended the scene. Andy actually looked a little scared. He didn't get up immediately, and when Mal moved away, he clung to her ankle, earning another sharp kick to free herself.

"Mistress, what's wrong? Have I offended you?"

Her jaws worked, her eyes dark with reproach. Victor came to her aid. "Sorry, Andy, she's upset with me. I need all my editors working through the night to make sure the pilot is ready. Do you have friends you can hang out with tonight? I thought I'd just have Mal sleep over in my guest room so I could work her as late as possible."

"Oh, sure, I was going to meet some friends after work tonight anyway. Are you going to have an opening night party, Mr. Connagher?"

"Of course," Victor smiled, and Shiloh couldn't help but shiver. Was Andy really that stupid? Couldn't he see the shark swimming beneath the surface, mighty jaws at the ready to swallow him whole? "It's tradition, isn't it? My place, Friday night. We'll watch the pilot together."

Hours and days flew by in a blur of frantic work. Shiloh, Mal and Victor worked long into the night managing the thousands of details that would make or break the show. Victor fielded all the countless phone calls and public relations. Mal proved to be a godsend in the editing room, and she was more than willing to spend every waking moment at work so she wouldn't think too much about Andy.

Shiloh worked herself into a stupor each day and then fell into Victor's bed for another kind of blissful stupor. They made love each night, sweet and slow or hard and passionate, but they didn't play BDSM games. She didn't feel any lack, and evidently his needs had been met—at least temporarily—on the show.

Watching the pilot was surreal. She didn't recognize herself masked and in costume, kneeling at the fierce masked man's feet. She'd known Victor would be incredibly hot on the screen, but watching him and seeing the tightening of his eyes and mouth, the darkness flickering in his eyes, the quick, hard tug on his hair, all signaled how much he wanted her. How much the little scenes they played out turned him on.

She became so unbearably aroused that she felt swollen and achy, as though they hadn't had sex for months. Years.

She suddenly understood why some people got off on voyeurism. Watching the trailer was enough to make her tremble and break out in a sweat. If he brought out his crop and smacked her with it, she'd come right here in the middle of thirty or more chatting guests. They couldn't leave soon enough. They all applauded wildly after the credits rolled, and Shiloh's eyes filled up with tears.

Her name, listed as creator and show runner. He'd given her full credit. She couldn't imagine what KDSX would do with that little tidbit. Would people leap to all sorts of conclusions about her relationship with Victor? Could the gossip be any worse than it already was? Although those words printed out in black and white on the screen were proof that she was real, that the blog was real, and so her relationship with Victor Connaghter, CEO of VCONN, must also be real.

Grueling hours at the office had taken a toll on Victor's knee. Grimacing, he rubbed it while he talked with Mal. Everyone else had left, but Shiloh couldn't begrudge the other woman his time. Not with the difficulties she was experiencing with Andy.

"How am I supposed to pretend like nothing's going on? Like I don't know what he's up to?"

Victor's upper lip curled slightly as though he smelled something bad. "Pretend. Use your anger and hurt to punish him better than ever. That's all he'll care about." He let out a short, harsh laugh. "You have the opposite problem I experienced with Kimberly. I don't know if it'll be easier to pretend you don't need to punish him, or to pretend you're punishing him with love and not real rage."

As unobtrusively as possible, Shiloh knelt before him and began rubbing his knee. With a grateful smile, he stretched his leg out, making it easier for her massage. She kept her touch light and gentle on those sore muscles, slowly building up intensity.

"I don't know how you did it for so long," Mal said, shaking her head. "At first, I admired your ability to keep the dark side under lock and key."

"And then?"

"Then I wanted to beat the shit out of you because I knew you couldn't possibly hide forever, and Kimberly wasn't the kind of woman who could deal with the Master."

Shiloh bit her tongue to keep from blurting out, *I can deal with the Master. I'll deal him all day, all night, any way he wants.*

She ran her fingers down the sides of his bad knee, stretching those tendons with firm, long strokes of her fingers. His eyes fluttered, his breathing caught, just a slight hesitation, but she heard it. Keeping her head down, she made herself concentrate on her work and not what he might be feeling. Fears and doubts raced and tumbled in her mind like a frantic hamster running on its wheel.

Does he love me? Will he accept our relationship, both the normal sex and the darker side of pain we both crave? Or will he keep pushing that need away? Will we have to run season after season of America's Next Top sub *to get the relief we both need? Will he ever see his handiwork and feel as much pride in those bruises as I do?*

As long as he kept the crop under lock and key, she knew

she'd never have his full heart.

"I can see myself out," Mal said as she stood. "Thanks for listening to me bitch and moan about Andy."

"You've certainly listened to me often enough."

Silent, Shiloh kept her head down and her fingers busy on Victor's knee. His voice had lowered to a silky rumbling timbre that spoke of arousal and long hours of pleasure.

Or pain.

Mal laughed softly and gave her a friendly squeeze to her shoulder. "You've got magic hands, Shiloh. I haven't seen the Master this relaxed in years."

"I may not need surgery after all."

At that compliment, she couldn't help but jerk her gaze up to his face. "Really? It's helping that much?"

His mouth quirked. "You're helping all sorts of things. VCONN's ratings. A shitty season with our front runner forced to cancel at the last minute. My bum knee."

"A Master with a crop and no sub to enjoy it," Mal added, with a slight emphasis on *enjoy*. "I'll see you two Monday morning at eight o'clock and not a moment earlier than that, okay?"

"Yes, ma'am," Victor retorted in a voice that made his friend snort. They both knew who would top the other if they were ever forced to play together.

Shiloh moved her hands up slightly higher and gripped his thigh, drawing her fingers firmly down the long lines of muscle to his knee. He let out a groan and dropped his head against the back of his chair. Listening to Mal's departing footsteps, the door shutting, his breathing deepening, Shiloh bit back the words and tears threatening to bubble up. Her heart ached in her chest, yearning to please him in all ways, even those he was too reluctant to bare. The same need gnawed deep inside her, sharp and relentless. Making love with him was wondrous, but sometimes...

Sometimes I need you to whip me with that wicked crop until I scream and beg and cry. I need you to hurt me, so good, so very, very good.

She couldn't ask him, though. Not when it was so difficult for him.

She pulled her fingers down the upper curve of his calf, but his boot interfered. She gripped the heel of the cowboy boot and pulled it off, then the other, and he made no protest. Now she could work his calf and the tight tendons running down to his ankle. Every muscle and tendon would be strained to compensate for the weakened ones at his knee, even if they didn't consciously hurt him.

When his leg was completely relaxed and putty in her hands, she leaned forward and pressed light, reverent kisses where she knew he bore the surgical scars. She rubbed her face on his thigh and trailed her fingers lightly up and down his calf, simply worshiping his strength and muscled power.

He dropped his hand to her head and rubbed her scalp gently. With silence in the house and the Master fully at ease before a romantic, dancing fire, she could cry for being so happy. So quickly, he'd become home to her. Family. This is where she belonged, and if he ever sent her away...

Her throat tightened and her eyes burned.

"What can I now do for you, baby?"

His voice sounded thick with sleep...or sex, although as relaxed as he felt beneath her hands and cheek, he was surely just tired. His fingers didn't tighten in her hair. He made no move to drag her mouth to better use.

Tightening her arms around his leg, she hugged his thigh

and relished the feel of muscle beneath her cheek. She hadn't worked so hard to relax him, only now to ask for something that would make him tense and worry about how far she might push him. "Love me?"

He reached down and pulled her up into his lap. She tried to burrow into his neck—so he wouldn't see the darkness in her eyes—but he wouldn't let her hide. No, the Master could hide all he wanted, but he would never tolerate such dishonesty in his submissive.

She tried to make herself angry with him, but it didn't work.

He kept his hands gentle, but she knew he had to see the truth written in her eyes. *If he doesn't...then he can't be my Master, no matter how much I want him to be.*

The thought made her want to throw her head back and screech with grief at the top of her lungs.

"I do love you, baby. I know I haven't said it out loud, but I've been trying to show you."

His words only made her agony worse. *Show me how much you love me by bringing that crop into your bed. Rip the mask away and give me the real you, all you, all night, all weekend, the rest of our lives.*

She smiled tremulously and fought to keep the stream of pleas dammed in her mind instead of reflected in her eyes. He was the Master, she the slave, at least in this. It wasn't about what *she* needed; she wanted to please *him*. She wanted to keep the lines of pain smoothed from his face, his knee loose and comfortable, and the shadows of guilt out of his eyes.

"You have shown me." *Every time you lift that crop.* "I love you, Victor."

He pulled her against his chest and nuzzled his face against her hair, his breath warm on her ear. "Do you know where I keep my crop?"

Tension rippled through her body. Of course she'd noticed where he put the crop after each taping. It hung on a hook inside his closet door. She'd wanted to ask him whether he'd always kept it there, for surely Kimberly would have noticed it. A good submissive would have taken careful note of where the Master kept his tools so they could be fetched at a moment's notice. How could the crop on the inside of his closet not have signaled what kind of Master he was?

"Yes, of course. Shall I get it and your cleaning supplies?"

"I'll clean it," he breathed heavily in her ear, his hand sliding up her back with enough pressure to send her heart galloping faster. "After I whip you while you suck my cock."

Chapter Nineteen

The flare of hope in her eyes made his heart hurt in his chest. *Intolerable*, he thought as she leaped from his lap to do his bidding, *for a woman I care about so very much to feel like she's unable to express her need for fear of upsetting me.*

A caring, attentive Dominant would never neglect his submissive's needs, not unless making a deliberate point or lesson in discipline. She would not ask for what she needed, for she knew all too well his struggles to keep the sadist at bay.

When it was the sadist she needed most of all.

I'm falling in love with an incredible submissive who knows what I need and want better than I do. I can—and want—to do this.

He couldn't deny the heavy thud of his heart, the coiling need building in his groin, or the fierce joy he felt at the sight awaiting him in his bedroom. Shiloh knelt beside his bed, nude, with his crop laid on the edge of the bed. Her eyes were large and dark with her need, the same shadows he knew must be reflected back at her as he raked his gaze over her body.

Stepping closer, he began undressing, forcing himself to go slowly and methodically. She didn't say a word but he noticed the tenseness in her shoulders and arms, as though she fought against her natural instincts to reach out and speed him out of his clothes. When he picked up the crop, she let out a sighing exhale, and that tension in her upper body simply melted away.

He pointed at the foot of the bed. "All fours, facing me."

"Yes, Master." She did as he ordered, making sure she kept close to the edge of the king-size bed so he had easy access to whatever body part he might wish to torment first. Without being told, she kept her legs parted, her back arched to show her breasts and ass to the best of her ability. She made an offering of herself, her eyes silently pleading with him to feast upon every inch.

Instead of fisting a hand in her hair and setting to work immediately, he forced himself to walk about the mattress and take a good, long, appreciative look at her from all angles.

Of course, he slapped the crop against his thigh, a stinging rhythm that made him hard and eager to mark her flesh. Her, too, if the gleam of moisture on her upper thighs was any indication.

"Let's get one thing very clear, Shiloh. If I'm failing to meet a need that you have, you must tell me. Even if you think it's something I don't want to hear."

She hung her head. "Yes, Master."

"So tell me all about that darkness I've noticed in your eyes tonight."

"I need you to hurt me, Master. Hurt me real good."

A red-hot iron poker jabbed through his spine and stirred his innards into a steaming, boiling pot ready to explode. Before he even realized his arm had cocked back over his shoulder, he landed a blow on her ass hard enough that she quivered and cried out with surprise.

Red bloomed on her skin, a hypnotic, addictive sight. He burned to lay Vs up and down her body, imprinting his will on every inch of her heart and soul until she was his.

He wanted his diamond V on her throat and red Vs of pain on her body.

Breathing too fast, he took a deep breath and held it for a long count of ten before he trusted himself to speak. "Too hard?"

"Never, Master." Her voice was as sultry as a Texas summer night and she bent her elbows so she could arch her ass higher in invitation. "Thank you, sir. Shall I count out loud?"

"No."

He hated "thank you, sir, may I have another" formal shit. It was too much like Patrick's demonstration, which ratcheted his lust up exponentially. He wanted her screaming and begging and crying for release, not calmly and coolly counting out his strokes. With that thought, he landed another blow on her other cheek.

She sucked in her breath and rocked back on her knees to meet the next blow.

He whipped her until her ass was hot, red and swollen, until he feared she might not be able to sit down for a week, and yet she lifted into every single stroke. Her moans of pained appreciation urged him onward, to strike harder, sharper, compelling him to give more pain. She'd buried her face in his bed, her cries muffled against the blankets, so he strode back around and jerked her head up by a handful of hair.

"Oh no you don't, baby. I want to hear every single cry you make. I want every response, everything you're feeling. Have I taken you high enough yet?"

"Please," she moaned, fighting against his grip. "No."

His gut twisted with a sharp thrust of fear that absolutely did not feel good. In fact, he thought he might actually puke on the carpet. "Shiloh, do you need me to stop?"

"Please don't stop! I meant no, you haven't taken me high enough yet. I can take more, V. I can take everything you need to give me."

She knows I'm still holding back.

The thought terrified him, even while lust exploded through him so hard and violent he felt like the top of his head had blown off. He thrust into her mouth, forcing her to take him all or choke, while he brought the crop down on her back.

Careful, he tried to remind himself. *Ribs. Spine. Not too low. Protect her kidneys.*

While demons shrieked and lit hellfire through his veins.

He kept the blows to her shoulders, slanting the crop so he could see the red Vs forming on her upper body. He drove into her mouth, his back arching with an orgasm that ripped out of his body, sandblasting every thought and doubt and fear from his mind.

Shaking, his bad knee weakened. He leaned against the bed, grateful for her steadying hands. She licked and sucked until he thought he might expire on the spot. Or come again, he wasn't sure. Laughing raggedly, he forced his eyes open and his amusement died.

Blood dripped from a deep slice of the crop, trickling down her lovely back.

"Lie down on your stomach," he ordered in a voice that froze her heart with dread. "I'll get the first-aid kit."

His face was hard, a statue of granite and guilt. She hated the way he averted his gaze. One minute, he was all Master, all sadist, taking his pleasure and sending her soaring into the ether, and the next, he buried her in a six-foot-deep hole in a tiny box that would suffocate them both.

She did as he ordered and tucked her face in the crook of her arm, trying to decide what to say. She still felt too good and high on endorphins to really feel any pain, but it must be bad. Why else would he clam up like that so quickly?

Nothing extraordinary or edgy had happened. Nothing had made her uncomfortable. She hadn't been afraid or in doubt one moment. In fact, she'd thought she was finally seeing the real Victor, the real Master, the real sadist. Exactly who she wanted. Exactly who she needed.

But the man who sat on the edge of the bed and carefully touched a gauze pad to her back was a cool, reserved stranger. He dabbed antiseptic on the cut and she sucked in her breath at the sting.

He made a low sound of regret that made her eyes burn with tears. "Victor—"

"Be still," he replied in a rough voice unlike anything she'd heard from him before.

"I'm not injured."

She felt the tremble in his fingers. "You're bleeding."

"That happens sometimes." She cocked her head back, twisting her shoulders so she could see his face. Pale, sweaty, and breathing short and fast, he looked like he might faint. "Are you all right?"

He let out a choked sound. "No. No, I'm not. I hurt you."

She scooted closer and laid her head on his thigh. "I bet that's when I came so hard I nearly passed out."

The stinging slashes were beginning to cut through the blissful haze, and she wanted nothing more than his arms around her. Maybe a soothing massage, his hands easing the pain he'd lovingly given her. A long soak in the Jacuzzi, cradled between his thighs.

The muscle beneath her cheek quivered with tension and his silence weighed heavily in the air. Maybe she could lighten his mood. On that thought, she lightly bit his thigh.

He jerked away and stood up to pace. Tightening his hair, limping on that knee, he radiated pain and guilt. His right hand slapped against his hip, and then his mouth twisted into a grimace of self hatred.

Throat aching, she sat up and crossed her arms over her chest. Her backside throbbed and it felt like it'd swollen to twice its size. It hurt too badly to sit, but she didn't want to stand here naked and hurting, aching for some cuddling, if he was only interested in punishing himself for hurting her.

When that's exactly what I wanted. What I needed. What he needed.

She pulled on her pants, not bothering with underwear. She had a feeling the elastic bands would hurt like a bitch. Same with her bra, so she simply jerked her T-shirt over her head.

"Where are you going?"

"Home." She grabbed her shoes and sat on the foot of the chaise. "And before you start in on your guilt trip, it's not because of my back. You hurt me, Victor, but not with your crop."

"I don't understand."

"I wanted this to happen. I asked you to bring your crop into your bed and show me what you could do with it when it's just you and me. I loved every minute. Don't you understand? I wasn't scared. I wasn't anywhere near begging you to stop. You were my Master, exactly what I wanted and needed you to be. So for you to shut down like this hurts me more than anything you could do with the crop in your hand."

"I hurt you too much."

"Not until I needed you to hold me and you pulled away."

He stared at her, his jaws grinding and the column of his throat working. "I didn't want to push myself on you after I'd just hurt you."

She snorted and jerked the laces of her shoes tight. "That's what I needed most of all, Victor. I needed you to hold me, and you were too busy feeling sorry for yourself."

His eyes flared with indignant surprise. "I wasn't—"

"Yes, you were. Every time I think I'm finally seeing the real you, you decide to flail yourself with guilt instead of my ass with your crop. Maybe you're a bigger masochist than I am. Admit it. You're sickened by what we just did."

He opened his mouth but no words would come. Eyes wide and dark, face pale, he looked stricken, as though she'd just announced his entire family had all been killed.

Swiping angrily at her tears, she turned away and scanned the room for the rest of her things. "I can see the guilt on your face, and I don't need that. I don't need you, not if you can't—"

Her voice broke, but it was her heart shattering into a million pieces. She'd sworn she wouldn't ever ask a man she cared about to hurt her if he couldn't stomach it. "I thought you needed the same thing, or I never would have asked."

"Shiloh, baby, don't leave. I swear I won't hurt you like that again."

She closed her eyes and struggled to draw in a breath against the crushing grief dragging her down to the depths of the ocean. "And that's exactly why I have to leave. I *want* you to hurt me like that again. I need it. When you take me to that dark, sharp place of pain, then that's where I find myself. I'm free there, freed by the pain and the pleasure it brings. I thought I'd found you there, too, but you hate it, don't you? You're always burying that side of you away, hiding it from me, and I can't stand it. Nobody hurts me as good as you, Victor, but I can't stand to see the guilt on your face. The shame. You'll hate me eventually, and I refuse to ask you to do something you hate so much."

Stumbling through the tears, she headed for the door, and he made no move to stop her. He didn't call out for her to stay. He didn't chase after her. And that told her more than anything that he must be relieved he wouldn't have to keep fighting her to hide the truth.

She paused at the door and looked back at him, memorizing the harsh lines of his face. Dark hunger still blazed in his eyes, stark and raw despite his reluctance to bare the Master. Every time she closed her eyes, she'd see him like this: naked, angry and desperate, but so fucking relieved to see her go.

"By the way," she ground out, determined to ease some of the guilt on his face. "Don't ever worry that you won't be able to stop in the middle of a scene. I was never once tempted to give you my safeword tonight, and yet you still had the control to pull back and make sure I was okay. No, if anything, you can't go far enough for a pain slut like me."

Chapter Twenty

Driving up to the Connagher ranch was like stepping back in time. Victor parked his Corvette beneath the mighty maple he'd planted with Daddy and his younger brother. Mama loved all sorts of plants, but especially roses. They'd dug so many holes over the years they'd begun to joke they'd run out of acreage, which was hardly a possibility with Daddy's thousand-acre spread.

He'd built the house with his own two hands, determined to make his own way and provide for the woman he loved who could have purchased the finest mansion in Dallas. A busted-up cowboy who'd ridden his first bronc before he could read, Tyrell Connagher had been a man of few words, hard hands and a heart as big as Texas itself.

Virginia Connagher waited on the wraparound porch as though she'd known her son was coming home, even though he hadn't made the hour drive up from Dallas in months. She wore the same thing she always did; riding jodhpurs, English riding boots and a spotless white shirt, even though her hands and knees were dirty from digging in her garden. Her black hair was sprinkled with a bit more gray, her face lined with a few more wrinkles, but her eyes still snapped with the fiery spirit that had captured Tyrell Connagher's heart forty years ago.

"Hi, Mama."

"Son." She looked him up and down and he couldn't help but straighten his shoulders and widen his stance. He braced for her to begin questioning him, but instead, she smiled. "Come on down to the stables and see the new foals."

Relieved, although he tried not to show it, Victor walked with her down the red-dirt road to the long horse barns behind the house. Proudly, she showed off the new stud she'd shipped in from Ireland and the yearlings in the paddock, and bit by bit, he managed to relax. The smells of sweet hay, feed and horse were as familiar to him as the two-story farmhouse where he'd grown up. He'd worked with Mama in the show ring and Daddy in the fields, rounding up the cattle and shipping them to market. He'd ridden every inch of their acreage and spent hours with Conn down at the creek fishing and swimming.

Standing at the fence and watching a sleek bay mare with her spindle-legged foal, he felt the last stone of guilt fall away. Here, he knew exactly who he was. He was *the* Victor, the oldest Connagher son, football champion and proud of his hard-working parents. Maybe he could convince Shiloh to drive out here with him. If she saw him here, the real Victor, then maybe...

"I saw your show last night," Mama said, her voice too careful for him to tell what she'd really thought about it.

He propped a boot up on the bottom rail but didn't turn to look at her. "What'd you think?"

"I was wishing your Daddy could watch it with me so we could recreate a few of those challenges ourselves."

Victor practically choked on his tongue.

Mama chuckled at the look on his face. "Surely you wondered where you got such an inclination. Did you think I'd be horrified at the thought of my boy with a crop in his hand?"

"Yeah, I did," he admitted sheepishly. "I guess I should

have known better when Conn called me a few years ago for help."

Nodding, Mama leaned against the fence and turned that steely blue gaze on him. "He's not as hard as you. He never was."

"Not as mean, neither."

"Oh, Victor, is that what you think? That you're mean?"

He ground his teeth and averted his gaze. *I'm one mean sonofabitch, Mama. I like to hurt people. Especially the woman I love.*

"I suppose you think I'm mean, then."

That made him jerk his gaze back to hers. Just a few inches over five feet tall, she possessed the kind of quiet, commanding presence that made people snap to attention whenever she walked into a room. No one would claim she was a ravishing beauty, but once someone met Virginia Connagher, it was hard to take their eyes off her.

Reluctantly, he had to admit it was the same kind of power he'd always had. People listened to him. He never had to raise his voice, and if he did, he scared the shit out of people. He'd always assumed he'd inherited that top-dog attitude from Daddy.

Thinking back over his childhood, he tried to remember a time when Mama had ever overruled Daddy. They'd always worked like a team, smooth and well-oiled. Daddy wasn't a big talker, but he'd always handled the discipline. A look from him could strike terror into the most recalcitrant boy's heart, so he'd never gotten into much trouble beyond the normal boyhood scrapes. They'd both been there for him, through heartache and disappointments, like when he'd blown his knee and kissed his future goodbye.

They'd seen him at the lowest point of his life. His dreams

turned to shame, his love lost, his victor's heart broken by the biggest loss in his life.

His gaze fell on the old barn in the distance. Worn gray wood still stood, lost and forgotten amidst the shiny redwood and white fences of the newer horse barns. When his last hope of returning as a pro-quality quarterback had died, he'd retreated to that old barn, too ashamed to come home and face Daddy. Too heartbroken to risk his pity.

"As soon as I noticed my old crop was missing from the barn, I should have had a talk with you." Mama's voice was as gentle as the hand she dropped onto his forearm braced on the fence. "But you'd been through so much already, and you didn't ask any questions. I watched, I waited, and you seemed to move on with your life. When Conn went to you for help, I thought you were settled and comfortable with your needs, but maybe I was wrong. Maybe I should have talked more openly with you."

"This isn't the kind of thing a man wants to discuss with his mother."

She laughed again, shaking her head. "You could have asked your Daddy, but he could have only helped you understand the other side."

That made him whip his head back to her face. "Daddy was a submissive?"

She snorted. "There wasn't a submissive bone in your Daddy's body. He never wanted to be conquered or tied up. He wasn't into that kind of game and neither was I."

Dreading her answer, Victor asked, "What were you into?"

"Pain," she answered simply. "I used to joke that a bronc rider would have to be a masochist to get back on after getting trampled a few times."

Victor tried to think of something to say, but he couldn't. He couldn't imagine his weathered father submitting to the sting of a lash, let alone asking for it. The man had worked from sunup to sundown every day of his life, raised three God-fearing respectful children and died loving only one woman his entire life. Victor had always thought him the strongest man in the world, fearless on a horse, even the wildest, rawest green broke mare. He just couldn't imagine the same man asking someone— a woman, his wife, no less—to whip him.

"Do you think I liked knowing that I yearned to hurt your Daddy?" Mama asked sharply, her fingers tightening on his arm. For a woman, she had a fearsome grip. He'd always assumed her strength came from a lifetime of training show horses, but now he wasn't so sure. "Do you think it made him feel like a man in our day and age? To lock the door of our bedroom, strip off his shirt, grip the bedpost and ask me to whip him within an inch of my life? I had to, son. He had to. The need was there, eating away at him constantly. He needed the pain as much as I needed to give it."

She turned away, but not before Victor saw the sheen of tears in her eyes. "He said once that he wished I were a man so my arm didn't give out quite so quickly. He'd meant it as a joke, but it hurt, son. He could have taken much more than I could ever give him. For years, I worked out with the whip and crop, training my arms and body to make sure I met his need to the best of my ability. So don't you look down on yourself, Victor Connagher, or you're looking down on me and his memory."

Victor hung his head. "I don't want to hurt anyone, least of all someone I love."

"The young lady on the show?" He nodded, so Mama asked, "When do I get to meet her?"

"Maybe never. She left me."

"I saw the way she looked at you, son. Even on TV, I could see that woman would give her heart and soul just to see you smile. So why would she leave you?"

"She needs more than I can give."

"Can, or will?"

He growled deep in his throat and jerked his hair tighter, but the pain didn't help. Not this time. Nothing would east the raw, aching need burning in his gut. Nothing but Shiloh.

"It's got to be difficult for a woman to find the right man when she needs to be hurt. Women in our society have fought tooth and nail to get to the place where they can demand what they want in bed, but pain is a different beast all together. It's not politically correct for a woman to play the submissive, but it's somehow even more horrible if she needs pain too. If someone had dared hurt Ty in a way he wasn't interested in, he would've plowed his fist into the bastard's face. What's your woman supposed to do, son? Walk up to a stranger and ask him to hurt her? How's she going to be able to get him to stop when she's had enough?"

Rage exploded in Victor at the thought of another man laying a hand on Shiloh. *He* wanted to hold her, love her, and yes, hurt her. Exactly the way she needed it.

"If she needs to be hurt, then it's better done by someone who loves and cares for her well-being than an arrogant fool with a whip who doesn't give a damn about anything but putting on a show. Do you love her?"

Victor clenched his jaws and nodded. God, yes, he loved her. He hadn't been able to sleep last night, tormenting himself with the memory of the pleasure she'd given him, mixed with the guilt of the cut on her back. He'd lain there all night, hating himself but rock hard and aching with the need to do it all over again. *All I could think about was how fucking good it'd felt to hurt her.*

"Give it up, then." At the flat, cold tone of Mama's voice, he jerked his gaze up to search her stern face. "If you hate that crop so much, then leave it here and go back to her without it."

His right hand flexed and clenched, aching to wrap around the leathered hilt. Could he give up the crop he'd carried all these years? Then what would he do in the dark hours of the night when need hammered inside his skull and vicious claws shredded at his control? When he couldn't bear it any longer? If he didn't have the crop to satisfy those urges...

Stunned, he realized that even without the crop he'd still have this need to hurt and ravage and punish. He'd always be on the cutting edge of pain, whether he wanted to admit it or not, whether he abandoned the crop here at the ranch, hid it in a drawer, or left it hanging in his closet so he could order his submissive—Shiloh, the only submissive for him—to fetch it and prepare for punishment.

Which she needs as much as I need to give.

"You can't deny this side of you, son. You're only lying to yourself." Mama reached out and gripped his upper arms, leaning closer so she could stare up into his eyes. He might be a foot taller, but she made him feel like a little boy again. "We didn't raise you to be a liar or a quitter. You might have lost a game, but everything's on the line now. This is the biggest game of your life. You've searched your whole life for a woman who could love you and accept the pain you need to give. Are you going to let her get away?"

He smiled, not the nice, gentle smile a son would give his mother, but the grin of a confident conqueror bent on razing his enemy to the ground. *Even—especially—my own stupid hang-ups.* "No, ma'am."

"You go get her, son, and you bring her home this very night. I want to meet the woman who finally claimed my Victor's heart."

"Soon," he promised, leaning down to kiss her cheek. "But not tonight. We have to finish taping the show first."

"Then you'll bring her to the ranch?"

"If she'll come, yes."

"Remember, give her the pain you both need, son, but hurt her with love and hold her when you're done." Mama smiled back and Victor felt a chill inch down his spine. "And don't worry, she'll come, or I'll fetch her myself."

Chapter Twenty One

Throughout the weekend, Shiloh's finger had hovered over the delete key of her blog a hundred times, but she couldn't bring herself to do it. Those filthy words and secret fantasies were all that she had left of him. She'd turned off the comment feature, but not before her in box was stuffed with responses from people she didn't know.

She stared at a blank post, trying to think of something, anything to say, but she felt frozen and numb. She'd lost him, and now hundreds of thousands of people would witness her misery.

She'd never considered herself a coward, but walking back into VCONN Tower Monday morning took considerably more courage than she possessed. After a weekend of lying around the apartment feeling sorry for herself with an ice pack on her ass, she didn't want to see Victor Connagher ever again.

No, really. She'd just pack up her office and sneak out the back door before he even knew she was in the building. She could move to California, live with her mother's stepchildren, and keep far, far away from her stepfather so Mom wouldn't bring up the past. Maybe they could use a BDSM reality show in Hollywood.

Who am I kidding? I want nothing and nobody else but Victor.

Lifting her chin, she marched into the building as though she owned the place. No one would ever take Victor's place in her heart, even though it felt like a herd of horses had trampled said heart and crushed it beyond repair. She'd waited all weekend for the phone to ring, or for Victor to drive up and beg forgiveness. She'd dreamed that he would come for her, dragging her kicking and screaming back to his penthouse and whipping her with his crop until she swore to never leave his bed again.

But that hope had died long before Monday morning. She'd loved him for so long that she'd never really thought about what her life would be like without him. Working with him would be pure hell. Acting out a scene with the Master, impossible. Yet her own stupid, aching heart refused to give up so easily. At least on set, he wore the mask of the Master. If that's all she could have of him, she'd take it, and hopefully those sweet moments of pain would last her the rest of her life.

She scanned the hallways as she made her way to her office, praying she wouldn't run into him until they were on set and their roles defined. There, she knew what he expected of her. They'd film the last few scenes and be done.

Her heart shriveled in her chest and died all over again at the thought of losing him. Never seeing him again. Never feeling the strength of his hands, the commanding way he gave pain, knowing she would take whatever he chose to give, without question or hesitation.

No, the hesitation was on his side, waiting like a starving wolf to devour him.

She made it to her office without incident, which ironically pissed her the hell off. The bastard couldn't even bring himself to come down to her office and say a few words to her before the most crucial scenes of the show. What if she'd chosen to blow him and *America's Next Top sub* off? Oh, but he'd known she'd never do that. This show was her baby, even if she couldn't be his.

She'd managed to work herself into full-blown rage by the time she changed into the corset and thicker petticoats—to hide the vibrant bruises on her ass and thighs. Fury was easier to handle than hurt. She'd rather punch him in the mouth and bloody his lip than let him see her crying or upset.

Somebody knocked on her door and her heart galloped up into her throat. "Yes?"

Andy stuck his head inside and she had to clench her hands at her sides to keep from ripping his head off. "V wants us to report to his office first and go over the next segment together."

She clamped her mouth shut and forced herself to count to ten...twenty...before she could respond without venom. "I'll be there in a few minutes."

Andy arched an eyebrow at her and propped his shoulder against the door. "Anything going on that I should know about?"

"Why would you say that?"

"Oh, no reason, other than Mal acted strange all weekend, and now you're fuming. Did Mal and V get into a fight over the weekend?"

"How should I know? I haven't seen Mr. Connagher since Friday night's premiere."

Andy snickered. "Of course. Like you didn't spend the entire weekend with him."

"I didn't." She grabbed the storyboards she'd prepared days ago—when she'd been so sure of earning Victor's collar—and stomped toward the elevator. "Like I said, I haven't seen him since Friday night."

"Wow, you're telling the truth." Andy rushed after her. "Did you two get into a fight or something?"

"It's really none of your business."

"Oh, come on, Shiloh, give me a break. Mal kept snapping at me all weekend and punished me for no damned good reason other than she was in a pissy mood. I thought she was mad at me, although I have no idea why."

Shiloh rolled her eyes. Yeah, of course he had no idea that his Mistress knew he was a lying sneak of a submissive who had betrayed her confidence and leaked details of her show.

"Is she mad because I cut out early from the party?"

She punched the button again and wished the elevator would hurry up. "I honestly don't know."

"So what's up with you and V?"

"Again, that's none of your business." Thank God, the elevator opened and she stepped inside. Too bad the door wouldn't zip shut and leave the nosy bastard behind.

"Did the Master finally freak you out? I've heard the rumors, you know. V's pretty nasty when he wants to be. Even Mal's afraid of him, although she won't admit it."

Shiloh turned and jabbed her finger into Andy's chest. "I'm not afraid of him, he didn't freak me out, and I like him nasty, all right? Now back off and leave me the hell alone." By the end of her tirade, she was yelling loudly enough to hurt her own ears.

"Sheesh, fine. Give a guy a break." Andy's eyes flared wide and he let out a little squeak. He squeezed past her and darted out of the elevator. "Sorry we're late. She had to get a few things from her office."

Slowly, Shiloh turned around. Victor stood outside the elevator, his big palm blocking the door from shutting. With the fierce glint in his eyes and the furrow on his brow, she couldn't tell whether he'd heard her entire tirade or not.

"You didn't blog this weekend."

She narrowed her eyes and cocked her head. "Is that right? So the Master wants Dallas to read about how his submissive walked out on him?"

"I want Dallas to hang on your every word."

Not an apology, no explanation, just a casual mention of a disagreement that had left her devastated and alone. Hurt, rage and betrayal roiled in her chest and she couldn't draw a breath. She couldn't look away from his face. Only now did she notice he'd left his hair loose about his shoulders. What did that mean?

Finally, she forced out, "Is that an order?" In a deliberately snide voice, she added, "Master?"

He locked his fingers around her upper arm and marched her toward his office. "Yes, it is. Blog about every nasty, dirty detail. Then you're going to read it aloud to me each and every morning before we tape. Start with how I whipped you so hard that I cut your back and then you walked out on me for the entire weekend. But here you are, baby, right where I want you, and everybody knows whose bed you'll be in tonight."

She sat where he put her, her cheeks burning with shame. Patrick, Mal and Andy stared at her with their mouths open, hanging on every word.

"Now that that's settled, let's start with what we're taping for this episode."

Her mind felt as empty and clean as a washed chalkboard on the first day of school. Her throat ached like she'd been strangled, her eyes hot and burning, but no one knew the next episode, not like she did. *I'm the show runner, and I'm not going to let him ruin my show, no matter how big a dick he is.*

Or has.

She swallowed the lump trying to choke her. Staring down at her neat storyboards, she began. "Today's taping is to show how a submissive can recognize the Master's hand, not just by weapon but by weight and technique. Each Dominant should test the remaining submissives and try to trick us by switching their favorite weapons around. At the end of this episode, we should have the three final submissives you wish to see compete for top sub."

Victor sat behind his desk and propped his boots on the edge. "Patrick, which sub are you taking through to the final?"

"Peppi."

"And you're taking Andy."

"Of course." Mal smiled and even managed a wink at her submissive. "I wouldn't miss the chance to come down to the final punishment round against you, V. I'm going to try and hang with you stroke for stroke."

Andy paled even more and gulped in a shaking breath. Even though Shiloh didn't like him at all, she knew exactly what he was feeling. "See you in the finals, Shiloh."

"I don't think so," Victor drawled out, tipping his chair back even further. "I don't want a top sub who walks out on me. I'll be taking Ruby to the final."

Shiloh kept her head down until she was fairly certain her eyes weren't spitting hateful flames any longer. She'd known he would relish hurting her, but she hadn't counted on such blatant humiliation games. *Mal said mind games weren't his thing, but maybe that all changed when I called him on his bullshit. Everything changed.*

"I need a couple of hours before I can begin taping, so let's take the morning to get through as much editing and production work as possible. New taping won't happen until this afternoon."

The CEO and Master had made his decree, so everyone stood up to leave. Shiloh followed, determined to escape without saying a word. He was waiting, judging every little look and word, but she refused to give him the pleasure of forcing a reaction from her.

"I'm not finished with you, Shiloh. I certainly didn't give you permission to leave."

A red-hot sheet of rage tore through her, but she held her breath and kept her mouth shut. Mal walked by and squeezed her shoulder, shooting a dark look at V. Even after the door shut, Shiloh didn't say a word.

His chair squeaked as he pulled his feet down off the desk. Idiot, risking scratches to such a lovely desk just to show off those ridiculous boots.

"Come here, baby."

"Fuck you," she retorted, jerking her head up with a snarl. "We're not in a scene and this isn't the show."

"Then I'll come to you."

"The hell you will. You come over here and I'm going to punch you."

He sat on the desk in front of her. "Go ahead. I deserve it."

She didn't have to be told twice. She stood up, reared back, and slammed her fist into his stomach as hard as she could. "Bastard. To sit there and humiliate me like that!" She punched him again, hard enough he grunted and his breath wheezed out. "You're the biggest dick I've ever met in my entire life, and if you think I'm going to let you treat me like this, well, come at me again, asshole. I'll rip that fucking crop out of your hand and lay into you instead."

"That could be interesting," he gasped out. "If you want to try the crop on me, I'm willing. It's in the top right-hand drawer."

"Yeah," she said slowly. "Yeah, I think I do."

She stomped around his desk, yanked the drawer open and wrapped her fingers around the hilt of his crop. It was heavier than she expected, a nice solid weight in her hand. A little too long and unwieldy for her, but she could make do with it.

Holding it in her hand, she felt a raw surge of power. Victor's eyes were dark, his breathing short and fast, his erection obvious in his pants. He rolled over and stretched out across his desk. "Go ahead, baby. Let's see how much arm you've got."

She stepped behind him and leaned against his thighs, rubbing herself against him. "Are you sure? You're the sadist, not the masochist."

"I like pain either way. I'd prefer to give it to you, but I'll take it, especially from your hand."

"Don't give me that shit." She backed away and brought the crop down across his buttocks. His breath caught but he didn't groan. She hadn't hit him hard enough for that. "You don't want to give me pain. We've already been over that."

"Give me more, baby. I can take it."

Gritting her teeth, she brought the crop down with all her strength. "That's my line."

"And a fine one it is." He hauled in a deep breath, air hissing between his teeth. "Do you really think you can take everything I want to give you?"

She gripped the crop in both hands and brought it down

again on his back instead of the luscious muscle of his ass. He definitely let out a groan this time, but no joy filled her. She didn't relish hurting him. The whistling crack of the crop made her sweat and her body clench tight, but hurting him only made her stomach churn.

Stepping back, she couldn't keep the anguish from escaping her lips. He rose and sat back down on the desk, wincing a little. She knew that feeling all too well, which helped take away some of her regret. Slowly, he reached out and took her hand holding the crop, drawing her closer. "I will never strike you in anger."

"I'm sorry," she whispered, blinking away tears. "You hurt me, and I didn't know how else to hurt you back."

"I didn't mind." Chuckling, he adjusted himself so the erection wasn't so painful. "I enjoyed it, but you didn't. That's the difference."

His arm slid around her shoulders, drawing her down against his chest. God help her, she went. His powerful arms locked around her, his scent filled her nose, and all the agony and grief she'd been struggling to bear just slid away.

"I'm sorry, baby. You're right. I should have held you like this Friday night, all weekend, whatever it takes to make you feel safe and secure with me."

Tears filled her eyes, but she refused to cry. Not yet. She didn't want to give him all her hurt and emotion, not so easily. A few words, that's all he'd given her. No promises, no hope they could actually be together without making each other miserable.

"Everything I just said in our meeting was a trap for Andy. You know no other sub will ever please me like you. I needed your reaction to be authentic and convincing, and I'll make sure Patrick and Mal are filled in before we actually start taping.

From the look on her face as she left, Mal is seriously contemplating trying out her flail on me."

More of Shiloh's anger melted away. Of course, it made sense. That's why no one else had been present. Victor would trust Mal and Patrick. A fight between Victor and his new sub would be irresistible to the media hounds, and if news of it broke, it'd prove once and for all that Andy was their leak. "Then we'd better go ahead and get the final taped too, before we lose him."

"Excellent plan," he murmured against her ear. "What else should we discuss?"

She pulled back and searched his gaze. "You have to trust me as much as you want me to trust you. I have a responsibility to tell you if I'm uncomfortable or scared or near my limit. If I get hurt because I fail to meet that responsibility, it's my fault, not yours. I have no doubt that you'll stop if I need you to. That's never been something I worry about."

He didn't avert his gaze, letting her see the fear darkening his eyes and the tightness of his lips. "I never want you to look at me like Kimberly did when I hurt her. After we'd made love countless times, she suddenly looked at me like I was Jack the Ripper. I'd rather lose you than ever see that fear and loathing in your eyes, even though losing you will kill me."

She cupped his face in both hands and leaned closer so he would feel her breath on his lips. "I don't know what my limits are. I guess if you bring knives into a scene or something scary like that, then I might freak out. But I know how to stop you, Victor, and I'm not afraid of you. Do you want to use knives on me?"

"No," he whispered hoarsely. "Just my crop. I don't even want a flail or paddle to touch you."

"A crop delivers a cutting blow. I may occasionally bleed.

And I'm okay with that."

A tremor shook his shoulders. "I'm not."

She brushed her lips against his. "Come on, now, V, tell me the truth. You didn't like knowing that you'd whipped me so hard you'd cut my skin open? Even a little? And I still got off on it? Not to mention the impressive load you blew in my mouth."

His big palms clenched on her hips repeatedly before he finally nodded. "You don't mind?"

"I'll bleed for you, V. When it comes to you, my answer is always going to be yes."

"That's exactly what I'm afraid of, baby. I don't want you to commit to something just because you think I want it."

"If you're seriously into something, then my answer is yes. No doubt, no hesitation. I won't refuse you outright and I'll always at least try it. I'm willing to do that for you, but you have to be willing to trust that I'll stop you when I've had enough."

"How can I know you'll stop me when you didn't even have a safeword?"

She draped her arms around his shoulders and gave him a wicked grin. "I have one now, don't I? I guess you'll just have to wait and see if you can make me use it or not."

"Now that is a challenge no Master can refuse."

Chapter Twenty Two

Blindfolded and bound to a St. Andrew's cross, Shiloh concentrated on breathing deeply and slowly despite her nerves. She was pretty sure she'd recognize Victor's touch, even if he chose to use something other than his crop, but she'd encouraged them to be tricky. She had no idea how Mal would approach her or whether Patrick would use his whip or not. Per the rules of the challenge, the Dominants weren't allowed to talk to the submissive once they entered the room nor to touch them with their bare hands.

If I screw up and claim Patrick's or Mal's hand instead of Victor's, I'll die of shame. Who's stupid idea was this anyway?

"Gift, are you ready?" Georgia asked.

"Yes." She strained her senses, listening for footsteps, anything that clue her to who approached. The small private room at Silken had carpeting, which made it practically impossible to tell what kind of shoes the Dominant might be wearing.

"For your first test, you must tell us which weapon the Dominant is using. Each Dominant will test you. If you answer all three correctly, you'll continue to the next round. Do you understand?"

"Yes." She tried not to sound impatient, but she really just wanted this over.

"Dominant number one, please begin."

Muscles straining and rigid, Shiloh couldn't help but brace for the blow. Shoulders, back, buttocks, thighs...?

The whisper-soft strike totally blew her mind. With not even a hint of pain, the blow had been so gentle that it could have been an accidental touch without the challenge. She concentrated on her skin and the delicate sensations that had brushed against her. Some submissives were perfectly happy with such a weapon in her Dominant's hand, but as far as she was concerned, Victor might as well use a feather to tickle her for all the arousal such a touch would give her. "Velvet flail."

"Very good, Gift, that's correct. Dominant number two, proceed."

This blow was sharp enough to make her suck in a breath. The double thud was unmistakable, the flexibility in the bamboo making it rebound against her buttock. A few blows from that weapon would likely push her to her nebulous limits, if Victor ever cared to pick up a "Cane."

"Excellent, Gift. Now for Dominant number three."

She braced, but the blow never came. Instead, something seared her right biceps. She flinched, instinctively reaching to swipe the pain away, but they'd bound her wrists to the cross bar. Heat pooled on her skin, spreading into a molten circle that made her twitch and moan. For once, it wasn't the kind of pain she liked. Not at all.

"Get it off," she gasped out, twisting her wrists.

"Answer the question, Gift."

She hated the uncomfortable sensation sticking to her skin, trapping heat that only grew in intensity. When they peeled it off, would it take a layer of skin too? Logically, she knew it wasn't really that hot. It probably wouldn't even leave burn marks. But it *hurt* and it creeped her out. "Wax! Hot wax!

Now please, get it off!"

A cool, wet cloth wiped the wax away. Victor whispered in her ear. "I believe we just found an unexpected limit, didn't we?"

Grateful for the blindfold—so he wouldn't see the tears that pooled in her eyes—she gave a little nod, unsure whether the cameras still rolled or not. She hadn't prepared a list of allowable torture items, never once thinking the Dominants might want to use something other than the standard hand-held weapons.

"Do you know what that does to me, baby? It makes me want to do it again and again, just to see how long you'll endure, simply because I ask it of you."

The thought made her tremble, her stomach fluttering with dread. Here, then, was the real sadist coming out, and yes, the real masochist, because she knew she'd endure a hell of a lot simply because he asked, even the kind of pain that brought her no pleasure at all. *And to think, I begged him to take the mask off and show me what he was capable of.*

He lifted a bottle to her mouth, giving her a drink of cool water. They must have moved on to filming the next contestant. He'd have to leave soon, but she savored the way he took care of her. Water had never tasted as good as that offered by his hand. It would taste even sweeter after he'd tortured her for awhile. She trembled harder, and there was nothing she could do about it.

One last touch to her cheek, and then he was gone, leaving her blinded and trembling, waiting for the next phase. Would he use the crop? Would his pride allow him to hand it off to someone else for the purpose of the show? The dime-sized burn on her arm stung, reminding her of his words.

Now, the pain began to bleed into arousal, because she

knew what that pain would mean for him. For the first time in her life, she felt pain for a Master that didn't give her pleasure but still managed to turn her on. The realization that she'd let him drop wax all over her body, burning her, giving her more of this kind of pain, just to please him, sent a rush of sensation through her. It felt like thousands of fire ants raced up and down her spine, nerve endings stinging, on fire. The top of her head crawled, her neck prickled, and worst of all, she felt a trickle down her inner thigh that confirmed she was aroused. So aroused, and so helpless, which only turned her on more.

Finally, Georgia returned for the next phase. Still nervous and afraid, at least Shiloh knew the challenge was almost over. This endless stewing and fantasizing about her wicked Master with a tub of hot wax in his hand would soon end.

"For this phase, Gift, you must correctly identify the Dominant behind the weapon. If you mistake your Dominant for someone else, you will be automatically disqualified from this challenge and you will not proceed to the final top sub round. Do you understand?"

Nodding, she didn't even try to speak—her teeth were chattering too hard.

"Each Dominant will punish you until you either call out your safeword or you identify Master P, Mistress M or Master V. If you do use your safeword, you will still be given the opportunity to identify the Dominant behind the weapon. No penalty will be given in this case. Don't assume the Dominants will proceed in the same order for this round, either. Do you understand the rules of this challenge?"

Shiloh nodded again impatiently.

"Dominant number one, please begin."

When she heard the sharp crack, she knew immediately which weapon it was. Leather licked her back, a delicate, precise stroke. Only a true Master with the bullwhip could give such a loud snap and gentle touch, but she waited another few strokes to make sure before calling out, "Master P."

"Very good, Gift," he replied.

Her heart pounded harder. Only two left. She had a fifty-fifty chance of getting this wrong. Would Victor go next to confuse her—or last despite going last before?

"Dominant number two, you may begin."

Someone neared, and the hair prickled on the back of her neck. This Dominant came much closer than Patrick. Shorter weapon? Or merely a trick?

A sharp blow landed on her buttocks. Crop, definitely. She'd know its biting cut anywhere. But was it Victor's hand? Would he hand his trusty weapon of choice over to Mal, arguably his best friend?

Another blow landed, setting a slow but steady pattern, all to her buttocks. Victor certainly liked her ass, as the bruises testified. The blows weren't as hard as what he typically gave, but he could be remembering the lingering soreness on her backside.

However, her body didn't seem to recognize him. She didn't feel especially aroused by the blows, even though the thought of Victor with that wicked crop in his hand, standing behind her bound and helpless body would normally have sent her into the stratosphere. The strokes felt shorter, less confident, less...Victor. He might try to fool her by tightening his grip on the hilt of the crop, forcing a shorter blow, but still, the rhythm seemed wrong.

The sense of command and power she sensed when he stepped into a room just wasn't there. *It has to be Mal.*

When the Dominant shifted to Shiloh's left, moving a bit closer, she knew without a doubt that the Dominant was Mal—

unless Victor had started wearing perfume. "Mistress M."

The blows stopped at once and Georgia applauded. "Very good, Gift. You correctly identified two of the three Dominants. By the process of elimination, Master V is the only Dominant left, so there's no need to continue. You are indeed Master V's Gift. But will you be top sub?"

Canned applause filled the room. Shiloh let her muscles relax, her head drooping. She'd done it. She hadn't made a stupid mistake. Victor hadn't been able to pull the wool over her eyes. She couldn't help but smile with relief. She'd made it. She'd done everything possible to show him how much she loved him. She'd managed to yank his mask away and find the real Victor hidden beneath.

After he freed her from the bonds, they'd talk about the final round and make their plans. He'd need to punish her as long as possible, while Mal and Patrick tortured their subs. The last sub standing would be the winner, and she had no doubt whatsoever that she'd win it. She'd win it for him.

"Leave her bound like this." Victor cupped her chin, his fingers hard on her face despite the hint of amusement in his voice. "We're going to tape the final punishment round. Now."

Victor paced while the other two submissives were bound as their Dominants wished for the final round. He slapped his thigh with the crop and made damned sure Shiloh heard every single blow, even though he had no intention of using the crop much at all for this round. No, that would be too easy. Too safe. He already knew how much she could endure, and that wouldn't be a test at all. It certainly wasn't top-sub worthy. Even though this show was their creation and set up from the beginning, his pride demanded that it be a true test.

He couldn't call himself the Master of *America's Next Top*

sub if he knew deep down that he hadn't tested her within an inch of her life.

The best test would be something that she wouldn't ordinarily enjoy at all. When he'd decided to try a little hot wax in the last challenge, he hadn't expected such a reaction from her; he'd just wanted to do something a little different. Would she understand the test, though, and forgive him later for using his newfound knowledge against her?

He squatted down before her and kept his voice low. It wasn't a private conversation, but it was the best he could do under the circumstances. "Do you trust me?"

"It's a little late to ask that question, isn't it?"

He heard the faint tremor in her voice and noted the rapid thump of the pulse in her neck. She was nervous, definitely, and trying not to show it. She knew he wasn't into bondage, so leaving her bound like this would throw her for a loop. The *first* loop. The next one would be a doozey.

"Can I trust *you?*" Solemnly, he brushed a damp strand of hair off her face. "Will you give me your safeword when you can't bear any more, even if it means we don't win?"

Her bottom lip trembled. "What are you going to do?"

"That's for the Master to know. You'll find out soon enough."

"Victor, what are you going to do?" Her voice rose slightly, her pulse thumping frantically. "I created this whole show for you. Don't you want to win it?"

"Of course I do." He untied the blindfold. For this, there was no reason to keep her blind. He needed to be able to see her eyes so he could gauge her true level of pain and fear so he'd know whether he should continue or not. "But I'm going to win it honestly, and that means pushing you to your limit. You set this show up to prove to me that you could take whatever I

245

choose to give you, right?"

She nodded, a short jerk of her head, and her gaze fell on the equipment set up beside him. Low-heat wax candles made an attractive Gothic decoration...and a very effective pain device.

"The title of top sub means nothing to me if you don't go to the very limits of your endurance for my sake."

"You have to tell me," she whispered in a ragged voice. "Tell me you want me to do this for you as my Master. Ask me to suffer for you. Because I love you, I will."

"I want to hurt you, baby. I want to see the fear in your eyes. I want to see how far you'll really let me go, even if you're afraid. But most of all, I need to know that I've done something for you that no other Dominant has ever done. I need to take you to your limits and hear your safeword given in ultimate trust that I'll stop, even though I'm enjoying every single tear and pleading cry."

"Yes, Master."

A fierce surge of pride welled within him. She'd do this for him and him alone. Even something that made her tremble with dread at the thought. He pressed a quick, hard kiss to her mouth and then stood, taking his position at her side.

Mal had Andy in a similar cross, dressed in the rough trousers of a laborer and naked from the waist up. By the hard glint in her eyes, she was going to exact every single wretched lie from him, every single penny he'd cost VCONN by forcing them to scrap the show.

Patrick's submissive knelt on all fours, complete in pony gear. With her reins looped about his left forearm, he stood several paces behind her, giving him plenty of room to work with his long-tailed whip. His pony girl shook her head and stomped her right hoof—hand.

Victor met Mal's gaze and shook his head, a bemused smile on his face. He didn't get that kink, but then again, he didn't get Mal's either. She liked treating Andy like a dog or a slave. She'd often made him sleep on the floor or eat from a dog bowl, and he'd obeyed without question.

All I want to do is make my submissive suffer for loving me. How sick is that?

But looking at Shiloh, he didn't feel sick at all. For the first time in his adult life as a sadist, he felt...glad. She had a need that only he could meet, and he knew without a doubt that she was the only submissive that would ever meet his need. She loved him enough to endure pain and fear simply because he asked it.

Hopefully the cameras didn't shoot too low, or his massive erection would be viewed all over Dallas. With the crop in his right hand, he waited for the signal to begin.

"Dominants, this is the final round. You've chosen your submissive after rigorous tests and challenges. They've proved their willingness to submit to your will alone. Now, one of you will prove your skill to Dallas and name one of these contestants as *America's Next Top sub*, the submissive most willing to give his or her heart and soul simply to please the Master. Are you ready?"

All three Dominants inclined their heads.

"Name your top subs and ask them if they're ready and willing to being this final test."

Patrick gave a little jerk on his pony girl's reins. "Peppi, are you ready for the final challenge?"

The girl whinnied and nodded her head in a very horsey manner, which made Victor choke back a laugh. Mal wasn't so lucky and actually snorted out loud.

"Are you ready for me to beat you like the dog you are,

247

Beau?"

"Yes, Mistress."

Victor stepped closer to Shiloh and used the tip of his crop to push her chin up higher, straining her neck, forcing her to meet his gaze even though she was bound. "What are you going to give me, Gift?"

"Everything I've got, Master."

He took the ponytail holder out of his pocket and pulled his hair tight. He needed the familiar pain to focus him and keep him in control.

"Let the final challenge begin!" Georgia cried out triumphantly.

Mal and Patrick had performed together often enough that they had a back-and-forth, give-and-take rhythm. She landed a blow to Andy's back, and then waited for the sharp crack of the whip against Patrick's sub before giving hers another. Victor provided syncopation, beginning with the crop and using enough force to make an impression on the audience. These blows were foreplay, warm up for the main endurance test. He wanted Shiloh feeling good and flying as high as possible before he turned to the real fear he intended to wield against her.

He kept the blows concentrated to her ass and the backs of her thighs, determined not to cut the more tender and vulnerable skin of her back. No, this time he intended to leave a mark of a different sort on her flesh.

Patrick's whip whistled through the air and made an impressive crack. His pony girl squealed and reared beneath his stroke, and like any skilled horse master, he used his voice and soothing touch to steady her. Andy was moaning and mumbling beneath his breath, but Mal had no kind words for him. In fact, by the whites showing in his eyes and the frantic babbling, she'd begun confronting him about where he spent his nights and how much he'd gotten for selling her show. Of course he'd deny it, but Victor had a feeling they'd know by the evening news for sure.

Tension coiled in the room. He knew cameras were rolling, capturing every whispered curse and grunting cry, every grimace, every tear, every plea. The lights made them all sweat even worse, and his shirt was already sticking to him. He swore he could smell the musky scent of Shiloh's desire, her need growing with every single blow.

She needed to please him, even if it meant pain or fear or humiliation. *Him*, not Patrick or her old mentor or any other Dominant.

Flicking his gaze over her, noting her breathing, her skin color, and the way she kept her back arched and hips lifted for his blows, he judged it time to take her to the next level. He slipped the crop through his belt and tore open the simple linen shift to bare her back.

Georgia gasped. If the camera guy was paying attention, he'd zoomed in for a good shot. Bruises covered Shiloh's back. His marks, her badges of honor. *Let everyone in Dallas see how much she loves me.*

He picked up a lit candle with melted wax pooled around the wick. Looking at the camera, he smiled, a heavy-lidded grin of anticipation as he slowly tipped the candle and allowed wax to drip onto her left shoulder.

Her breath hissed and she jerked, arcing up against the bonds and fighting like she'd never done before. Her breathing was loud in the room despite the rising sounds of weapons hitting flesh and the deeper guttural cries of submissives in the throes of punishment.

"Give me your pain, baby. Give it all to me." Shaking, she let out a moan that winched him to a fevered pitch. The sharp edge of fear and true pain fed his lust like nothing else. "Remember what I want. It's my will to hear your safeword tonight, but first, I want you to endure as long as possible."

He dribbled a thin trail of hot wax down toward the small of her back, spacing each drop, each pain, with deliberate precision. Not too much wax—he didn't want to hurt her too much, too quickly. But he built the pain into a simmering volcano.

She shook, she sweated, she cried, and yes, she screamed, but she didn't beg him to stop.

Not his Gift.

"Mistress!" Andy howled in a shrill, high voice. "Forgive me! I'm innocent!"

Mal only whipped him harder, sliding her blows lower against the back of his legs. "If you're innocent, then why do you need forgiveness, boy?"

Evidently he didn't enjoy strikes to the backs of his knees at all. He bellowed out a word—*red*, Victor thought, but it was too guttural for him to know for sure. Mal lowered her arm and turned her back on him.

"Mistress M, your sub has surrendered," Georgia said. "He will not be top sub."

Mal bowed to the cameras and took her place on the lowest step of the dais.

Patrick commanded his pony girl to her feet, and she ran around him like a horse on a lunge line. He flashed a challenging grin toward Victor. "Are you willing to trade blow for blow?"

"Sure, as long as I can count pain as a blow."

"Works for me."

Victor stepped around in front of Shiloh and ran a critical

eye over her. The slight pause had let her catch her breath. Her eyes had a glazed fuzziness of a pain-induced trance. He stroked her cheek and whispered her stage name until she focused on him. "Are you ready for round two?"

"Did you finish the V?"

He couldn't help but smile. She'd known exactly what mark he was putting into her back, even though she couldn't see it.

Her voice sounded hoarse, so he gave her another drink of water. Patrick took the opportunity to do the same, although he'd made his submissive kneel and drink out of a plastic bucket that Mama would have thrown out of her stables in disgust. "Not yet. I'll do the second half now, mixed heavily with the crop. I'm going blow for blow with Master P, if you're up for that."

Sharply, she said, "I haven't asked you to stop yet, have I?"

He saw through her bravado. Her chin trembled, her eyes rolled white, and her pulse thumped frantically in her throat. "I'm proud of you, baby. You're so fucking hot I can't stand it. I'd give anything to be far away from these cameras right about now."

She lowered her voice. "So you're enjoying it?"

Smiling, he pressed against her thigh, letting her feel exactly how turned on he was. She groaned out a deep pleading sigh that fisted around his heart and tugged so hard he couldn't breathe.

"Will you do one thing for me?"

"Anything," he said intently.

"Take out the ponytail."

She knew very well what that pain in his scalp meant. It was a barrier, a reminder for him to keep his control, a lock he'd often placed on his darker urges. No wonder she'd want him to take it out, in this, their greatest challenge yet. Leaning over her, he pulled the holder out so she could feel his hair tumbling down against her cheek. "I expect to hear your safeword very soon, Gift."

Why did he have to bring her down from the haze just to tell her what the next nightmare would be? Shiloh knew all too well. He wanted her aware. He wanted her to let him do this with full knowledge of the pain that was going to come. Her left shoulder blade felt like a blanket of molten lava had coated it, melting her skin and bones, her body just slipping away, falling off her like a hunk of meat. She knew the burns weren't that bad—they just felt like she'd fallen into a stew pot.

Patrick tapped his pony girl on the shoulder and she went to all fours before him. Eyes bright with excitement, he called over to Victor. "Ready?"

"Are you ready, baby?" He slid his hand down her unmarred shoulder. At her nod, he whispered, "I want your safeword, baby. I want it so bad I can taste it."

The crop descended on her sore backside, immediately shooting her body with endorphins. Instead of the vicious bite of the crop, she felt a buzzing heat that sent her soaring. Distantly, she heard him talking with Patrick, egging each other on. The sharp crack of the whip, followed by the slash of fire across her backside, back and forth, until she could swear that she felt both weapons. She remembered the feel of Patrick's whip dancing along her back, licking at Victor's bruises.

Fire puddled on her right shoulder, a searing glow of heat that blazed in the darkness of her mind. That fire tried to tug her back down, coiling around her like a molten snake of flame. Pain intruded, jagged glass slicing at her mind. Another blow thudded on her buttocks, warring against the wax on her shoulder, but the burn was winning.

The crop descended again and she could hear Victor's breathing, deep and labored. She smelled his raw heat, the masculine scent of a warrior after battle. No, the muddy, battered quarterback leading his team to victory. Only she was the one who felt battered.

Merciless, he drove her closer to that end zone, the place he wanted her to be. A place of endless pain. A place where she needed him to simply stop. To make all the pain, all the darkness go away with just a gentle touch of his hand.

And, oh, God, it felt so good. Too good. She hurt all over, the soles of her feet, the strands of her hair. She couldn't take any more.

She didn't want it to stop.

"Give it to me," Victor growled, punctuating the words with another glob of wax at the base of her spine.

His V had branded her, seared into her flesh. *His.* He'd made her his and it didn't take a collar. It didn't take a ring. All it took was the pain surging through her, tying her to him forever. He'd branded her with pain, addicted her with his crop, possessed her with his body. If she lost him now, she'd simply wither up and die. She wouldn't know how to breathe.

"I'm your Master, Gift, and I want you to give me everything. Give it to me!"

She sank into the red-hot core of pain and let it dissolve her into nothing.

He gripped her chin, his fingers drilling into her skull. "Give it to me now!"

She let the last of the air spill from her lungs on the word he wanted to hear. "Christmas."

Chapter Twenty Three

Shiloh didn't have to open her eyes to know she was in Victor's arms. His chest cradled her, his arms solid and safe about her, his body snug at her back. She was aware enough to know that she ought to hurt, but all she felt was heat. Perhaps because he held her, acting as a sort of soothing drug.

"You shouldn't hold her like that," Mal said in a low voice, tight and shaking. With worry? Still fogged in that secret world he'd taken her, Shiloh couldn't understand why. "At least put some ice on her back."

"I promised I would hold her."

Shiloh fought to open her eyes, peeling back the layers of exhaustion. Moving her head hurt, but she craned her neck, trying to see his face. "No, you didn't."

"I promised Mama." He cupped her face and eased her away from his chest. Air hit her back and her eyes flared open wide. She felt blistered from her neck to her ass. Quickly, he brought her down to lie on her stomach across his lap.

Mal dropped cool cloths and ice packs on her back, but Shiloh still fought back tears. Her breath hissed between her teeth on a long, shaking, "Shit."

"I'm so sorry, baby." Victor smoothed her hair, probably the only body part that wasn't swollen and sore. His voice roughened, his thighs tensing beneath her, transmitting his anguish to her. She knew he had to have enjoyed the scene as much as she had, but just as she was suffering with the after effects, so was he, only his was internal guilt. "Do you regret it?"

"That depends."

His hand stilled, heavy on her head and unmoving. He didn't breathe, waiting for her answer.

"Did we win?"

"Girl, do you honestly have to ask that question?" Mal snorted. "Of course *the* Victor won the challenge. He always wins." She stood and headed for the door. "I'm sending everyone home. We can tape the final award session later."

"Actually, hold that thought," Victor ordered. "Keep everyone on hand until KDSX news runs. Gather everyone in the main room to watch and keep Andy close."

"Oh, he'll be close all right. Beneath my boot."

The door shut. Victor shifted the ice packs so he could examine her back. Somber, he traced the V he'd burned into her skin.

She felt his fingers trembling. "Don't start—"

"I'm not," he broke in. "I don't have a single regret. You were incredible, Shiloh. You took everything I dished out and kept begging for more. You should have seen Patrick limping off set, his arm practically dragging the ground and his pony girl with her tail between her legs."

She had to see his face. Sitting up carefully, she shifted on his lap and draped her arms around his shoulders. "*You* were incredible. No one has ever been able to make me phase out like that. You kept me high on pain with the crop, and then balanced it with the wax, dragging me back down enough where it hurt and I knew it hurt and I still didn't want it to stop. I admit, though, if you hadn't kept using your crop, I wouldn't have been able to endure the whole V."

A slow, toe-curling smile curved his lips. "Now that is something I never dreamed to hear. Are you honestly saying my crop kept you from giving your safeword earlier?"

She nodded with a sheepish shrug. "After protesting that I didn't need one at all, I certainly learned the value of a safeword tonight. I can take your crop as long as you want to give it, but wax..." She shuddered and pressed closer to him. Every little movement made her skin scream with pain, but she didn't care. She needed to be close to him, feel him, touch him. He'd given the pain. Only he could take it away. "It was hard, V. Harder than I expected."

He cupped the back of her head, mindful of the tender skin on her back. "And that's why it meant so much to me."

She shifted her weight to her knees so her ass didn't throb. She didn't think about the implications, until she felt one of his hands settle on her backside while the other...

"Mmm, you're still wet. Were you this wet while I was whipping you?"

"No," she whispered against his mouth. "I was wetter."

He slid a finger inside her, while his other hand lightly danced across the welts still burning in her flesh. Her muscles clamped down on him so savagely and suddenly that she cried out against his mouth, her fingers clutching at his shoulders.

Jerking his pants open, he pushed inside and clamped his hands on her hips, bringing her solidly against his thighs. Bliss to be filled, agony to press her swollen backside against his rock-hard body, and the two together sent her pleasure cascading higher in intensity, fed by his own explosive climax.

"Two in less than five minutes," he purred against her lips. "I would've tried for a dozen if we didn't have a whole roomful of people waiting on us."

Now her face blazed as hot as her bruised ass. She couldn't remember exactly how loudly she might have cried out. From the smugness on his face, she'd done just a bit more than *cry out.*

If they were all just outside the door...

Chuckling, Victor gave one last tender squeeze to her ass and helped her stand. Mal had left a new shift and the dreaded corset. The thought of that torturous contraption biting into her sore back made her shiver.

So of course he slipped it over her head, although he took some pity on her and didn't lace it tightly. "One of the hazards—and rewards—of a really good scene is the making up part after the fact. Nobody will be surprised that I needed to be inside you or else die on the spot." He laced his fingers with hers and drew her close to his side. "Though they may be surprised that I was able to make you scream that loud without my crop."

He threw open the door and their production crew burst into cheers.

Leaning against the bar with Shiloh tucked against his side and the large television playing above and behind his head on the wall, Victor watched Andy waver between shame, guilt and downright terror. Mal stood beside her lover, stiff and cold, her gaze averted from the KDSX announcer.

"According to our source, Master V had a massive falling out with Ms. Holmes this weekend and has rejected her as his top sub choice," Frank Firkuss said in that oil-slick voice that made Victor grit his teeth. "Ironic, isn't it, when she created the whole show to gain his interest?"

His co-anchor, a chesty blonde, smiled. "Maybe we should offer her a job at KDSX. I'm sure she'll have all sorts of interesting insights into VCONN's CEO. She might not be *America's Next Top sub*, but she could make a name for herself as the Master's discarded trash."

Fury made a vein throb in Victor's forehead, but he kept his touch light and easy on Shiloh. He hadn't expected them to drag her name through the gutter like this or he never would have given Andy the rope to hang himself. He should have just fired the little prick and been done with him, instead of letting his ego get in the way.

She leaned up on her tiptoes and whispered into his ear. "I don't give a damn what they say, as long as you're my Master."

"I am your Master," he said louder, leveling a cutting glare on the other man. "And you will never be my discarded trash."

Pale with fear, Andy bolted toward the door. Mal reached out and snagged a handful of his shirt, whirled him around and forced him to his knees. If Victor had tried such a stunt, he might have enjoyed more of a struggle, but Andy was used to obeying Mal. He knew her touch and instinctively obeyed his Mistress.

Victor paced a slow, deliberate circle about the kneeling man. "Let's do a little math, shall we? There were three people in my office this morning, other than Shiloh and myself. Only three people who heard that Shiloh and I had a disagreement over the weekend. Only three people heard me say I was going to take a different sub to the final round. Which we just taped, coincidentally, and I did indeed choose Shiloh. I will always choose her. Mal and Patrick both knew that I had only said otherwise in my office to see if we could ferret out the leak. So who do you think our leak is, Andy?"

"I'm sorry." He bowed his head and wrung his hands. "I needed the money, and KDSX was willing to pay. I was desperate, sir."

"Desperate enough to give up my submissive's name to the media hounds? Desperate enough to spread malicious gossip about our private life? Desperate enough to announce to all of Dallas that Victor Connagher is the meanest sadist in Dallas?"

"All of Texas," Mal corrected.

"No, in America." Moving to stand beside him, Shiloh smiled and squeezed his arm. "We should have named the show *America's Only Top Master*."

Pride swelled his heart until he felt like his ribcage would simply bust open. *How could I ever be conflicted about who or what I am, when I'm her Master?*

Andy looked from him to Mal and back with a flinch. "What are you going to do to me?"

"I'm going to fire you," Victor replied calmly. "What Mal chooses to do with you is up to her."

"Mistress..."

"How can you possibly call me that when you've done nothing but lie to me?" Mal fisted her hands at her sides, her jaws tight and her voice thick with emotion. "I loved you, Andy. We shared more than I ever thought possible, and then I found out you've kept this kind of secret from me? That you betrayed me? My show was ruined. You seriously damaged my career as well as endangered VCONN's season. All for a little poker money?"

"I love you, Mistress." He sobbed and pressed his face to the floor, his hand stretching out toward her ankles, but she sidestepped out of reach. "Forgive me. I never meant to hurt you."

"Get help, Andy, from someone other than me. You can't be my submissive any longer. I expect your things to be gone by the time I get home tonight."

Victor leaned down to whisper against Shiloh's ear. "Do you mind if she stays with us tonight?"

"It's your home."

"And I want it to be yours too."

Her eyes went wide and dark, her mouth soft and open on a little sound of surprise that drew him like a moth to a flame. He kissed her, a gentle persuasion of lips and tongue that insisted she belonged with him. Forever.

He felt a sudden, fierce desire to see his collar on her throat. "Let's film the final awards."

"Now?" Mal brushed surreptitiously at her cheeks. "Can't we do it tomorrow?"

He looped his arm around her waist and drew both her and Shiloh with him toward the dais. "It'll just take a few minutes and then we can all sleep in tomorrow. Besides, we're all here. We might as well take advantage of it. Let's get the proof of this season's success on film so we can sit back and laugh at KDSX and their erroneous stories."

Raising his voice, Victor called over two of the dungeon assistants and motioned them toward Andy. "Bring him over to the bottom step."

Patrick and his pony girl took the second dais, looking frankly battered and worse for wear. The submissive was still sweaty and shaky, like a horse rode hard and put away in the stable still wet.

Victor led Shiloh to the top of the platform and helped her with her mask. Dropping to her knees, she still looked dazed from his casual announcement that he wanted her to move in with him. *So the rest of what I intend will totally blow her mind.*

As soon as the cameras started rolling, Mal planted her stiletto on Andy's back and pinned him face down to the floor.

"You are no longer my submissive. Find a new Mistress, slave." She gave a little twist with her heel, digging into his flesh, and then she turned and stepped off the dais, walking away without a backward glance.

Patrick stroked his pony girl's cheek and smiled at the cameras. "We didn't win top sub this time, but we'll be back for next season."

From the whites rolling in the submissive's eyes, Victor didn't think it too likely that she'd ever consider coming back to the show.

The music rose to a crescendo and the lights dropped so that a single beam focused on him. He lightly tugged on Shiloh's hair so she rocked back and lifted her gaze to his. "Gift, you have pleased me beyond my wildest dreams. You are indeed *America's Next Top sub.*"

He waited while the crew and other contestants cheered.

"Do you want to be V's Gift?"

She smiled tremulously. "More than anything, Master."

Georgia brought the black-velvet tray up the dais as grandly as any empress's royal jewels. She even inclined her head to Gift and then backed down a step, still in the shot but lower than the stars of the show.

He picked up his collar and held up the necklace for the cameras. "The Master's collar is not worn lightly. It's a symbol of ownership, yes, but also the most solemn commitment. I hereby commit myself to Gift. I commit to taking care of her needs, ensuring that she receives the pleasure, and yes, the pain, that she needs. I commit to improving my skills so that I can continually rise to the challenges she presents me. Most of all, I commit my heart to her. Gift, I love you and only you. Will you be my submissive?"

She smiled with such joy that his heart thudded, sore and

261

wounded by her love. "Yes, with all my heart."

He bent down and latched the collar about her neck. It looked like high-end jewelry, but the latch was actually a tiny lock, ensuring the only hand that would remove the collar was his. He didn't intend her to wear it all the time by any means, but the commitment and permanence were important to him, and to her, by the shining tears in her eyes.

Victor drew Shiloh to her feet and sealed his mouth over hers in a fierce kiss of possession, dangling the crop prominently down her back.

Georgia applauded. *"America's Next Top sub* is Master V's Gift!"

Chapter Twenty Four

V's Gift Blog

Waking up in V's bed, I always feel like a kid walking into the world's largest, most fantastic candy shop. I hope I never lose that sense of wonder.

But this morning is even more wondrous, because I wake up with His crop beneath my cheek. Yes, He brought it to bed last night, without me asking. What's funny is that we didn't even use it. There was no need. Just the act of Him trusting Himself—and me—enough to bring it to bed and have that wicked crop at hand meant the world to me.

By the smoldering fire in His eyes, He's been awake for quite some time. "Good morning, sleepy head."

I glance at the clock and it's only nine, surely not late enough for that comment...but then I realize it's a work day. I shoot up like someone goosed me with that crop, but He snags my wrist and tumbles me back down beside Him. "Your boss decided you weren't working today. Neither of us."

I can talk like a phone-sex worker and beg Him to whip me within an inch of my life, but the innuendo inherent in my very inappropriate relationship with my boss, my Master, still makes me blush.

Which He thinks is hilarious. By the time He stops laughing at me, I'm far from the mood to cuddle beneath the blankets. I start to get up, but He's still got my wrist trapped in His big hand.

He's got the most powerful, punishing grip. "You're not going anywhere."

I can't help but notice as He picks up the crop with his other hand, and my body goes into instant meltdown. I try not to let my voice shake. "I'm not?"

"I need something, baby. I need it so badly I've been watching you sleep for the last hour and thinking about nothing else. What do you think that might be, hmmm?"

I rise up on my hands and knees. "Hurt me, V. Hurt me so good."

Filled with so much pride and love he felt like his heart might burst, Victor pressed a kiss to Shiloh's neck and trailed his fingers down the deep-cut back of her gown. "You look fantastic."

Arm in arm, he escorted her toward the exclusive cocktail reception to benefit a Dallas children's charity group. Mal and Patrick walked just ahead of them, but what really made Victor smile was the two young men making eyes at each other. Léon and Brandon had really hit it off. "Is this one of my sister's designs?"

"She insisted that I pick out a formal gown for tonight and mention to everyone where I got it."

The dress was made from brazen red silk that hugged her body to perfection, but in his opinion, what made the gown so mouth-wateringly gorgeous was the deeply slashed back. He knew that the barest width of silk covered the marks he'd left in her flesh. His brand, his V of bruises, lay there, barely hidden.

She was proud of every single one of those bruises. She

admired them in the mirror each and every morning, so he couldn't be guilty. Not when she met his gaze, her eyes as warm as molten chocolate and full of aching love.

Cameras flashed all about them, and KDSX anchor Frank Firkuss shoved a microphone in his face. "Mr. Connagher, are you really a sadist?"

Victor gave his meanest smile. "Did you hear that I fired an employee this week who admitted to leaking confidential information about VCONN's highest rated new show, *America's Next Top sub*?"

"Indeed? Who was he?"

"I think you know his name all too well. Maybe he can go from the Mistress's top sub to KDSX's trashy spy."

"Ms. Malinda Kannes has been more than open about her sexuality, and we all know she's your friend and partner at VCONN." Firkuss leaned closer. "Does Ms. Holmes really let you whip her with a riding crop? Is she really Gift? Or is this all a promotional scam to fool Dallas viewers into watching your show?"

Ignoring the clamor of flashing cameras and those annoying but amusing questions, Victor leaned down to kiss her neck again and noticed the sleeve of her gown had slipped a little. He nudged it with his mouth so the bruise beneath was revealed.

Eyes heavy lidded, he smiled into the camera and ran his mouth over the bruise. Shivering, Shiloh turned toward him. Her eyes were dilated, her mouth open and soft, and yes, her nipples were hard against the silk. Her hand fluttered up to touch the glittering diamond V at her throat, unconsciously displaying the large engagement ring on her hand.

"Watch the show and see if you can decide."

About the Author

Joely always has her nose buried in a book, especially one with mythology, fairy tales and romance. She, her husband, and their three monsters live in Missouri. By day, she's a computer programmer with a Master of Science degree in Mathematics. When night falls, she bespells the monsters so she can write. Read more about her current projects on her website, www.joelysueburkhart.com. Hurt Me So Good is Joely's seventh published title.

When the screen fades to black, all that remains is love.

Rough Cut
© *2010 Mari Carr*
A Black & White Collection story

Ty Ransome. Reigning king of Hollywood, producer, actor, Look Magazine's Hottest Man Alive. He has it all—until he reads a book of short stories that touches him in places kept carefully hidden from the tabloid gossip mill. There's only one way to meet the introverted writer—invite her to Tinseltown to work on a script. The moment he sees her, he realizes why her work haunts him. There's something missing in his life, and it's her.

Gwen steps off the plane with reservations. For one thing, her darkly sexual stories are hardly movie material. Then there's Ty's reputation as a ladies' man. Yet she's won over by his charm and agrees to stay on for a week to get to know him before making her decision. And as the days go by, she discovers there's far more to Ty than a handsome face.

They eat, drink and breathe the characters in their screenplay, re-enacting scenes that delve into the BDSM realm, setting Ty free to unleash his powerful cravings and exposing Gwen's deepest needs. Needs she set free on paper...but is not sure she's ready to make a reality.

Warning: This title contains all the following Tinseltown essentials: explicit sex on a movie set, anal play in a mansion, BDSM with a hot movie star, capture fantasies while writing a screenplay, bondage in a limo, and, oh yeah, some graphic language—sorry about that.

Available now in ebook and print from Samhain Publishing.

Enjoy the following excerpt for *Rough Cut...*

"Now this is the way I like to wake up," a deep voice said beside her.

Gwen opened her eyes, briefly surprised to find her face only inches away from Ty's. She blinked a few times to make sure she wasn't dreaming, then their nighttime conversation drifted back through her consciousness.

"You were supposed to stay on your own side." Her voice was gruff with sleep. As she came fully awake, she became aware of his hand lightly rubbing a bare bit of skin at her waist, beneath her T-shirt.

"So sue me." He leaned so close to her the only air she could feel was that of his soft breath on her cheek. His hand stopped caressing her waist and instead gripped it, pulling her even closer to him.

"I don't think this is a good idea," she whispered, despite the fact her hands were resting, unresisting, on his chest. She'd placed them there to push him away, but instead the traitorous things were exploring the rock-hard definitions of his pecs.

"I think a kiss in the morning is always a good idea."

"Just a kiss?" She cursed her sudden breathlessness.

"Just a kiss, Gwen." She was shocked by her disappointment until he added, "for now."

His lips brushed hers and her body shuddered at the impact. His mouth wasn't gentle, it wasn't easy. He took her lips with a roughness that proclaimed his possession. He took everything she offered with her lips and tongue and demanded more. His hands drifted up to her face, engulfing her cheeks in his firm grip, turning her head exactly the way he wanted it. His teeth nipped at her lower lip and she thought for a moment she heard him growl before his tongue plunged into her mouth, tangling with hers. She'd never been kissed like this in her life and the feeling was heady. It made her dizzy, giddy, reckless and she suddenly realized she wanted more. Hell, she wanted all.

She reached up and held his face to hers, twisting her fingers in his hair. He mimicked the action with her own long tresses and she was amazed by her reaction to his rough touch. Each time he pulled her hair, the sensation of pain flowed pleasurably down her body, causing her hips to flex, searching for relief. Her body felt as if he'd set it aflame and she found her reactions shockingly animalistic.

"Harder. Pull harder," she begged and he responded in turn. His lips trailed along her face, his rough beard scratching her sensitive skin until he reached her ear. He bit her earlobe, pulling her hair at the same time and she cried out, her hips gyrating wildly.

His hard body came over hers as he took control of her wrists, dragging them above her head and holding them firmly in place with one of his hands. She sensed he knew what his actions were doing to her as he pressed his covered cock firmly between her legs, letting her feel the proof of the desire they shared. She wanted to scream at him to take off his pants and give her what she needed, but instinctively she knew he would refuse her.

"Shhh." He tightened his grip on her wrists while planting soft, sweet kisses on her face. "Calm down, gorgeous."

She was panting, frustrated, and she foolishly felt as if she were on the verge of tears.

He leaned back at the sound of her soft cry, the look on his face a perfect mixture of shock, awe and naked, red-hot desire.

He smiled as she struggled to regain composure, her body screaming for relief.

"I can see there will be no such thing as innocent kisses with you," he said.

She blinked rapidly, determined he shouldn't see the tears threatening to fall. Christ, she was a fool.

"I-I, shit." She struggled to free her hands. He released her and she pushed him away. He moved over easily and she realized she wouldn't have been able to budge him if he hadn't permitted it. She walked away from the bed, pressing her back against the wall for support.

"This is not, I mean, I don't—" She was gasping for air and her voice and her body betrayed her, shaking uncontrollably.

He sat up slowly and she knew he was deliberately keeping his movements unhurried lest he frighten her. "Gwen, you didn't do anything wrong."

She wanted to laugh at the understatement of his words. He'd pulled her hair, held her down and she'd responded like a bitch in heat. He didn't think that was wrong, weird?

"I told you before, Ty. I want us to keep our relationship professional. Sex muddies the water. You know that."

"No, I don't think I do. Gwen, there's nothing wrong with admitting that we're attracted to each other sexually. Shit, I can't think of anything I want more than to tie your lovely body to that bed and bury myself between those hot thighs of yours."

"Stop it! Stop saying stuff like that. It isn't going to happen. Ever."

He scowled at her words and rose from the bed, crossing to where she stood, trembling. "Well, I think you and I are about to have our first disagreement."

He leaned toward her as she pressed her body flat against

the wall. He caged her in, grasping her hands by the wrists once again and pressing them against the flat surface, just above her head. "You and I are most certainly going to have sex, Gwen. Hard, hot, incredibly intense sex and you're going to love every minute of it."

"You smug, conceited—"

"Pull your pants down," he said as he loosened his grip.

She wanted to deny him, wanted to drive her fists against his chest and tell him to get the hell away from her, but his deep voice, his demanding words spoke to the loneliest part of her soul and she felt as if she'd been sunk neck-deep in quicksand.

"Pull them down now," he repeated, his voice commanding. Clearly he expected her to comply. This was so wrong. God dammit, it was wrong. And yet her body felt alive for the first time ever.

She reached for the waistband of her pajama bottoms and she slowly shimmied the soft cotton over her hips. The material fell to her ankles and she stepped out of it, never taking her gaze off his determined face.

"Good girl," he murmured and she raised her hand to slap him for his condescending comment. He caught her wrist and pressed it against the wall. "You don't want to do that."

She closed her eyes in surrender and he released her hand.

His dominant actions, his powerful words, were truly soothing her weary soul, despite the fact her head was demanding she run away from him. Ty Ransome was the one man who could be her complete and utter downfall, yet rather than escape, she found herself relishing every touch, every word he offered.

CPSIA information can be obtained at www.ICGtesting.com
Printed in the USA
LVOW060245211011

251401LV00001BA/56/P